THE TANNENBAUM CHRISTMAS QUILT

Third Novel in the
Door County Quilts Series

ANN HAZELWOOD

Publisher: Amy Barrett-Daffin
Creative Director: Gailen Runge
Acquisitions Editor: Roxane Cerda
Managing Editor: Liz Aneloski
Executive Book Editors: Elaine H. Brelsford and Karen Davis of Gill Editorial Services
Copyeditor: Managed Editing
Cover Designer: Michael Buckingham
Book Designer: April Mostek
Production Coordinator: Zinnia Heinzmann
Production Editor: Jennifer Warren
Portrait photography owned by Michael Schlueter

Published by C&T Publishing, Inc., P.O. Box 1456, Lafayette, CA 94549

Library of Congress Control Number: 2021945550

Printed in the USA
10 9 8 7 6 5 4 3 2

Dedication and Thanks

To Those We Lost

Having to write this third novel during the pandemic of 2020 was indeed a challenge. I was determined not to introduce the horrible COVID crisis into the lives of my characters, who were trying to function under normal circumstances. The response from my readers during this time was one of relief and gratitude for them to have a place to escape.

This escape was necessary for me as well. My real world became smaller and smaller as I became limited in seeing my family, my close friends, and my dedicated readers at book signings. My husband and my closest contacts became my only source of communication.

During the pandemic, I transferred to another wonderful publisher and said goodbye to my AQS family, whom I dearly loved. I will always be grateful to them as well as my new family at C&T Publishing.

So, I said goodbye to 2020 with gratitude for staying healthy and managing to keep writing.

This has been a year like no other, so I would be remiss if I didn't dedicate this book to those who didn't make it to the end of 2020. If your family was touched by a lost loved one, I want you to know I was praying for you as I wrote this book. May you continue to be safe. God bless.

—Ann Hazelwood

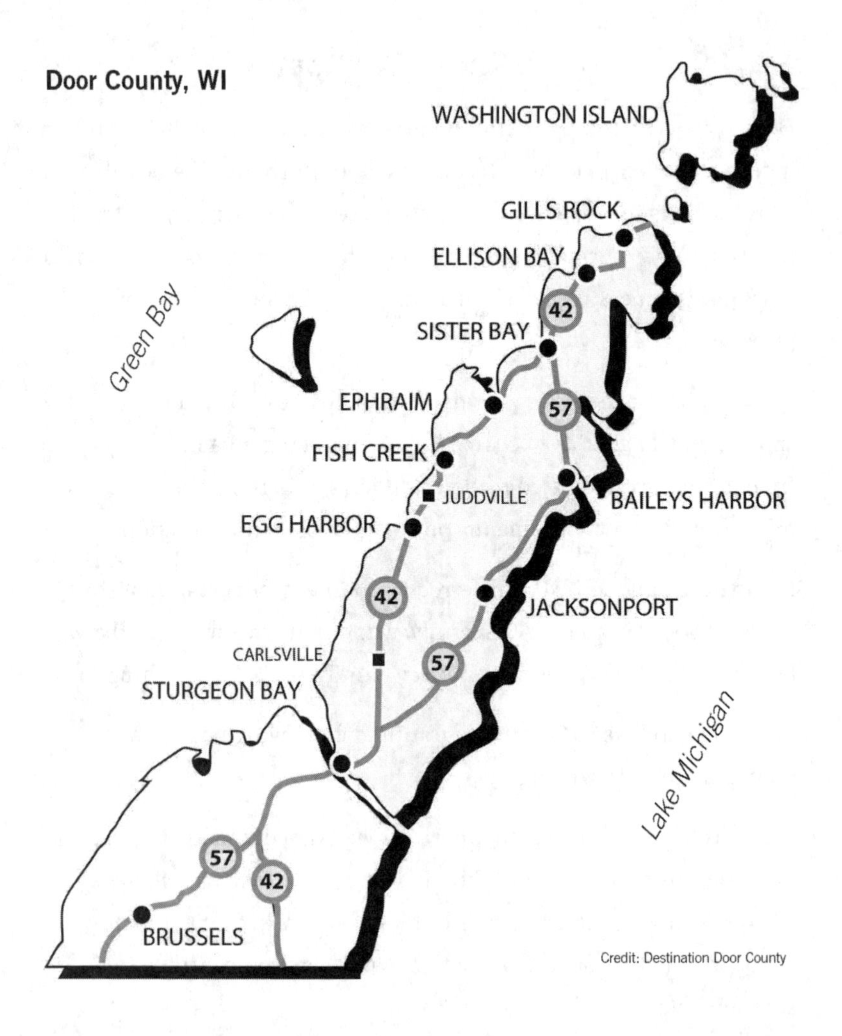

Door County, WI
WASHINGTON ISLAND
GILLS ROCK
ELLISON BAY
42
SISTER BAY
Green Bay
EPHRAIM
57
FISH CREEK
JUDDVILLE
BAILEYS HARBOR
EGG HARBOR
42
JACKSONPORT
CARLSVILLE
57
STURGEON BAY
Lake Michigan
57
42
BRUSSELS
Credit: Destination Door County

WHO ARE THE QUILTERS OF THE DOOR?

GRETA GREENSBURG is Swedish, in her sixties, and is one of the charter members of the club. As she leads the group, she holds firm in keeping to the tradition of only nine members who are diverse in their quilting styles. Greta makes quick and easy quilts and is one of the few members in the club who machine quilts.

MARTA BACHMAN is German. She's 57 and lives in Baileys Harbor. Her family owns a large orchard and dairy farm. Marta makes traditional quilts by hand. She typically has a large quilt frame set up in her home.

AVA MARIE CHANDLER is 54 and loves any kind of music. She served in the Army where she sang for anyone who would listen to her. She's blonde, vivacious, and likes to make quilts that tell a story. She loves her alcohol, so no one knows when her flamboyant behavior will erupt. She lives in a Victorian house in Egg Harbor.

FRANCES McCRAKEN is the eldest member of the group at 78 years old. She regularly spends time in the local cemetery where her husband is buried. She lives in the historic Corner House in Sturgeon Bay and has a pristine antique quilt collection that she inherited. The quilts she makes use old blocks to make new designs.

LEE SUE CHAN is Filipina and is married to a cardiologist. They live in an ornate home in Ephraim. She is 48 years old and belongs to the Moravian Church, also in Ephraim. Lee is an art quilter who loves flowers and landscapes. She is an award-winning quilter who is known for her fine hand appliqué.

OLIVIA WILLIAMS is Black and lives in an apartment over the Novel Bay Booksellers in Sturgeon Bay. She is 40, single, and likes to tout the styles of the Gee's Bend quilts as well as quilts from the South. She is quiet in nature, but the quilts she makes are scrappy, bright, and bold.

RACHAEL McCARTHY and her husband, Charlie, live on a farm between Egg Harbor and Fish Creek. She is 50 years old and has a part-time job bartending at the Bayside Tavern in Fish Creek. They have a successful barn quilt business and sell Christmas trees in season. Rachael makes their business unique by giving each customer a small wall quilt to match their purchased barn quilt.

GINGER GREENSBURG is a 39-year-old redhead who is Greta's niece. She and her husband own a shop in Sister Bay where they sell vintage and antique items. They reside upstairs and have two children. While she works in the shop, Ginger likes to make quilted crafts to sell and takes old quilt tops and repurposes them.

AMY BURRIS, 40, owns the Jacksonport Cottage in Jacksonport, Wisconsin. She sells Amish quilts and other items made by the Amish. She lives in the same building with her husband.

ANNA MARIE MEYER, 45, is the niece and goddaughter of Marta. She just moved to Door County from Ludwigsburg, Germany. She does dimensional quilting and is a fabulous baker. She buys a building in Baileys Harbor, where she opens Anna's Bake Shop and lives upstairs. She's single.

CLAIRE STEWART, 55, is single and is the main character of the series. She is the newest member of the quilting club because her friend Cher moved back to Missouri to take care of her mother. Claire was eager to leave Missouri and moved into Cher's cabin in Fish Creek. Greta and the club made a rare exception to let Claire replace Cher until Cher moved back to Door County. Claire, a blonde who is showing some gray streaks, is a quilter and watercolor artist who sells her artwork in galleries and on her website. Claire has a brother in Missouri who is a journalist and author, and her mother also lives in Missouri.

Chapter 1

A shower of golden leaves gathered at my feet as I waited for Carole to answer the phone. It was a beautiful day, and I relished being able to stand outside my front door and watch the fall wind stir the remaining leaves into activity.

"Hi, Claire. I'm sorry I couldn't return your call sooner, but I didn't hear from Jill at the hospital until just now. Her shift ran late."

"I hate to be a pest, but your daughter is my only connection to what's really going on with Austen. Thanks so much for getting back to me."

"Well, Jill said there hasn't been much change. He's still in a wheelchair when he comes for therapy twice a week. They say he doesn't have much feeling in his legs right now. I'm sure it'll take some time before he walks again."

"It's hard to believe all this is happening. It's been four weeks since the accident. Shouldn't there be more improvement by now?"

"Well, he also had other injuries. He appears to have recovered from those pretty well."

"I hope that's the case," I responded.

"Are you still coming home for Thanksgiving?" Carole inquired.

"Well, I should probably come before then to see him. I feel like it's the right thing to do."

"And just what do you expect to happen? You haven't heard from him since he called to say he was on his way to see you, right?"

"No, I haven't heard anything more from him. I sent a card telling him how sorry I was to hear about the accident, but he never responded. I suspect that he blames me for everything."

"Stop it, Claire! He made the decision to get on the road even though you told him not to." Carole paused, softening her tone. "I saw your mother at Rozier's yesterday, and she's counting on you being here for Thanksgiving. You'd better tell her otherwise if you're not."

"I will. She's pretty upset about Austen's accident. She wonders if there's anything she should do, but I told her it's best if she doesn't do anything. Please thank Jill for all her help."

"I certainly will," Carole agreed. "Tell Cher hello for me when you see her."

"Of course," I assured her, disappointed that I hadn't learned any more than I had about the man who'd been driving to see me but ended up in the hospital instead.

As soon as I hung up, I called Cher to tell her about Austen's progress. I didn't get an answer, so I left a message. Then I remembered that it was her day to work at Carl's gallery, a unique store that specializes in Door County artwork. He'd just expanded his retail space, and Cher lucked out by being in the shop when he announced that he'd need some help.

Disappointed that I couldn't speak with Cher right away, I went to the enclosed porch to continue painting. My subject matter for this piece was going to be fun, but challenging. The idea had come to me after Cher and I organized and executed Door County's first outdoor quilt show that featured quilts hanging from the buildings of many of the local businesses. The show had been an enormous success, and one of the more attractive displays had been at the White Gull Inn located down the street from me. The banisters across the second floor had proven to be a perfect spot for hanging quilts. Inspired by the visual beauty of the outdoor quilt show, I thought it would be appropriate to paint a series of Door County buildings with quilts hanging from them. I was working from a photograph I'd taken the day of the show. My current painting project was ambitious, but because of the popularity of the building featured in it, I had a decent chance of someone wanting to buy this piece.

It was hard to concentrate as I thought of poor Austen. When I left him to move to Door County, I didn't hear from him at all for an entire year. I assumed he'd moved on, just as I had. I should've known better. As controlling as he was, it was just like him to try to make my life miserable because I'd left him. He'd even tried suing me for studio space I had while living with him. When he got nowhere legally, he attempted to woo me back, assuming I'd weaken. His most recent attempt was a phone call announcing that he was on his way to Fish Creek. He said he'd arrive in time to take me to dinner, and I emphatically told him not to come. He hung up suddenly, and I couldn't get him to answer his phone again. He got as far as Springfield, Illinois, where he collided with a tractor trailer. The truck driver died, and Austen was severely injured. I wouldn't have known the details had it not been for Jill, Carole's daughter, who works at the hospital in Perryville, Missouri, where Austen is a pediatrician.

Chapter 2

Late in the morning, the phone rang. It was Cher.

"Hey, I'm about to leave for lunch. Have you eaten?"

"No, I'm just cleaning my brushes."

"How about meeting up at Gibraltar Grill? I'm hungry for their chicken quesadillas."

"Sounds like a good plan! I'll need some time to freshen up," I replied, feeling better knowing that Cher and I would have an opportunity to talk. Being with Cher always cheered me up. We'd been friends since elementary school in Perryville. We were nicknamed Cher Bear and Claire Bear because we'd been so close. We'd attended art school together and managed to remain friends through the various seasons of our lives.

When Cher found herself newly divorced several years ago, she moved to Door County and made her living as an artist. In fact, the cabin I now live in was hers. She left Fish Creek and moved to Perryville when her mother became ill with Alzheimer's. When she knew I was leaving Austen and wanted out of Perryville, she suggested that I move into her cabin.

After her mother passed, Cher decided to come back to Door County and make a fresh start in a condo in nearby Egg Harbor. When I moved to Door County, I told Cher I needed to live in her cabin a year before deciding whether to buy it. I loved it dearly, but living in its tiny confines was challenging at times.

The autumn air felt good as I climbed in my Subaru to meet up with Cher. When I pulled into the restaurant parking lot, I spotted her sitting at one of the tables by the outdoor fire. We didn't have many more days left on the calendar that would be warm enough to sit outside.

"Cher Bear, I can't wait to hear about your morning," I said, smiling at her.

"I've had a great day so far, and you're going to love what I'm about to tell you."

"What?" I asked, suddenly curious.

"Well, I sold one of your Quilted Snow pieces to a woman from Canada!"

"That's great! I can barely keep up with making those quilted seasons. Quilted Snow seems to be the favorite. I guess I'd better use my time at night for quilting."

"You still have one Quilted Blooms, a Quilted Sun, and two of the Quilted Leaves, so no rush. You have a good thing going there with that series."

"Well, Carl gets credit for the idea."

"He's good at knowing what tourists are looking for," Cher said. "I like to think I'm helping him increase his knowledge of quilts."

"I've never asked him, but do you think he's married?" I asked.

"I've always wondered, but from the way his sister talks, he must live alone."

"Then why don't you ask him out?" I asked abruptly. I could've guessed Cher's immediate reaction. Predictably, she looked horror stricken.

"Exactly what are you thinking, Claire Bear?" she asked, reaching for her drink while giving me a look I'd seen dozens of times before.

"Well, he's good looking and certainly is nice enough. I know he may be a bit older than you, but at our age, that doesn't matter anymore," I explained matter-of-factly.

"Do you want to get me fired?"

I chuckled. "I'm just pointing out that he has many fine qualities. He's so kind," I continued. "Remember the way he helped out with our quilt show?"

"I sure do. He was a big help," she agreed. "I hope he doesn't regret taking on the additional shop space next to him."

"Do you know when he plans to close for the season? Everyone on the street seems to be on different schedules."

"He'll start the process by just being open on the weekends, and then he'll close after Christmas. That'll give me time to make more items to sell. By the way, I saw that you called earlier. What was on your mind?"

Our food arrived and we dug in. I replied, "I need your help in deciding when to see Austen."

"I thought you were planning to do that at Thanksgiving."

"I was, but I'm reconsidering. I'm beginning to think that's a bit too far out to take care of this. It's been gnawing at me, and I have to put it to rest."

"For heaven's sake, why do you feel so guilty?"

"Cher, he may never walk again. He'll be in therapy for goodness knows how long, and he's probably not practicing medicine now. Can you imagine how depressed he must be?"

"It's all very sad, but remember that it was his choice to come see you."

"I know, but I still care about him, Cher. I never wished him harm."

"Even though he didn't treat you well?"

"Yes, even though."

Chapter 3

"What does Grayson think about your concern for Austen?"

"I haven't discussed it with him. I'm uncomfortable talking about Austen with him."

"Well, if you're going out of town, you may have to mention something to him eventually."

"I realize that, but my decision to go won't depend on what Grayson says."

Cher laughed at my candor and decided to move to another subject. "Don't forget that we have quilt club coming up. Lee is supposed to recommend approving Amy from the Jacksonport Cottage as a new member."

"Good news there. It'll be interesting to see if Greta was actually sincere about us taking on new members. The fact that we have to vote in secret is a bit reminiscent of high school, don't you think?"

"I agree, but I bet Marta had to do some dancing around to get Greta on board with the recent changes. I like Amy and her shop filled with Amish-inspired selections. She'll fit right in," Cher said.

"I agree," I replied. Taking a deep breath, I returned to our conversation about Austen. "Well, I'd better call Mom and let her know when I'm coming. I have to check on flight times, too."

"You're flying?" Cher asked, surprised.

"I think I am. My vertigo has been in check, and I did okay when I flew home last Thanksgiving."

"Just remember to take some meclizine before you go. Are you going to see Carole and Linda while you're there?"

"I'm not sure. My main objective is to talk with Austen. Then I just want to visit with Mom."

We continued chatting throughout our delicious meal. After a two-hour lunch, we knew we had to be on our way.

As I pulled in the driveway at the cabin, I saw Tom, my shared handyman, raking leaves at the Bittners' house next door. He waved and kept working. Their leaves had to be raked before mine, but he'd get to my yard as soon as he could. He'd proven himself a reliable helper since I'd been at the cabin.

Puff, the cat I'd inherited from Cher, jumped off her favorite wicker chair to greet me.

"Hey there," I said, picking her up and stroking her fur. After a few minutes, she jumped out of my arms and returned to the chair. I'd never had a cat before, and my behavior early on truly showed my ignorance. Over time, Puff and I settled into a familiar routine.

When I checked to see what I might have for dinner later, the choices were slim. It was obvious that I needed to make a trip to the Piggly Wiggly in Sister Bay. The Pig, as the locals called it, was the only full-fledged grocery store in the county. It was a beautiful fall day, so off I went.

The drive did me good and gave me an opportunity to think about my upcoming trip. When I passed the Nelson Shopping Center, I spotted some mums that piqued my interest. Since we hadn't had a hard freeze yet, my geraniums were still bright red, but the mums offered beautiful fall colors that would be pretty outside my door.

My thoughts returned to the trip. What would be the worst that could happen? Would Austen just flat-out refuse to see me? He had every right to since I had done that to him. Should I go to his house alone?

I arrived at the grocery store with my mind elsewhere. When someone bumped into me with their cart, I was surprised to see that it was my good friend Rachael.

"Hey, watch where you're going!" she joked, laughing at my bewildered expression.

"I'm so sorry," I said, shaking my head. "I was deep in thought."

"Are you okay?" Rachael asked, furrowing her brow while giving me a closer look.

"Yes, I'm fine," I assured her.

"I'm still planning on your help this Christmas season at the farm," she said.

"I wouldn't miss it," I answered. "It made my Christmas last year. I'm so glad you asked me to come back."

"Great!" she responded, clearly happy that we had an understanding. "Harry and I are trying to think about what we could add or do differently this year. You're so good at suggestions. I bet you have some ideas."

"Oh, it's dangerous to ask me!" I laughingly warned. "You know how I like special events!"

"I know. I'm still thinking about the chili festival idea you proposed last year. Maybe we need to talk more about that. I also need to see what Harry thinks."

Chapter 4

Rachael and I turned out to be instant friends when I moved to Door County. She's a member of quilt club. When she and her husband, Charlie, needed an extra hand at their Christmas tree farm store during the holidays, she asked me to help. I enjoyed being involved and got to know them better in the process. Unfortunately, Charlie died of a heart attack soon afterward, but Charlie's best friend, Harry, stepped in to help Rachael. Harry is a big teddy bear of a man with a huge heart. It's been nearly a year since Charlie's passing, and Rachael and Harry have become inseparable. He's been helping her with the heavy work on the farm and offering some financial direction as she's starting a new life without her beloved Charlie.

As I drove away from the grocery store, I decided to stop by Nelson's. As always, I was distracted by all their other merchandise rather than focusing on why I stopped in the first place. This was Door County's go-to store for everything from soup to nuts. I counted on them to have the plants I needed for the season. After I was done browsing, I settled on four of their pretty yellow mums and headed home.

When I arrived home and looked objectively at the landscaping, I decided that the herbs looked overgrown and neglected. I wasn't the cook or gardener they deserved. Eager to brighten up the exterior of the cabin, I planted the mums out front. Every time I added a personal touch to the cabin, I loved it more. Still, I remained undecided about whether to purchase the cabin from Cher. There was nothing unlikeable about it except its tiny size.

I stared at my front yard firepit, piled with wood just waiting for a wonderful fall fire. Tom kept tossing in smaller branches whenever he cleaned up my yard. Thinking what a perfect idea a campfire would be, I impulsively called Grayson.

"Hey, Claire. What's up?"

I dove into my invitation with enthusiasm, convinced that it was a wonderful idea. "I was working in the yard and decided that tonight would be a grand time to build a fire in my firepit. Do you have any interest in sharing some burned hot dogs and s'mores?"

There was a lengthy pause, followed by, "I find your offer most intriguing, and I think Kelly would love it."

"Wonderful!" I replied. "Do you need to check with her first?"

"I think you can count on a positive reply. What time?"

"Around five or six. That's when it gets dark."

"Sounds good. Can I bring anything?"

"Yes. Have Kelly pick out items to make the s'mores. She'll know exactly what we need. Thank you!"

"Glad to do it. See you soon."

I wanted to do a happy dance right there in the yard. I loved having pop-up events like this. I was never quite sure how forward to be with Grayson. He was a widower raising a teenager, so many things could go wrong. I still smile to myself when I think about noticing him the first time at the Blue Horse Beach Cafe soon after I'd moved to the area. He'd been wearing a red neck scarf that drew my attention to his dark complexion. We'd exchanged glances with one another and somehow I knew we'd be getting to know each other better.

I quickly cleaned off the handsome vintage wooden lawn chairs that Cher had left behind and arranged them around the firepit. I got the table from my porch and placed it nearby to hold the food we were going to fix. What fun this would be!

Chapter 5

Living at the cabin was like playing house as a kid. It all still felt so new as I experienced each season and participated in Door County activities. My life had been quite different before I moved here. Austen's house in Perryville had been luxurious. I had a beautiful, spacious studio, and entertaining was so easy there. Early in our relationship, we entertained a lot. We catered the best food, provided the best wine, and invited those on the current who's-who list. People were eager to see the exquisite home of the area's most popular pediatrician. The contrast here was stark, yet I feel so much happier living in my modest cabin with Puff.

I went inside to spruce up the place in case Grayson and Kelly came indoors. I decided to warm up some apple cider for Kelly to enjoy. If Grayson didn't want wine tonight, he'd probably like the warmed cider as well. After a bit, I took a deep breath and gave the cabin another quick glance. I smiled and felt good about the evening ahead.

Later, when I saw the two of them drive up, I was surprised to see that Kelly was carrying her new cat, Spot. I chuckled to myself remembering how she'd managed to become the cat's owner despite Grayson's protests. Several of us were attending a BBQ at Rachael's house when a stray cat appeared. Rachael didn't know the owner but told Kelly she could have the cat if the owner failed to show up to claim it. When no one did, Kelly became its new owner. When she heard my cat was named Puff, she named hers Spot, mimicking the pet names from vintage Dick and Jane books. I was pretty certain that Kelly didn't have a clue about what those early readers were like, but she knew the character names of Dick, Jane, Spot, and Puff.

"Well, look who's here! Welcome, Spot!" I exclaimed.

Kelly grinned, and Grayson only shook his head slowly.

"I hope you don't mind, but I wanted Spot to meet Puff," Kelly explained. "Dad said I should've asked you first."

"I don't mind a bit!" I responded. "How are you, Mr. Wills?"

He grinned at my use of his formal name and offered me a quick peck on the cheek. "I'm pretty good, and I'm certainly looking forward to those burned hot dogs," he teased.

"Well, let's go inside first and meet Puff," I suggested.

When we entered the cabin, Puff took one look at Spot in Kelly's arms, jumped off the chair, and dashed upstairs. We all burst into laughter. Then Spot jumped out of Kelly's arms and landed on the floor. It seemed that every hair he owned was standing on end. Instead of going upstairs, he started checking out the rest of the cabin in case other creatures were lurking about.

"Well, what do you make of that?" Kelly asked, laughing. "Puff must be afraid of Spot!"

"She's just not used to someone being in her territory," I explained. "I'll bet she'll eventually come back downstairs."

"Well, I'm going to get that fire started," Grayson announced.

"Great idea," I agreed. "Kelly, how about some hot cider?"

"Yum!" Kelly responded.

"That sounds good to me too, Claire," Grayson chimed in.

"You two get started out there while I pour the cider," I said, going into the kitchen. "Kelly, you might want to find Spot and take him with you."

Kelly laughed and agreed, beginning the search. Once she found Spot, the two of us took our mugs of cider and joined Grayson outside.

As Grayson built the fire, he noticed the new mums and mentioned how nice the yard looked. I explained that Tom deserved all the credit since he's the one who cares for it after he maintains the Bittners' yard. The three of us settled into chairs and welcomed the heat from the blossoming fire.

"Grayson, I think I'm going to buy this place," I announced, quite out of the blue. "With winter coming, I want to feel settled somewhere. I think I owe it to Cher to finally make a decision."

Grayson looked deep in thought. "This is a mighty good piece of real estate," he stated. "It'll be a sound investment. Have the two of you talked terms?"

I shook my head. "No, but I know she really wants me to have it, and she'll be reasonable about it," I replied.

"Well, if you need some help, let me know. I can put you in touch with a good appraiser if you need one."

"Thanks," I responded. "I appreciate that."

Chapter 6

The cookout was everything I hoped it would be. The hot dogs were burned to a crisp, and Kelly made us the best s'mores ever. We shared stories about when we'd each had our first s'mores. We laughed together, and one story seemed to fuel the next. My first campfire was a success, and it made me feel even more connected to the cabin and its property.

When we went back into the house to clean up, we saw that Puff had returned to her favorite chair. Kelly held on to Spot tightly, but Spot still managed to climb from her arms. He immediately headed toward Puff. We braced ourselves for a good cat fight, but instead we watched a contest where they stared each other down with neither cat making a move. It was a sight to see.

"I think they're working out a compromise," Grayson surmised, smiling. "Well, we need to grab Spot and head on home, Kelly. Be sure to thank Claire for this fun invitation."

"It was my pleasure. Now that Spot and Puff have been introduced, I'm sure the next time will be better," I stated.

After a sweet goodbye, they left. I'd felt the warmth of both Grayson and Kelly tonight. The campfire had turned out to be a good way to get to know both of them better.

From the enclosed porch, I watched the last of the fire go out before I headed to the shower. Later, safely snuggled under the covers, I replayed the evening in my head. Then, like a dream that returns again and again, my mind drifted to the image of Austen in a wheelchair. I couldn't ignore that I still had feelings for him, but now, those feelings were turning into pity and guilt. I knew I had to do something about seeing Austen and decided to call Mom tomorrow to tell her I'd be coming home.

I woke up after a good night's sleep with Puff stretched alongside me. I realized it was later than I'd thought and then remembered that I had to get ready for quilt club. I hurriedly dressed, fixed a cup of coffee, and fed Puff. In no time, I was off to the library.

Looking forward to my second cup of coffee, I walked into the Door County library with Ginger, a fellow club member. I quickly noticed that she wasn't as chipper as usual.

"Good morning, ladies!" Marta greeted as the meeting began.

Marta had recently been installed as the new president. Greta had historically led the group and did so with precision and a keen sense of personal ownership. I watched for any reaction from Greta as she placed herself in the front row. I was curious to see how she'd tolerate the new leadership and changes that would necessarily follow.

"Good morning!" everyone responded.

"I only have a short program today because we have some new business to discuss," she began. "I have asked Lee to give us a bit of information about what's involved if anyone wants to enter a quilt in a major show. As you know, Lee has quite a lot of experience doing just that. She also has experience as a winner. Lee, you may have the floor."

"Thank you, Marta," she began, her voice quiet. "I started entering shows about ten years ago. I had no idea what I was doing, but in time, I learned a lot about the process."

Most of us responded by smiling at her. Lee was known for beautiful, quilted landscapes. She was able to produce lovely handwork, so we were eager to hear more about her quilting journey.

Lee held up a typical entry form and read some of the requirements and instructions aloud. She then explained how important good photos, slides, and CDs were to being accepted into shows. She recommended using a professional photographer and then talked about how being accepted into a juried show was a significant accomplishment for an entrant. From what she shared, it seemed that each judge has their own take and opinion on things, but she's learned something from each comment she's ever received on a judging sheet.

"Some shows have a printed guide for their judges to follow, and many companies use a point system," she told us. "Most shows make sure that you receive the judges' comments about your quilt whether they're good or bad. They can truly vary from judge to judge."

As Lee was winding down her portion of the program, there were a lot of questions, but none from Greta. She sat there, silent.

"Thank you, Lee," Marta said graciously. "I certainly learned some new things, didn't you?"

In response to the program, everyone clapped. Greta would've been banging her gavel by now, but Marta went seamlessly into the next item on the agenda.

"As you know, ladies," Marta continued, "we've decided to open our club to new members. Lee would like to nominate someone. At our next meeting, we'll vote by secret ballot. Lee, please proceed."

"I think everyone here knows Amy Burris from the Jacksonport Cottage," Lee began. "She not only has a popular business but does an annual Amish quilt show that draws many folks from all over the country. She has expressed interest in our club for some time, but we had a closed-membership rule until just recently. I think she'd be a wonderful addition to the club as a quilt retailer and as someone who offers a diverse perspective of the quilting industry in general. I do hope you'll give her a positive vote."

Chapter 7

"Thank you," Marta said. She looked at Lee, who responded with a smile. "Everyone will have time until the next meeting to decide how to vote." Marta glanced at her notes and continued, "Amy did ask that I mention the Amish quilt show coming up on October 7 at Mr. G's. Ending on October 10, it's a great beginning to your Christmas shopping." Marta glanced at her notes again and then looked up with a smile. "I'm excited to tell you that at our next meeting, I'll be bringing my niece, Anna Marie Meyer, as a guest. She's coming from Germany to live in Door County, and you'll notice right away how polished her English is. Naturally, I'm very excited, and until she finds her own place, she'll be living with us on the farm."

"Marta, that's wonderful," I said.

"Is she a quilter?" Olivia asked.

"She certainly is," Marta said enthusiastically. "She uses a technique that we don't see much of here. I would say that she's a dimensional quilter. She quilts pieces that are more like objects. She makes houses, vases, and bowls. She's quite a baker as well. I'm looking forward to having her create wonderful aromas in my home."

Everyone chuckled.

"How lucky for you!" Rachael responded.

"I'll have her bring some of her quilt samples," Marta said. "I plan to nominate her to be a part of our club."

Everyone except Greta expressed their pleasure at the prospect of welcoming the new resident into the group. Greta was squirming in her seat.

"Now, does anyone have a show-and-tell piece?"

"I made this vest using some of my old doilies, lace, and buttons," Ava said. She stood and held up her creation. "I've used this vest pattern often because I like to make seasonal vests."

"Very clever, Ava," Marta acknowledged. "Some of you may want to take a closer look at her vest, but time has gotten away from us, so I'll entertain a motion to adjourn."

Greta made the motion, and Rachael seconded it. When the meeting ended, no one seemed to rush out the door like we typically did. Marta was making the meetings more interesting, and we wanted to know more about her niece.

"I'm really excited to meet Anna," I said as Marta was getting her things together.

"I'm so excited. She's my goddaughter, and we have so few family members left in Germany. She's alone, and I know she'll do well in the art community we have here in Door County. She's good at many things, but it's been her dream to own her own bakery where she can also live upstairs. She's young enough that she could make that happen."

"She sounds very talented," Rachael, who was also listening, said.

"She learned it all from her mother, God bless her soul."

"When you say she's alone, what do you mean?" I asked, curious to know more about her.

"She hasn't been married and has no children, but she always appears to be happy," Marta said, shaking her head like she couldn't imagine such a thing.

"Makes sense to me," Ava said jokingly. We snickered at her remark since several of us in the group were neither married nor had children.

"Well, she was a wonderful caretaker for her parents, but it's time she made her own life," Marta said, summing up her young niece's situation.

"For sure!" I responded. "Let me know how I can help. I'd love to have her in this group."

"Thanks, Claire," Marta said with a smile.

No one was available to go to lunch, so I stopped by Pelletier's to pick up a sandwich. It seemed that everything was turning to pumpkin wherever I looked. When I surveyed the menu, there was a definite pumpkin theme. I settled for the ham sandwich special but broke down and added a slice of pumpkin pie with extra whipped cream.

Even though it was chilly, I sat on the front doorstep of the cabin to eat my sandwich. The fall sun kept me warm as I thought about calling Mom when I finished. When I took the last bite, I tapped her number into my phone.

"Honey, what a nice surprise! What's going on?" she answered.

"How would you like to see me before Thanksgiving?"

She paused and then answered, "I hope nothing's wrong. You know you're welcome to come home anytime."

"I keep thinking of Austen, and I want to see him." I received another pause.

"Well, it's a most unfortunate situation."

"He hasn't responded to anything I've sent him since the accident, and I feel terrible. I guess I really don't blame him."

"It's nice that you reached out."

"I've thought about this for a while, but I wanted to talk to you before I made an airplane reservation."

"I see. You just listen to your heart, Claire. I told you that when you left for Door County. I'd love to see you, though."

"I can fly out this weekend, so maybe we can have an early Thanksgiving."

"Well, you could also come back then."

"I can't do that, but I sure would like some of your home cooking. Maybe Michael will even show up if he knows I'm coming," I suggested.

"Well, don't get your hopes up about that, but we'll make it a nice visit. I sure miss you!"

"I miss you too, Mom."

Chapter 8

I hung up with mixed feelings, but in my heart, I knew I had to make peace with Austen. I immediately went to the computer to make my reservation. Once that was done, I wondered who I needed to tell. It wasn't yet time to start work at the farm, so I didn't have to tell Rachael, but I'd have to say something to Grayson. Just then my phone rang, and it was Ericka.

"Hey, stranger!" I answered.

"Hey," Ericka replied. "Are you loving this fall weather? I told George I wanted to have a cookout by the fire before we get our first snow. Are you and Grayson free on Saturday night?"

"Thanks for the heartwarming invitation, but I've made plans to go home this weekend."

"Is everything okay?"

"Yes, everything's fine. I've decided to go home earlier instead of at Thanksgiving, but I sure will miss coming to your cookout."

"Well, call me when you return. We'll have lunch. George is sitting here, and he says to tell you hello."

"Tell him hello for me, and have fun at the party."

When I hung up, I felt sad about having to decline their invitation. Ericka and her brother, George, had been so supportive of me when I'd arrived in Door County. George immediately became too friendly, but we'd continued to be friends even after I turned down his advances. Having just left a relationship, starting a new one was the last thing I'd wanted to do after arriving at my new home.

I did have George's good friend Rob do some projects around the cabin when I first arrived. He helped me hook up my computer and put up a light in the backyard for my safety. Unfortunately, Rob became a servant to his drug habit and got into trouble robbing places here in Door County. It caught up with him, and now he's serving time for his mistakes.

Cher and Ericka are close friends, so Ericka was naturally delighted when Cher moved back here. Ericka isn't a quilter. She works at an urgent care facility in Sister Bay. She's a determined person who's quite civic minded. She feels strongly about protecting the environment in Door County and works to make it a better place to live.

As I planned my trip, I made a fire in the stone fireplace. The process of starting and enjoying a fire in the fireplace always seemed to calm me down. Last winter was my first living in Door County, and fires were comforting on those chilly nights. Tom always made sure I had plenty of firewood, so I thought I might as well make use of it. I wasn't the only one who appreciated the comfort and warmth it provided. Puff always took notice when I began building the fire, managing to find a warm, snuggly place where she could take her next nap.

I poured myself a glass of wine, and when I returned to the couch, I received a text from Kelly.

[Kelly]
Isn't this photo too cute of Puff and Spot?

Pleased that she'd sent me the adorable picture, I smiled and hoped that I was winning Kelly over.

[Claire]
I love it. Do you think they'll ever be friends?

[Kelly]
Of course! Dad wants to know if you can meet for coffee tomorrow morning at the Blue Horse at eight thirty.

I smiled again.

[Claire]
Tell him I'd love to.

[Kelly]
Done!

Hands down, that was the best part of my evening. Meeting Grayson in the morning would be the best time to tell him I was going to Perryville.

Chapter 9

As I saw the first evidence of daylight the next morning, I heard the patter of raindrops on the roof. I checked my phone, draped my robe around me, and headed downstairs for coffee. Puff was more than ready to follow. I sat at the kitchen table and watched the rain pour down outside. I felt anxious about meeting Grayson. I went upstairs to dress and found an old, bright yellow wool sweater I hadn't worn in ages. It made me smile, and it contradicted the gloominess of the day. Before I left the cabin, I received a text from Cher.

[Cher]
You're going home on Saturday???

I knew it had to be Ericka who told her.

[Claire]
Yes, Mom's expecting me. I'll let you know how it goes.

[Cher]
Be careful. You know how controlling Austen can be.

[Claire]
I know. Have fun at Ericka's party.

Cher always had my back, and I appreciated her warning.

I quickly checked my makeup and pulled my hair into a ponytail. To be prepared for the rainy day, I grabbed my umbrella and threw on a raincoat. When I reached the coffee shop, I spotted Grayson's SUV and parked nearby. Gathering my purse, keys, and umbrella, I quickly darted inside. He was sitting at a table, and I knew that he likely saw me run in. He motioned me toward him after I placed my order.

"Your order has been paid for by the man in the red scarf," the young man said as he handed me my hazelnut coffee and cinnamon bagel. I blushed because I knew all about the man with the red scarf.

"I like your red umbrella," Grayson teased.

"And I like your red scarf," I teased back. "It's a good thing we can spot each other."

He chuckled. "So, do you have plans today?" he asked innocently, unaware of my arrangements to head back to Missouri.

"Actually, I have lots to do because I finally made the decision to go home this Saturday instead of at Thanksgiving."

"That's news!" he said as he took a sip of coffee.

"That also means that I'll be in Door County for Thanksgiving."

"Why the change?"

"I'll be honest. It's because of Austen. I still feel tremendous guilt about his accident and want to go see him."

"Guilt about what?" Grayson said, using an even tone.

"I told you that despite my reluctance to see him, he was making the trip anyway."

"Yes, and that was a bad judgment call on his part, I think."

"I know, but Grayson, he may never walk again."

Grayson's expression tightened. "Seriously?"

I nodded. "He's wheelchair bound and has to get himself to therapy sessions. I know that dealing with his situation has to be difficult for him both physically and emotionally," I explained.

"How will your visit change anything?"

"I feel the need to make peace with him. We had a legal battle and shared some pretty harsh conversations. I don't wish him ill. I can't imagine all the feelings he must be experiencing."

"So, do I have anything to worry about?" Grayson asked.

His question had a shyness to it that surprised me. "You? Worry?" I smiled at him but then said, "I think you have to trust me on this. I can't let these bad feelings continue. It's not like me, and it's not how I was raised."

"That's commendable, but I doubt that it's going to change much on his end. I'm sure he's a proud person who doesn't want to be pitied. If he doesn't greet you warmly, don't be surprised," Grayson warned.

"I feel as if I've thought of every possible response. I just want to come across as a caring friend."

"Has he been able to return to his medical practice?"

"I doubt it. Also, you have to understand I'm getting my information about him secondhand from an employee at the hospital."

"Claire, I wish you well, and I'm pleased you'll be here for the holidays."

"I am, too," I agreed. I felt that it was time to move on to another subject and asked, "So, do you have a busy day ahead of you?"

"A pretty busy one, I'm afraid. A lot of boats are going into storage now and some need servicing."

"Good luck. Oh, I loved that Kelly sent me a photo of Puff and Spot."

Chapter 10

"Don't get me started on that cat," Grayson complained, shaking his head.

"Spot is becoming part of your extended family," I stated in a serious tone. "Is he fulfilling his responsibilities?" I asked, winking at him so he'd know I was teasing him.

He grinned and replied, "Spot can't control everything, of course, but I certainly don't appreciate him jumping up on my desk and messing up my sense of place. I really don't want him in the kitchen at all, but I'm losing that battle. When Kelly goes away to college, that darned cat is going with her."

"She's got another year to go, so you'd better suck it up."

"Hey, whose side are you on, anyway?" he protested while he smiled at me.

"I didn't want Puff either, but in time, we came to understand one another. We compromised, or should I say that *I* compromised?"

He laughed.

"I really thought that when Cher returned, Puff would be happy to see her, but instead, her own cat ignored her."

"They know the hand that feeds them," Grayson offered.

I smiled and nodded as we continued to chat. Our coffee visit lasted longer than I'd imagined. Surprisingly, he gave me a long kiss and hug before we dashed out into the rain. I got the feeling that he was hoping I'd remember that kiss and hug while on my trip.

I stopped by the post office to get my mail on the way home. I was pleased to see Ginger, who was just leaving.

"Long time no see," I joked. "That was quite a different quilt club meeting we had this week, wasn't it?"

"It sure was! I hope everyone supports those who want to come into the group."

"Well, I know I will. I'm eager to meet this Anna Meyer."

"Me, too! Claire, if you have time to grab a coffee or go to lunch this week, I'd like to talk to you about something."

"Well, it might be a while because I'm leaving for Perryville tomorrow. I don't know when I'll be returning, but we'll make that happen when I get back. Is everything okay?"

"It's nothing that can't wait," she assured me. "I hope you have a good trip."

"I have a mission for this trip. It's not for fun," I admitted.

"Well, give me a call when you return," Ginger requested.

"I promise," I assured her.

On the way home, I wondered what in the world could be happening with Ginger. She and Allen had always seemed happy. They had a wonderful vintage shop in Sister Bay, and both had helped with our quilt show. I hoped that whatever she wanted to share was not too serious.

When I returned home, I started packing. As Puff watched me intently, I wondered what I should do about leaving her. I decided to ask Cher to check on her.

[Claire]
Would you take Puff while I'm gone or at least check on her?

Within a short time, I received a rather unexpected response.

[Cher]
Puff does just fine by herself. Make sure there's plenty of food and water, and clean her box before you go.

I responded just as quickly.

[Claire]
You're cruel, Cher Bear.

I was even more surprised by her next response.

[Cher]
You're her owner, Claire Bear!

I didn't respond but instead talked directly to the cat who'd become mine. She gave me a meow in response, so I was good with that.

I put away my painting supplies and made sure there wasn't any food on the counters that Puff might get into. I gathered her toys in the middle of the room. When I returned from Perryville the last time, I came home to find my Christmas tree knocked over thanks to her antics. Luckily, I'd placed a chair in front of the tree to keep it from hitting the ground.

I happened to notice Tom bringing in wood for the Bittners, so I went outside to tell him I'd be out of town. He could keep an eye on my cabin while he was working nearby.

I had an early flight in the morning from Green Bay, so I needed to turn in early. I crawled into bed at eight thirty in the evening but wasn't really tired. Puff had no problem with that, so I patted her back as I watched her drift off to sleep. Everything was by the door and ready to go, so I tried to relax and fall asleep.

Chapter 11

My mixed feelings about this trip followed me all the way to the airport. After I parked the car, I took some medicine to control my vertigo while I was on the airplane. I didn't pack many clothes, so my bag fit easily in the overhead compartment. The seat next to me was occupied by someone immersed in his work, and I was grateful to be left alone. I was able to catch a nap on the way to the St. Louis airport, which was helpful since I'd gotten up so early. It took a while to secure a rental car, and then I was on my way to Perryville.

I arrived around four o'clock, and before I went inside Mom's house, I glanced around, surveying the condition of her yard. It looked unkempt, and her mums had spent blooms on them. The fall leaves weren't under control, and they blew into the neighbors' yards. Mom usually kept her yard looking nice.

I gave a slight knock, and Mom came to the door with her welcoming smile and a warm hug. She wore her red-checked apron, which was a sure sign she was cooking today.

"I'm so glad you arrived safely," she said as she took my hand and led me to the couch, where we sat down.

"Everything went well. How are things here? It sure smells good!" I exclaimed.

"I have one of your favorite meals in the oven, so I hope you brought a good appetite."

"Don't tell me it's a roast with carrots, onions, and potatoes," I said, hopeful that I was correct.

"That's right! They still had some fresh tomatoes at the farmers market, so we'll have those, too," she said.

"Next year, I'm going to have to put out a plant or two. There's nothing better than a newly ripened tomato."

"My gardening days are over, I'm afraid. Every year, things get a little harder. My flowers need to be cut back so badly, but I may not get to it."

"Maybe I can help. Are you feeling okay?" I asked, leaning toward her. She nodded, but there was a sadness to her demeanor that was troubling.

"Bill and I were just saying the other day how difficult it is to relinquish things we loved to do. He gets frustrated watching how the young lawyers practice today, but I quickly reminded him that he was a young lawyer, too, at one time." She smiled as she remembered their conversation.

"I'm so glad the two of you are friends. You have a great history together. Did he tell his daughter when she visited that the two of you have become close friends?"

"He did."

"What was her reaction?" I asked, curious.

She chuckled. "She was a little more outspoken than you and Michael have been."

"Really? How so?"

She blushed as she said, "Well, she told him she thinks he should marry again."

"Marry? That's being outspoken alright!"

"We both got a kick out of it. No one will ever replace your father. We're too old to be thinking about such a thing. However, we were both at the senior center last week, and they had a small musical group that played some of our old songs. Some folks got up and started dancing. Bill's knee bothers him, but do you know, he asked me to dance! I never thought I'd see that day!"

To my delight, her face lit up as she told her story of the good time at the senior center. "That's wonderful. Did he do okay?"

"He's still got a few moves left in him," she joked.

We laughed heartily. "Never give up on those pleasant moments, Mom."

"What about you? How is Mr. Wills these days?"

"He's wonderful, and I'm getting to know his daughter a little better."

"Oh, I hope it works out with him. A mother wants to know her daughter will be happy for the long haul."

"There are no guarantees, Mom. Look at what happened to me and Austen."

"So, will you see Austen tomorrow?"

"If he'll let me."

Chapter 12

"Oh, for heaven's sake, I hope he does," Mom said in disgust.

"What if he never walks again, Mom? How can I live with that?"

"Don't even think that way, child. Now take your things to your room while I get dinner on the table."

"Is this the same bottle of wine you opened when I was here last?" I joked as I poured myself a glass.

"Probably so. It's in the same place that your father used to put what he called 'the good stuff,'" she laughed.

As I drank my wine, I watched Mom move around the kitchen putting the finishing touches on the meal. Watching her make gravy from the roast broth was spellbinding. It magically appeared as she added just enough water and flour. I was sad to notice that she was moving much more slowly than I'd remembered. She'd already set the table with her fine china and made a beautiful centerpiece. I wanted to keep this memory of her and her thoughtfulness forever.

"You should wear some of your other aprons occasionally, Mom. You have a whole drawer full of them that your mother made," I suggested.

"Oh, but I like this one," she explained. "I used to wear some of the others when I helped at the church suppers."

"Do they still do that wonderful turkey sausage supper?"

"They sure do. If you're still here next weekend, we could go to it."

I smiled, thinking back on the annual event. "I sure remember how delicious that meal was, especially the dressing," I recalled. "No, I need to get back home before then, but while I'm here, I need to visit Austen."

"Honey, I just have to ask. Do you still have feelings for him? If you do, this is the time to do something about it."

I wasn't at all shocked by her question. To be honest, I'd asked myself the same question.

"I do have feelings for him, but not the good, healthy kind. Does that make sense? Of course, it did my ego good when he regretted my leaving, but the more I thought about him and his ways, I knew I just couldn't go back. Honestly, if I hadn't started a new relationship, I might have weakened and gone back to him."

"Well, call me old-fashioned, but you'd better think about all that before you see him."

"Do you think I'm going to change my mind?"

She sighed as she placed the platter of tomatoes on the table. "He won't be that tall, handsome, confident man you knew before. Your pity could even be confused with love. Please be careful of every word you say, because he may interpret it differently."

"You're saying these things like you've had a similar experience."

"Never you mind," she said, giving me a smile. "Just have a clear head before you go. If he's still controlling, you may not have the outcome you planned."

"You're right about everything as always, Mom. Thank you. I just have to tell him how bad I feel for him, or I can't move forward."

She nodded like she understood. Her eyes scanned the table. "Well, I think we have everything on the table, so let's enjoy our dinner."

After we said our usual table prayer, we both dug in. Mom's comfort food was just what I needed. What would I do without her words of wisdom and her good cooking?

After we cleaned up in the kitchen, I stepped out onto the front porch for a breath of fresh air. Mom always kept the house so much warmer than what I was used to. I received a text just then and saw that it was from Grayson.

[Grayson]
Hope you arrived safely. Thinking of you. Gray

Hmm, he called himself Gray. Did anyone else ever call him that?

[Claire]
Just finished comfort food with Mom. Thinking of you as well.

And that was it. There was no other response. I could only wonder what was going through his mind.

I went to bed early in the same bed I'd had since grade school. I chuckled when I pulled back the covers and saw the same flowered sheets I'd had in high school. My pillows had been replaced in the past few years, but they smelled of roses, like everything else in the room.

Chapter 13

The next morning, I awoke to the aroma of coffee. What a rare treat to have it waiting for me, plus a hearty breakfast, which Mom always insisted on. After I showered and dressed, I joined her at the kitchen table as she was reading the local paper.

"Good morning! Any news I should know about?" I asked.

"No, but I did save the paper that announced Austen's accident if you'd like to have it."

"I'll take it with me and read it when I get home."

"How about a blueberry pancake? I just finished frying the bacon. It's nice and crispy, like you prefer."

I grinned. "I'd love some of both." Mom was always of the mind that food made everything better. Right now, it did.

"Would you like me to prepare dinner for Carole and Linda this evening?"

"Thank you, but no, not tonight. I don't know how my day will go with Austen. They know I'm in town, but I didn't want to commit to anything."

It was ten o'clock, and I debated about whether to call Austen's house before I left. In the end, I decided to go without calling. If I contacted him, he'd have the opportunity to refuse to see me.

As I drove into his neighborhood, I marveled once again at the nice lifestyle I'd left behind. I pulled into the driveway, and it appeared that nothing about the home had changed in my absence. I noticed an unfamiliar car in his driveway. Another visitor wasn't going to stop me from seeing him.

I got out of the car and took a deep breath before ringing the doorbell. I waited and then rang the bell again after a couple minutes. No response. Was he watching out the window? Disappointed, I turned and walked toward my car.

"Claire! Claire!" a voice called out.

I turned around and recognized a familiar face from Austen's office. Remembering her name was Bernice, I walked back toward the door.

"I'm Bernice. Do you remember me?" she asked kindly. "I'm so sorry we kept you waiting. How are you?"

"Fine, fine," I answered, feeling awkward. "I came to see Austen. Is he up to seeing visitors?"

She paused. "He's having coffee on the sunporch. He knows you're here, so come on in. Do you know anything about his condition?"

"If you're referring to his being confined to a wheelchair, yes. I'm in town and really would like to see him."

"Of course. Come on in."

The large entryway and living area looked the same. I'd decorated much of it myself. I knew exactly where Austen would be. He liked to have his morning coffee at the breakfast table on the back porch because of its spectacular view.

"Hello, Austen," I greeted. Bernice had disappeared, and I felt an unexpected shyness wash over me.

"Coffee?" he asked without returning my greeting.

"Sure, I'll have some," I said as I walked closer.

"Have a seat," he said as he poured me a cup. "Black, if I recall."

"Yes, thank you. Look, I know you're not thrilled to see me, but I had to see you."

"So you could see for yourself that I really am in a wheelchair?"

"Austen, that's not fair," I said quietly.

"Not fair?" he repeated, his voice sounding tense.

"I'm so sorry about the accident."

"Well, it is what it is. Isn't that where things stand between us?"

I ignored the question, not quite certain what he meant. "I understand you've recovered nicely from some other injuries."

"I'll be fine. They're doing some remodeling to accommodate this chair at the office, so I can start seeing patients again after the construction is complete."

"That's great news!"

"Great news? Really?"

Again, I ignored his questions. "How's the therapy going? Will they have you walking soon?"

"It's slow and quite painful. I'm not too hopeful, but as you remember, I don't give up easily."

"Yes, I know," I said, smiling. "Is there anything I can do?"

He gave me a quizzical look and then replied, "Now look, Claire. I know you don't mean that. I'll adjust as time goes along. Is everything going well with you? Did you come to get some things you left behind?"

"Don't be rude, Austen," I said. "It's not necessary. You know I care about you, and I feel terrible that all this has happened to you. Things are fine in Fish Creek. I had an outdoor quilt show in the spring that I was very proud of. Cher and I did it together."

Austen smiled. "I remember when you wanted to have a quilt show and hang quilts all around the courthouse square here in Perryville."

I nodded and smiled. "Perhaps someone will do that one day."

"Well, are there any other questions you have for me?"

I didn't know what to say. I was unprepared for his shortness with me. I paused for a moment and then said, "Okay, I guess I've overstayed my welcome, so I'll be going. Austen, I wish you all the best, and I hope you believe that."

He looked down at the floor while I rose from my chair and headed toward the door.

"Claire," he called out. "Take care of yourself."

My eyes teared up.

Chapter 14

I couldn't help myself. I turned, walked back to him, and kissed him on the cheek, smelling the oh-so-familiar fragrance of his aftershave. My action took him by surprise, and when he looked up at me, I saw enormous sadness in his eyes. I turned around and started to walk out of the room.

"Thanks for coming, Claire," he said from behind me.

I turned around and smiled. Then I couldn't get to the front door fast enough because tears had sprung in my eyes. Flashbacks of the day I left this home reverberated through my mind. I knew for certain that I could never, ever come back to this.

Once I pulled away from Austen's, I headed to the town square and drove around. I wasn't ready to go back to Mom's. When I looked at my phone, I saw that Linda had called, so I returned her call.

"Hey, girlfriend! Where are you?" she asked.

"Can you meet me at Villainous Grounds for a quick cup of coffee?"

"Now?"

"Yes."

"Sure. Should I call Carole?"

"Please. I just came from seeing Austen."

"Okay. We're on it."

Seeing the charming new coffee shop on the corner of the town square was just what I needed. I longed to relax with friends who understood my situation. The aroma was divine from the first step inside. Oh, what I would've given to have had this place when I lived here!

I placed an order and found a table where I hoped to be joined by my longtime friends. The place was terribly busy, which was good to see. I didn't want to run into anyone I knew because I wasn't in a very good mood and suspected that my unexpected crying had ruined my makeup. I stared at a large, beautiful quilt on the wall and wondered who might have made it.

Fifteen minutes later, Carole and Linda entered together and headed my way. They each gave me big hug.

"Let's get our coffee, Linda," Carole suggested. "You just sit here and relax for a bit, Claire."

I smiled as I watched them order. It was obvious they were no strangers to this new business endeavor and even seemed to know the folks behind the counter. Armed with their specialty coffees, they joined me.

"Just start from the beginning," Linda instructed as they got seated.

I took a deep breath and tried to retrace my steps. They listened intently without interruption. When I told them that I went over and kissed Austen on the cheek, I could see Linda tear up.

"How do you feel now?" Linda asked, concerned.

I paused and then said, "That's a good question. I do feel like my mission has been accomplished. There isn't much more I can do. He knows I'm not angry with him, and he knows I care. My actions could've easily been interpreted as pity."

"I remember Bernice," Carole mentioned. "She must be helping him. She's a sweetheart."

"You always know everyone," I teased, giving us a much-needed laugh.

"I'm sure he needs help," Linda said.

"He said the office was being remodeled, which means he could go back to work. That's a good thing."

"Actually, that would be a good thing for his patients to see, don't you think?" Linda expressed.

We nodded in agreement, knowing that Austen's determination could be an inspiration to the young people he served.

A woman came out from behind the counter and stopped by to ask, "Can I get you ladies anything?"

"Claire, this is Mary Jo, the owner," Carole said. "Claire used to live here but moved to Wisconsin."

"Nice to meet you, Claire," she responded, "and welcome back. The girls have mentioned you often. I hope to get to Door County one day."

"I really like your shop! What a wonderful addition to downtown!" I said enthusiastically.

"Thank you. We're grateful for how the community has responded," she said graciously.

"I love the quilt on the wall," I mentioned.

"Oh, my mother did that. She's a quilter who never stops!"

"Claire is an art quilter," Linda added.

"Well, tell her I like it very much," I said, glancing back at the beautifully quilted piece.

"Will do. She never gets tired of compliments," Mary Jo said laughingly before she returned to the counter to serve the next customer.

Chapter 15

"So, what would you like to do this evening?" Carole asked with excitement. "Do you want to come over to my house for dinner?"

"Thanks, but I need to spend some time with Mom," I responded. "I may try to fly back tomorrow."

"Tomorrow? You just got here," Carole replied in disbelief.

"Yes, I know, but I did what I came to do," I admitted. "I feel the need to get home and see Grayson."

"I can understand that," Linda said. "Was he supportive of your reasoning for seeing Austen?"

"He was," I replied. "I guess I wasn't prepared to enjoy any of this visit. You both have been wonderful about it, as has Mom. I hope you understand."

"Sure," Carole said kindly. "We're just glad we got to visit with you at all."

"Before I leave you gals, do you have any updates about how your sales are going in Door County?" I asked. Both had come to Door County to help with the outdoor quilt show. While in the area, they also made contacts with shops to consign some handmade items and a cookbook.

They started talking at once about the failures and successes they'd had after having met with businesses in Door County while in town for the quilt show. It seemed to have been good exposure for both of them.

"I'm so glad you've had some success," I said, smiling. "Someday, I'll find out the real reason Carole ended up limping as she left Door County."

They burst into laughter, exchanging knowing glances.

"We followed the rule!" Carole said boisterously.

Together we chanted, "What happens in Door County stays in Door County!" We laughed even harder at ourselves.

Before I said goodbye, I called Mom to see if I could bring something home for dinner.

"Honey, I made my homemade chicken and dumplings this afternoon, but we can have that another time if you've made other plans."

"My goodness! Did you roll out the dumplings like you used to?"

"Of course. You give me too much credit. It's not that hard," she protested.

"Keep it on the stove. I'll be right home."

"Well, it appears that she's still spoiling you," Linda teased. "You know how much she loves doing that for you."

I nodded in agreement and smiled. "I wish she lived closer," I said, feeling sad. "It means a lot to me that the two of you look out for her."

"You know you can count on us to do anything for her, don't you?" Carole said, gently touching my hand.

"Thank you both," I said, realizing I was about to cry. "I love you, and I promise the next time I come home, I'll stay longer." As I hugged them, they promised they'd come to Door County for the next quilt show in July.

Tears sprung to my eyes as I drove home. When I pulled into Mom's driveway, I saw a large Cadillac that I didn't recognize. When I walked inside, there sat Mr. Vogel.

"Well, hello, Claire," he said warmly as he stood. "I haven't seen you in a long time."

"My goodness, it has been a while," I replied. "How've you been? Mom tries to keep me informed. Are you doing well?"

"I'm fine, and we can talk about that later, but we're both just concerned about how your day has gone," he said, looking at me with a kind expression. "I understand that you went to see Dr. Page."

"I did," I said, emitting a big sigh as I collected my thoughts. "I guess I'd say he's progressing. He plans to go back to the office when they finish making some renovations there."

"That's good news!" Mom exclaimed.

"Are you staying for dinner?" I asked Mr. Vogel. "If not, you'll miss a great meal."

"I'm sorry, but I have another engagement, so I just stopped by to say hello," he explained. "Now, I have to say, I've enjoyed her chicken and dumplings a time or two, and I can only hope there might be some left over," he said, chuckling.

"I'm sure there will be," Mom said.

"You know, your mother and I have a lot of memories that we share," he said. "But when one of us can't remember something, the other one tries to help out." They laughed. "Your dad was a lucky man. I was, too, with my wife. There aren't many of us left here in town from our original group of friends."

"I'm sure that's a strange feeling," I said softly. "Having a supportive group of friends is so important. I'm so happy you have one another."

"We try to keep each other informed with the goings-on in town, and I'm lucky enough to enjoy some delicious home cooking every now and then."

Mom blushed, but I noticed how carefully she listened to the things Mr. Vogel said.

"Mr. Vogel, if you're ever up for traveling, I'd love for you to visit Door County," I shared.

"Your mother never stops talking about how charming it is," he replied. "I'm glad you're happy there. I have an old friend in Green Bay I haven't seen in a long time, so I suppose it's not out of the question. Well, I need to be on my way now. It was good to see you, Claire. Next time you're in town, I'd love to take the two of you to dinner."

"I'll look forward to that!" I said.

Mom walked him to the porch, and I smiled as I observed the two of them. I watched to see if there would be an embrace or a kiss, but they parted with only a friendly wave to say goodbye.

Chapter 16

"It was nice of him to stop by," I said to Mom when she came back in the house.

"It was. We were both curious to hear how your visit with Austen went."

With that, we went into the kitchen, where I poured some wine and Mom checked on the dumplings.

"It went better than expected," I said softly.

"You don't have to tell me every detail, honey."

"Well, I almost walked away when no one answered, but Bernice from his office was there and finally answered the door."

"Well, I'm glad he has someone there to help him. You mentioned a Bernice when you lived with him."

"She wasn't present for our talk, but with my visit there today, she now knows that Austen and I are still friends."

We sat down to enjoy the delicious dumplings. Mom had also stopped and gotten bread from Hoeckele's Bakery & Deli.

"Remember when I used to make that Jell-O and banana dessert for you? Is it still your favorite dessert?"

I giggled. "I hope not, but I did love it, didn't I?"

"Well, I have some in the refrigerator, and I still have some chocolate chip cookies left from last week. How about it?"

I laughed and gave her a nod of approval.

My first bite of the familiar dessert brought back many memories of our family sitting around the kitchen table as I was growing up. I had forgotten how delicious Jell-O was. It's funny how the simplest things often seem to be the best. Tonight I'd eaten like this would be my last meal. It was tempting to think about taking the leftovers on the plane.

After we cleaned up, I checked the computer for flights going out of St. Louis. There was one leaving tomorrow afternoon, so I booked it.

Mom usually turned in early, and I did the same since I had a big day tomorrow. Instead of sleeping, I found myself wide awake reflecting on my visit with Austen. I envisioned what my life would be like if I'd agreed to go back to him while he was in a wheelchair. I tried to shake the thought. I had a lot to look forward to in Fish Creek. Thanksgiving was coming, followed by Christmas, my favorite season. I was looking forward to spending time at Rachael's tree farm. Perhaps Grayson and I could share the coming holidays as a couple. I had two big to-dos before Christmas arrived. Kelly needed a red-and-white quilt, and Grayson needed a painting. Finally, I wanted to convince Mom to join me at Christmastime. Michael could easily drive her to Door County. The three of us were all we had, and I'd love to have them join me for the holiday. I finally dozed off, feeling like I was pulled between two different worlds.

Chapter 17

I slept in the next morning, which also brought back memories of my teenage years. I could still remember hearing Mom fuss at me for sleeping too late. I also remember that when my dad died, I stretched across this bed and cried like never before. It's funny how smells, sights, and sounds can take you back to the past so quickly.

Saying goodbye to Mom wasn't easy, but it helped that she held back her emotions and agreed that visiting at Christmas wasn't completely out of the question.

I texted Cher that I was returning early since things had gone well with Austen. She suggested that we get together at the Bayside when Rachael was working again. We'd done that several times before, and it sounded like just the comfort I needed. Door County was my new life, and the thought of that made me smile.

My flight to Green Bay was delayed by an hour, but I had a great time people watching. The time flew by, and then I heard the call to board the plane. It was interesting to see whether people were joyful or sad to be taking this particular flight. There were business folks who worked from their phones and computers like their lives depended on it.

Unfortunately, when I arrived in Green Bay, it was dark. That meant I'd miss the beautiful scenery as I entered Door County. I stopped for coffee at a fast-food place in Sturgeon Bay. The caffeine would help keep me awake on my drive to Fish Creek. There was little traffic, which offered another chance to reflect on my trip.

When I pulled into my driveway, it felt like the whole neighborhood was asleep. I turned on the lights, and Puff was nowhere to be found. Had Cher picked her up and taken her home with her after all? Her food and water bowls showed me she'd been using them, so I kept calling her name. I took my suitcase upstairs and thought perhaps she'd be waiting for me on the bed, but she wasn't there. I looked in the other rooms, continuing to call her name. Finally, when I went back to my bedroom, I spied her coming out from under the bed. I swooped her up and gave her a hug.

"Why were you hiding? I told you I'd return."

Her sweet little face looked up at me like she didn't believe a word I'd said. I placed her in her spot on the bed to let her know she'd be there for the rest of the night. When I undressed and joined her, I wondered to myself whether she'd stayed under the bed the whole time I was gone. I quickly drifted off to sleep, happy to be in my own bed.

The next morning, Puff walked across my face, which naturally woke me up. What a welcome home! It was time to feed her and fall into my typical routine. I proceeded downstairs, fed Puff, made a cup of coffee, and headed back upstairs to unpack. While there, I dove into pulling out my fall and winter clothes. This seasonal task always took more time than I imagined it would. My phone rang, and I could see that it was Frances from the quilt club.

"Well, what a nice surprise to hear from you," I answered.

"It's so nice to talk to you," she said pleasantly. "I'm calling to invite you to a little gathering I'm having at my house."

"Oh, how nice."

"I typically invite my book club for such a meeting, but instead, I'm having the Quilters of the Door, whom I am quite fond of, as you know."

"Well, I'll look forward to it. Tell me more."

"I'll have it next week when my medium is free. Have you ever been to a séance, Claire?"

"A séance, like where someone tells your fortune?" I asked innocently.

"Kind of. It's not a scary thing by any means. The medium is quite delightful and has a good reputation for being accurate in her readings. Rachael asked to meet her because she knew I was aware of someone who could put people in touch with a person who had passed. When I arranged for them to meet, Rachael suggested that I invite the rest of the club."

"Oh, I see. I guess I'm open to anything. If Rachael's comfortable with it, I suppose I am as well."

Chapter 18

"That's the spirit!" she said. "No pun intended, of course."

"Can I bring anything? I'm excited to see your beautiful home. I hear that you have some lovely antiques."

"Yes, way too many, I'm afraid. The house has been in the family for generations. Just bring yourself. I'm located in downtown Sturgeon Bay, so I'm easy to find. I live close to Olivia."

"Is she coming?"

"Yes, she is. Perhaps you and Cher can drive together."

"Good idea. Thanks for the invitation."

I hung up in absolute wonder. What did Rachael have in mind? Was she hoping to connect with Charlie? I didn't know Frances well, but I knew she had an interest in the supernatural and loved spending time at the graveyard visiting her deceased husband.

As soon as I'd had a little something to eat, I called Cher.

"Welcome back!" she answered. "How was your trip? Can you meet at the Bayside tonight? Rachael is working."

"Yes, of course, but I'm dying to find out more about this séance Frances invited the quilt club to attend."

"What? Are you serious?"

"Yes. She knows a medium, and when Rachael requested to meet with her, Frances decided to invite all of us."

"Rachael wants to do this?"

"It seems so. It probably has to do with Charlie. I think Olivia is coming, but I'm not sure who else. I want to go. Are you in?"

"Are you sure you want to go? It could be a real downer. Honestly, I don't know if I'm up for it."

"How do you know that it's going to be a downer? I look at these things as entertainment. You can't take it seriously. Cher, what if she tells you that she sees a tall, handsome man in your future?"

Cher sighed. "Okay, okay. I'll go. I sure don't want to hear about what happens secondhand."

"Surely Marta and Greta won't come."

"I guess we'll know more when we talk to Rachael tonight. Can you meet at seven o'clock?"

"Sounds good. Okay, see you there," I said, hanging up.

I busied myself by getting out all my painting supplies and setting up my easel. I took my time since the enclosed porch was an inviting space this time of year. Once setup was complete, I took a break, prepared a cup of hot tea, and let my mind drift back in time to when I'd met a fortune-teller while in art school. We'd had an overnight party, and my friend invited a person who'd boasted that she could read our fortunes. I'd just broken up with my boyfriend, so I was anxious to know what my future looked like. When it was my turn, she looked at my palm, and I told her I was totally done with men for a long time. She started laughing hysterically. She said, "Girl, I can tell you right now that without a man in your life, you'd be like a wild woman in the streets." I've never forgotten that. Thankfully, I've never had to find out if she'd been telling the truth.

As I got back to my easel, I felt a sense of calmness. It felt good to get Austen out of my thoughts. I wanted to call Grayson to make myself feel even better but decided against it. He sure didn't need to know my personal thoughts about Austen. I was set up to begin painting but then looked at my watch. I had to get cleaned up for my big night out at the Bayside. Just then I got a text and was delighted to see that it was from Grayson.

[Grayson]
Back home?

[Claire]
Yes, late last night.

[Grayson]
I'm glad to hear it. I know someone who would like to meet you sometime. Let's get together soon.

[Claire]
Sure. Anytime.

That was the end of the texting. Who could Grayson have in mind for me to meet? It made me curious, but I guess I'd just have to wait until he was ready to let me know.

I showered and dressed, slipping on another pair of blue jeans. I hadn't had much food to speak of during the day, so a Bayside burger would taste wonderful. I could feel that the temperature had dropped, so I decided to drive instead of walk.

When I arrived, it was another full house at the Bayside Tavern. Walking in, I waved to Rachael. She blew me a kiss and pointed to the table where Cher was waiting. I passed a few other tables of locals enjoying their meals and sat down next to my best friend. Within a short time, Rachael walked our way and said we needed a group hug since we hadn't seen one another for a while.

"How was the meeting with Austen?" Rachael asked.

"Bittersweet, but all in all, I accomplished what I went to do. It wasn't ugly, which was a relief, but it was awkward. I even gave him a kiss on the cheek before I left."

"How did that go over?" Cher asked.

"I don't know." I shrugged. "I didn't turn around to see his reaction."

"Good for you, Claire Bear."

"He must've been a real jerk for you to feel that you had to run away from him," Rachael stated. "Hey, let me get you started on drinks."

Rachael put in our drink orders and took our food order when she returned with the drinks. We decided to talk to her about the séance when she took her break.

Chapter 19

My hamburger was better than ever, and Door County's Spotted Cow beer hit the mark. I looked across the room and saw Bayside regulars Nettie and Fred sitting at the bar. It was also interesting to see the younger crowd around the bar flirting with one another.

Finally, it was time for Rachael's break, and she joined us as we finished eating.

"We wanted to talk to you about the invitation we got from Frances about the séance she's going to have," I stated.

"Are you going?" she asked.

"Yes," Cher responded. "We're quite curious about it."

Rachael took a deep breath. "Well, I haven't shared with you about some of the strange things that have been happening around the farm each day that only Charlie would do or know about," Rachael explained.

"You're serious?" I questioned.

She nodded. "Even Harry is baffled at times," she added.

"So, you believe Charlie's spirit is around?" Cher asked.

"There's something going on. At first, I thought it was my imagination, but when Harry picked up on some things, I knew it wasn't just me. He doesn't want to talk about it much. I know Frances has connections to that sort of thing, so what do I have to lose?"

"I suppose I'd do the same thing," I admitted.

"Ginger called and said she's coming," Rachael shared. "I think there's something going on between Ginger and Allen. She seems rather stressed."

I thought of Ginger's recent request to have lunch with me. "I hope not," I said, concerned. "I sure like them both."

"I'd bet everyone will come to the séance except Marta and Greta," Rachael guessed. "We'll most likely be expelled after this."

"Don't be silly," I laughed. "We have to make sure we vote in some new members!"

"We will," Cher agreed. "The Bears are back, and things are going to change."

That gave me a chuckle.

"Well, I'd better get back on the clock," Rachael said as she looked at her watch. "I sure appreciate both of you coming in."

When she walked away, Cher and I looked at each other in disbelief.

"So, Charlie is alive and well, huh?" Cher joked. "Maybe he's not all that happy about the relationship between Rachael and Harry."

"You know, you have to believe folks when they tell you about these experiences. What if something like that happened to you and no one believed you?"

"I'm not going to answer that," Cher said, shaking her head. "So, do you want to have another drink or go home?"

"Whatever you want to do."

"Well, there's nothing to attract my fancy over there at the bar, so I may as well go home and read one of my trashy romance novels."

I chuckled. "Good heavens. Are you still reading that stuff?"

"Hey, don't knock it. I don't have Grayson Wills knocking at my door like you do."

At that, we gathered our things and headed outside.

Chapter 20

The next day, all I could think about was what our evening would be like at the séance. I saw Tom bagging leaves out front, so I motioned for him to come to the porch.

"Can you hang my Christmas lights again this year?" I asked.

"Sure. You want everything outlined on the cabin just like last year?"

"Yes, and I think you did a few bushes. The lights are in the shed, but if you need more, just let me know."

"Are you going to get another big tree to put on your porch again? That sure was something to see from the road."

I smiled. "Yes, I am. It helps working at the Christmas tree farm because they deliver it."

"It must be fun to work there. If they need any extra help, I might be available. Otherwise, I just do snow removal for some folks on Cottage Row."

"I'll remember that."

"Say, I noticed that you finally had a fire out here in your pit."

I smiled. "It was wonderful. I should've done it sooner. Thanks for having the kindling set up."

"No problem! Well, I'd better go. I'll get those lights up before Thanksgiving. How about that?"

"That would be great!"

As my day flew by, it wasn't long before it was time to get dressed for the atypical evening at Frances's house. For once, I didn't wear jeans. I didn't want to come across as a country bumpkin to the medium. I was sure she could easily make judgments about us based on our appearances. I made a quick call to Cher and offered to drive. First, I fixed us a snack of grapes and cheese to munch on our way to Sturgeon Bay since we had no idea whether there would be food or not. Cher had just gotten off work, so she left her car parked in front of the gallery.

"How was your day?" I asked. "Were you busy?"

She nodded. "Yes, but today's customers had little interest in quilts, which makes me sad. It's hard for me to sell some of the other things when I know so little about the artist or how the product's made."

"Well, Carl needs to build a clientele of people who are quilt buyers, and that takes time. I'm almost done with the White Gull Inn painting with the quilts on it. Hopefully, it'll sell quickly."

We chatted about the rest of her day as I drove. With the aid of my GPS, the house was easy to find. Parking was not a problem, and we soon found ourselves at the front door.

"Welcome, welcome!" Frances said when we arrived. "We're meeting around the dining room table, but feel free to tour the rest of the house."

"Frances, this is like a museum," Cher said as she stepped inside. "Your Victorian décor is perfect for this lovely house. I'd love to hear more about some of these beautiful pieces."

"I grew up in this house, and some of these antique pieces haven't been moved since I was a girl," Frances stated. "I don't know what'll happen to all of this when I'm gone. Ladies, there's punch on the sideboard in the dining room. Please help yourself. Olivia and Ginger are already here, and I see Rachael heading to the door now."

Frances's fancy place was darker than I preferred, and it reminded me a lot of a funeral parlor. Cher and I got some refreshments and continued to look around the dining room. The cranberry punch in the huge crystal bowl was delicious, and there were trays of candy displayed on various pieces of furniture.

"Hey!" Olivia cried out to us. "Are you ready for this?"

"I guess we'll find out," I said as Rachael joined us. I wondered where Lee and Ava were. We had nervous laughter in our voices as we chatted. Suddenly, Frances and someone unfamiliar entered the room.

"Ladies, please welcome my friend and guest, Celest Morgan," she said. "She's going to entertain you this evening and perhaps be able to answer some questions. Celest, these are my fellow Quilters of the Door."

With that simple introduction, we went around the table telling Celest our first names.

"Nice to meet you all," she responded.

Celest was a short, round woman who appeared to be in her sixties. Her dark hair had gray streaks that were pronounced in her unkempt bun. Her face was heavily made up, and her lacy dress showed plenty of cleavage underneath her strands of jewelry. She seemed pleasant enough and struck me as someone who would be fun to be around.

The doorbell rang, and Frances left to greet Ava, who was always late. We made small talk until Ava was settled at the table.

"I'm sorry to be late," she said apologetically. "I took a wrong turn or two on the way here. Frances, I just love coming here. This house speaks to me. I just love it."

I had to chuckle to myself. Ava always made a grand entrance.

"Thank you, Ava," Frances responded. "It's such a privilege to have you all here. A few minutes ago, I heard from Lee. She had something come up and won't be able to join us. As you know, we're here tonight to learn some things about ourselves. Celest has quite a reputation for being able to reach those who have left us and for reading personalities. She's available for private sessions, so before you ask your questions, you might consider that more private venue. Her cards are here in the center of the table."

"Thank you for inviting me, Frances," she began. "We've had some interesting gatherings in this lively dining room. I never know how successful an evening will be. Some folks are easier to read than others, and some put up defenses when it comes to their past. There isn't anything magical about what I do, but I know it's a gift that most don't have. When I was a child, I could read individuals' minds and actions. At that young age, I didn't realize how unique my gift was. I want to assure you that I'll keep my comments light and positive under these circumstances."

"That's good to know," Cher replied. "I've never been to one of these meetings."

Chapter 21

"In a group such as this, I'll ask Frances to dim the lights, so you won't be distracted by all the beautiful things in the room. Concentrate on her lovely chandelier so I can pick up any vibes from you. I may get vibrations from some but not others. Frances hasn't shared details about any of you other than that you are members of her quilt club."

"That's true," Frances concurred.

Celest looked to the ceiling and closed her eyes. The room became quiet. "My first sound is music from a big band. Someone in this room is quite the singer and loves to have a good time. You've had a disappointment lately, but your happy soul will sustain you, despite some fear that lingers on."

Of course, we transferred our gazes from the chandelier to Ava, and her face looked like she'd seen a ghost. She lowered her head and stared into her lap. One by one, we looked at the chandelier again.

"I know you're all quilters, but the only visual I'm getting in that regard is that there's a man holding a framed Blue Star quilt pattern of some kind. He's trying to get the attention of someone in this room. He appears concerned and is sending a warning of some kind. He's holding the item over his head and swaying it back and forth like he wants attention." She paused as we waited for more. "I'm sorry. He just went away."

We then looked around the table at one another, and I saw Rachael wipe a tear from her eye. I didn't know what to make of it. The block Celest described could've been a barn quilt. At this point, none of us were looking at the light fixture anymore.

Suddenly, Celest continued with, "Oh, he's returned and is standing in a grove of evergreen trees. If that means anything to someone, please see me later." Celest paused. Then she said, "Is there someone here searching for one of their parents? He's smiling and wants you to know he's now on the other side but thinks of you every day."

Suddenly, Olivia stood up and retreated to the kitchen. That led me to believe that Celest had struck a nerve with her. Despite the disruption, Celest forged ahead.

"One of you really doesn't want to be here tonight," Celest said slowly. "You're afraid of some secret coming out. I won't reveal it even if I discover it. We all have secrets of some kind. One of you has a special relationship with a man, but I see only half of him. He has a woman standing far behind him. Now he's gone."

Well, that could be Grayson, but it was so general that it could be any of us. Cher looked at me with wide eyes.

"I think I need to look closer and more directly into some of you," Celest announced as she stared at Ginger. "You're hurting inside, but don't fear. Your future looks extremely bright."

Celest's gaze landed on Cher. After a moment, Celest said, "I smell the fragrance of an iris in bloom," she began. "The person has faded, but the fragrance remains. You loved this person very much. It's a female who cares for you and wants you to notice someone who has a handicap of some kind."

Cher looked upset. I knew her mother loved irises and had collected many varieties in her garden over the years.

Celest then looked at Rachael. "I think you're the one who's connected to the Blue Star pattern," Celest said, as if it had appeared again.

Celest then looked at Frances. "Frances, as you know, I have shared more than one vision with you. You are an open book and very receptive to the spirits that try to contact you. The rest of you, please remember that if you feel a connection, you shouldn't be afraid."

"Well, Celest, would you like to take a break for folks to ask questions?" Frances suggested.

We heard the door close. Olivia still hadn't returned, so she must be going home.

"I'll be happy to visit a bit with any of you," she reassured us. "Don't forget to take one of my cards. If you want further information, I'll try to help you. A group setting can be intimidating."

We nodded in agreement, but there wasn't one question brought forth at the table. However, Ava followed Celest to the buffet. I watched to see if she was going to ask Celest a question, but what I thought I saw was disturbing. When Celest walked away, Ava picked up a small silver Christmas bell that was sitting by the floral arrangement. She actually put it in her purse! I blinked and tried to convince myself that I didn't really see Ava steal something from Frances.

Cher was trying to catch my eye. She already had our coats over her arm and was prepared to leave. We thanked Frances and Celest for a nice evening and told Frances we'd see her soon at quilt club. I kept watching Ava, who seemed to lag behind the rest of us. When Cher and I got in the car, we checked our phones before getting on the road.

"Poor Olivia," Cher said. "That news tonight had to be difficult for her. I'm not sure that should've been revealed in front of all of us."

"Well, Celest was just doing her job, I guess. The vision of half a man in my life with a woman standing behind him sure puzzles me."

"Yeah, and so did the irises, but I don't know anyone handicapped, so that part didn't make sense to me."

"Maybe you haven't met him yet," I teased. "On another note, I shouldn't say anything, but I think I saw Ava put something in her purse. I hope I'm wrong."

"What? Are you sure?"

I nodded. "Now I'm thinking that Ericka's missing rings might be at Ava's house."

"No, Claire. Remember? She found them."

"She did?" I asked in disbelief.

"Yes, I thought I told you. Ericka had to have the plumber in to fix her drain, and one of the rings was stuck in the kitchen drain. They didn't find the other one."

"Oh, thank heavens. I sure didn't want to think it was Ava."

"Ericka feels bad about mentioning Ava as the possible thief. At least she found the more valuable one."

"Then what did I just see?"

Chapter 22

"I guess all I can take from this evening is that Austen is supposed to be on my mind. Celest does have a gift, but how seriously we can take what she says is another thing entirely," I commented.

"Poor Ginger. I hope she was encouraged by the message of her having a bright future," Cher said. "I'm not sure this exercise was a good idea for our club, though. I want to get to know everyone better, but I'm fine not knowing their dark secrets."

"I think Frances has a gift, too. Remember when she told me to see the guy who looked like Clark Gable? That was Carl, and she was right about him taking my work."

We arrived at the gallery. I dropped Cher off by her car and headed back to the cabin. Once inside, I got a call. It was Rachael.

"Hey, is everything okay?"

"It's Charlie. It must be Charlie. I knew immediately when Celest said there was a Blue Star quilt pattern that it was Charlie. It was his favorite barn quilt pattern that I made. I sense he's concerned about what might be happening between Harry and me."

"Oh, my. I hope you're not reading too much into this."

"We have a red and green star that we put on the barn at Christmas. Otherwise, it's a blue-and-white star that always hangs on the barn."

"I see. Well, I wouldn't dwell on it if I were you. Has anyone heard from Olivia? Celest hit a nerve, I guess. I felt bad for her."

"I haven't heard from her, but I'll call her tomorrow. I'm going to make a private appointment with Celest. I want to know about anything involving Charlie."

"Oh, Rachael, be careful," I warned.

"I will be," she assured me. "Hey, don't forget that Black Friday is your first day of work. Harry is coming tomorrow to set up the tree stands."

"I'm ready."

I said good night and got ready for bed. What an unusual night. I had a lot to think about, including what I witnessed from Ava. Could I have been mistaken? It was a relief to know that she didn't have a part in stealing Ericka's rings, but what happened tonight? I finally said my prayers and fell into a deep sleep.

The next morning as I was having coffee and reading my emails, I got a call from Michael. Hearing from him unexpectedly always caused me to worry that it meant something had happened to Mom.

"Hey, Sis. I'm sorry I missed your Missouri visit. I was away on a business trip. You sure didn't stay long."

"I know, but my main reason for visiting was to see Austen. I guess by now you've heard about his accident. He's in a wheelchair."

"Yes, I heard about it from several sources."

"Oh, I'm sure you did. Did you hear it from the same person who told you I was having financial difficulties?"

He laughed good-naturedly at my sarcasm and then asked, "Well, how did it go?"

"It went as well as could be expected. At least I got to express my feelings."

"Feelings?"

"All this time, I've felt guilty that he had the accident on his way to see me. I'm still concerned about whether he will walk again or not."

"I know. It had to be surreal to see him in that condition. So, Mom was good?"

"Yes. I got my fix of comfort food, which was great."

"Boy, I could use some of that right now."

"I told Mom that both of you need to come to Door County for Christmas. I don't think I want her going on an airplane without a companion."

"I agree. We'll see."

"She really enjoyed it here last Christmas. Truly, you would, too."

"Let me see how things shake out here at work this fall. If we come, we'll drive."

"It's not a bad drive unless you run into a snowstorm or two," I joked.

"Let's not worry about that now," he responded, laughing. "I'm glad you called, Michael. Have a good Thanksgiving!"

"You, too!"

Chapter 23

A week went by without a word from my quilting friends or Grayson. I still wondered who he wanted me to meet. At this point, it was the peak of color in Door County. There were events happening all around, and echoes of the Fall Harvest Fest occurring in Fish Creek were reverberating everywhere. The traffic was endless! Cher was working more and more hours at the gallery as a result.

I was trimming herbs in the backyard when my cell rang. My heart stopped when I saw it was Grayson.

"How's my sweetheart? Is she still speaking to me?"

"She's missing you, that's for sure," I replied.

"I feel bad I didn't tell you about flying to Miami for a boat show," he confessed.

"Miami? I'll bet you're getting a lot of sunshine there."

"I'm seeing it from the inside, I'm afraid. We're in a great hotel and convention center, but there isn't any beach time, unfortunately. How are things going with you?"

"Well, it's definitely fall, and I don't know if Tom will ever be able to keep up with all the leaves that have accumulated in my yard. When are you returning?"

"In a couple of days. Marsha's sister is staying with Kelly. Have you made any Thanksgiving plans?"

"Not really, but I work the next day at the Christmas tree farm, so I might spend it with Harry and Rachael. Are you going to Marsha's sister's home like last year?"

"Yes, that's our plan. Kelly really looks forward to seeing all her cousins."

We chatted for a few more minutes, but the conversation served as a reminder that I was only a girlfriend to Grayson and wasn't quite ready for a prime-time spot in his family activities.

I went inside, cleaned myself up, and decided to go for a walk. I hadn't been to the post office in a couple of days, and I could stop at the gallery and say hello to Carl and Cher on my way there. As I was getting ready to leave, Puff kept following me around. I wondered if Cher ever took Puff anywhere. I picked the furry bundle up and put her on the wicker chair on the porch that she claimed. She looked at me sadly as I made my exit. We've come a long way, Puff and I.

Once outside, I was immediately glad I'd worn a hoodie. The wind was brisk as I wove in and out of the crowd making my way to the gallery.

"Well, look who's here," Cher exclaimed when I entered. "Did you bring us something to sell?"

"Now, what kind of greeting is that?" I asked.

"Hey, Claire!" Carl greeted.

"Carl has a birthday today, Claire," Cher said teasingly, as if she'd been reminding him of it all day.

"Well, happy birthday, Carl!" I said, matching Cher's exuberance about Carl's special day.

"It's just another day," he murmured. Changing the subject, he asked, "How's that painting coming along?"

"Great!" I assured him. "I think I can bring it in next week. I'm pleased with it, but in the future, I think I need to do smaller ones."

"It'll give the customers more choices as well," Carl agreed.

After the three of us chatted for a while, I said, "I'm off to get my mail, and then I might treat myself to a cup of joe at the coffee shop. I'll let you two get back to work."

"Why don't you take a break and join her?" Carl suggested to Cher.

"Are you sure?" Cher responded, surprised.

"Go!" Carl reassured her as he waved his hand.

"Happy birthday!" I repeated as we made our exit.

"Nice boss, huh?" Cher said as we began walking.

"I'll say," I agreed. "Does he ever talk about family other than his sister? I'm still assuming he's single."

"I don't think there's a wife, but honestly, his private life is just that. Very private. When I heard he didn't have any plans for his birthday, I suggested that we get a drink after work."

I looked at Cher with an expression of surprise on my face. "Oh, really? And what did he have to say to that?"

She laughed. "It definitely caught him off guard. He hesitated, but after I teased him about being an old scrooge, he agreed to a quick drink at Alexander's. He seems to like that place. He drew the line at dinner, though."

"I have to admit that Alexander's is a step up from our Bayside Tavern. So, Cher Bear, you have a date tonight!"

"I hardly think of it that way, but I do owe him a lot for giving me this job. I have to admit, what little money I make is coming in handy."

"I'm happy for you. Let me know how the evening goes. Now, don't drink more than two glasses of wine. You know how you get, and I won't be there to warn you."

She giggled.

"Carl is your boss, remember?" I asked, giving her a mock-stern look.

"Who's bossy here?" she laughed, shaking her head.

Chapter 24

Late the next day, I put the last stroke on my White Gull Inn painting. As I stepped back to admire it, I got a call from Cher.

"Do you have dinner plans tonight?" she asked, sounding upset.

"No, but I do have a wonderful pot of chili going if you want to join me. I can whip up some corn bread."

"Wow, what a stroke of luck! I wasn't going to call, but I'll take you up on that if I can bring some wine."

"I have plenty of that, so don't bother. How about around five since it gets dark so early now?"

"Sure! I'll see you then."

I finished cleaning my paintbrushes and then cleared off the small wicker table I kept on the porch. This porch offered the only area large enough for entertainment in the cabin. I had to admit, the view was wonderful. When it was warm in the spring and summer, I opened all the windows so I could enjoy the breeze. I'd just finished setting the table when Cher arrived carrying a bag of something in her arms.

"Oh, it smells so good in here, Claire Bear. What a perfect meal for a chilly night. I brought us some cheese curds because they're great with chili. It's a Wisconsin thing, you know."

"Well, it makes sense to me. Thank you. What else is in here?"

She grinned. "I had an extra cherry pie in the freezer. I actually made it myself."

"No kidding? I'm proud of you. I've been wanting to make a cherry custard pie like Mom makes."

Cher turned her attention to the cat that was comfortably curled up on the chair on the porch. "Puff, your mama's here. Don't you want to come and say hello?" As she spoke, Cher bent down to be a little closer to Puff. Just like that, Puff made a dash upstairs, leaving us both surprised. We looked at each other and laughed at how quickly Cher had been replaced in Puff's eyes.

"What have you told her about me?" Cher joked.

"You failed to teach Puff manners, that's what," I retorted, still laughing.

"I'll bring the wine out while you fill our bowls. I'm so glad you were free to talk."

"Well, I figure it's about last night, right?"

Cher blushed. "The evening started out so awkward, but then Carl loosened up after he had a drink. That's when he decided we should just stay and have dinner."

"Dinner? Oh! What did you talk about?"

"Very little about work, which surprised me. I let him do most of the talking."

"Did he talk about other people?"

She nodded. "Yes, mostly about people who've had something to do with the gallery more than about personal friends."

"Am I detecting some personal attraction here, Cher Bear?"

"I think I could really fall for him, Claire, but there's so much I don't know."

"I'd just say to go cautiously since he's your boss, and you like your job."

"Do you think he's attractive?"

"Well, if you think Clark Gable is attractive, I'd have to say yes."

We shared a laugh at my remark but then Cher said, "It's funny how someone becomes more attractive as you get to know them. I don't think I'd look twice at him if he were someone just coming into the gallery."

"Sometimes an attraction grows. With Grayson, I first saw the red scarf and a very private man. After some time passed, I wanted to see him more and more."

"So true, and you're very lucky," Cher sighed. Then her face brightened as she looked at me and said, "So how about some of that chili?"

We dug into our meal and never stopped talking. Girl talk was always the best between the two of us. We could almost finish each other's sentences since we'd known each other so long. We discussed Thanksgiving. Cher said she'd accepted Ericka's invitation to join her family. I told her I was likely to join Rachael and Harry at the farm.

Chapter 25

The next morning, I was determined to take the completed painting to Carl. My plan was to pick up my mail on the same trip. I already felt excited to start the next painting once this one was in Carl's gallery. Carl always seemed happy to see me, but the experience of someone judging my work made me a bit nervous.

Once I was inside the gallery, Carl greeted me in his usual kind manner. I held my breath as I waited for his response after I unwrapped the painting.

"Claire, this is charming, appealing, and highly detailed," he responded.

I smiled. Whew! He liked it!

"That's all?" I joked. "I loved doing it and can't wait to start on the next one."

"I think you're onto something here, just like your small quilts."

Just then, as he held up the painting to get a closer look, he accidently knocked over a piece of pottery that was sitting on the counter. It shattered, making a loud noise, and sent shards of clay in all directions.

"Darn! I can't believe I did that," he lamented as he placed the painting on the counter.

"Don't worry," I said as I bent down and began picking up the pieces. Carl bent down to help me with the mess. It was then that I noticed something peculiar about him that I'd never observed before. His left arm wasn't moving with the same usefulness as his right. His range of motion in that arm wasn't fluid.

"Carl, I've got this," I assured him. "Go ahead and take care of business while I clean this up. You may want to vacuum later to get the fine pieces, though. I hope this piece of pottery wasn't too expensive."

"It was just plain awkward of me," he lamented. "Anyway, what do you think about us hanging your new piece right over here?"

"I'd be honored to have that spot," I replied. "So, Carl, how was the rest of your birthday?"

"It was fine. At my age, it's just another day."

He didn't mention the extended date with Cher, but I hadn't really expected him to. Now that my painting was hung, it was clear that Carl needed to attend to other customers. I said goodbye and made my way to the post office to retrieve my mail.

My mind wandered back to Carl as I walked along the charming Main Street shops of Fish Creek. Was I imagining his inability to use his left arm, or was there something else to it? What would cause such a thing? I might ask Cher if she's noticed anything.

My thoughts then left Carl and his arm and moved on to the joy of seeing my painting hanging in the gallery just minutes before. I felt proud to see it there. Since the success of our Door-to-Door quilt show last July, I'd been excited about my idea to paint local buildings with quilts hanging from them. What building should I choose for my next painting? I'd taken a lot of photos during the quilt show, but one of my favorites was of O'Meara's Irish House. I loved the green Irish chain quilt hanging alongside their sign. It seems I'd made up my mind to feature the Irish shop for my next turn at the easel.

When I returned to the cabin, I spotted Puff on the counter licking up some leftover corn bread. Darned cat! When I reprimanded her, which I rarely do, she jumped and hit the sugar bowl, which nearly landed on the kitchen floor. I wasn't ready to clean up after another accident, so I hastily placed the bowl inside the cabinet. My mind returned to the condition of Carl's arm. Surely, Cher had noticed it, too.

I fixed some iced tea and made my way out to the porch to call Rachael. "What are you up to, barn lady?" I teased.

"Just that. I finished two barn quilts to complement the signs, so now it's time to call the customers and tell them their merchandise is ready. Customers really like being gifted a small quilt to match their larger barn quilt order. It's a great sales incentive. I don't think I'll ever change that facet of the business."

"I'd hoped to be able to help you with those, but painting is keeping me pretty occupied these days."

"I'm still counting on you, my dear," she reminded me.

"Good. Now, if your invitation to join you on Thanksgiving is still open, I think I'll accept."

"Glory be!" she shouted. "Harry will be thrilled! He's deep frying a turkey and has already claimed it will be the best ever. His son and the girls will be here as well. I'm thrilled you can come, Claire! What about Grayson? Do you want to ask him to join us?"

"He'll be with Marsha's family. It's their family tradition."

"Well, he's always welcome."

"I appreciate that. Since you pawned off your stray cat on Kelly, I'm not sure he feels safe to come around again!"

She laughed heartily at my observation.

"Kelly brought him over here to meet Puff, and it was something to see. I'm sure the two cats will have another date at some point."

"I'm so glad he found a good home."

Chapter 26

As the week went on, I realized I still hadn't heard anything from Grayson. Surely, he was back from his trip by now. It was Saturday, and time for another quilt club meeting. Today we'd be voting on whether to allow Amy from the Jacksonport Cottage to be a new member. Hopefully, Anna Marie Meyer, Marta's niece, would be the second new member joining us. Greta was likely shaking her head at the thought. She was all about keeping the group at just nine members when she was in charge.

Before I left for the club, I had just enough time to make a few sketches on my new art piece. The photo was definitely helpful, but I'd try to catch a few more details as I passed by the quaint shop.

There was a cold, light rain today, so Cher would be picking me up. We both agreed we'd have rather stayed in for the day.

"So, do you ask off work for these quilt meeting days?" I curiously asked Cher.

"He knows what days we meet, and frankly, he's starting to realize that this quilt club is important to the gallery. Lee came in last week and brought a lovely appliquéd piece to sell. She wants a lot for it, but Carl was happy to try for that price."

"Olivia should really bring in some of her work. It's modern Amish, I'd say. By the way, have you seen her since the séance?" Cher shook her head.

"I haven't either. Hey, how about lunch after the meeting?"

"Absolutely! We might as well make the most of this rainy day. Grayson said we'd get together when he got back from his trip, but I haven't heard a thing from him. We talked about going to The Waterfront."

"That's a romantic place. I hope you hear from him."

Cher and I dashed into the library from the rain to keep as dry as possible. I was glad to see Olivia after her quiet disappearance at the séance. I sat down next to Frances after I got my coffee.

"Good morning, ladies!" Marta greeted. "It's nice to see this turnout on such a gloomy day. I mentioned last month that I'd be bringing my niece, Anna Marie Meyer, to this meeting, so please give her a nice Door County welcome." We all clapped and turned our gaze toward Anna.

When she noticed all eyes on her, the poor woman turned completely red. Her blushing was in sharp contrast to her nearly white hair, which was long and pulled back in a braided bun. She wore no makeup, and her round face and blue eyes complemented her big smile. I guessed she was in her forties. Marta and Anna looked at each other so affectionately that I immediately liked her.

"Thank you, or *danke schoen*, as we say in Germany." Her words were spoken quietly, as if she were afraid she'd say something wrong. I was impressed with the fluidity of her English, though.

"We're delighted to have Anna living with us on the farm for now, especially with her baking skills," Marta explained. Everyone chuckled. "I've told her so much about the club and how diverse we are with our talents. We would learn so much from each other. When you see her delicate dimensional quilting, you'll see for yourself what I'm talking about. I asked Anna to bring the gingerbread house she made for me to enjoy during the Christmas season." We gathered closer to look.

Marta gingerly unveiled a precious calico and brown gingerbread house around twelve inches in diameter. It was embellished perfectly with rickrack, lace, and beading. The details were exquisite! She explained how Anna works on each quilted piece before she constructs the object. Anna listened and nodded at the description of her work.

"It's amazing," Lee immediately said.

"Her batting is thicker than what we'd use under normal circumstances, as she uses cardboard. Just look at her tiny stitches where she joins the pieces!"

Anna kept smiling. I thought perhaps Marta was doing all the talking because of Anna's shyness at her first meeting. We all wanted to ask questions and hear more about her work, but Marta kept us on schedule. Greta made sure of that as she stared at Marta and kept checking her watch.

"Oh, Anna, your work is wonderful," I managed to say before everyone sat back in their seat. "Thank you for bringing this." Everyone clapped as they sat down.

"Our first order of business today is to vote on Amy Burris from Jacksonport Cottage." Marta's voice was firm to get our attention and assert her new role as president of quilt club. "Here is your secret ballot to fill out. Olivia, can you collect the completed ballots from the group please? You and I can count them. Out of respect, we'll just announce whether any potential new members have been accepted or not without going into detail about the voting tallies."

I watched Greta during the process and couldn't help but wonder if she was going to vote no since she'd been so set on not introducing new members to the group when she was in charge. Greta had made it clear that when Cher moved back to town, I'd have to leave, as per the initial agreement. Cher and I were both going to drop the group, but much to Greta's disappointment, the rest rallied together to keep us both in.

Chapter 27

Everyone remained silent during the ritual of either blackballing or accepting the new member. It was a momentous occasion for this historic quilt club. While Olivia and Marta counted the votes, some refilled their coffee cups. Anna gazed only at the floor. I'm sure the process was uncomfortable for her.

When Marta and Olivia returned, I noticed the smile on Olivia's face.

"We're delighted that Amy Burris has been accepted into the Quilters of the Door," Marta announced. Everyone except Greta clapped, but she did smile.

"Now if I may, Marta, I'd like to nominate Anna Marie Meyer as our next perspective member to be voted on next month." Lee suggested. "As you saw here today, she's very diverse in what she has to offer in her quilting."

"I'll second that," chimed in Rachael.

"If there are no objections, I'd like to start the show-and-tell," Marta stated.

Greta began by showing a blue-and-white Jacob's Ladder quilt top that she was about to put in the frame. Then Olivia pulled out a table runner in all solids that she'd hand quilted in black thread. Finally, Rachael took a turn to show two Feather Star blocks she'd just completed for two barn quilt customers.

"Now you ladies are in for a rare treat," Marta announced. "When Anna arrived, much to my delight, she brought with her a family quilt that's so appropriate for this time of year. Anna, would you show the group what's in your bag?" The room fell silent in anticipation.

"This is my family's Tannenbaum Christmas quilt," she began. "According to an embroidery date on the quilt, it was completed in 1880." Everyone gathered around the table while Anna and Marta put on gloves to tenderly unwrap the quilt.

The medallion quilt was like nothing I'd ever seen. In the center was a feather tree that was delicately embroidered in a dark hunter green.

"For those of you who are not familiar with the feather tree, I'll explain," Marta offered. "These are actually dyed goose feathers wrapped around wires to create the look of pine. They get quite fragile with age, as you can imagine. The feather tree also happens to be the first artificial Christmas tree, developed in Germany. Of course, Germany is also known for its fine glass ornaments and use of natural things like strung cranberries for decorating the trees."

Frances spoke up, "I have a feather tree. It's not in good shape, though, so I haven't displayed it for years. I just can't bear to part with it because it's been in the family for so long. I used to hang antique ornaments on it, but now it's tucked away in a box."

"How lovely, Frances, that you have a real feather tree," Marta shared. She then moved her hand to another area of the quilt. “As you can see, the other blocks of this quilt are also quite something, but some are showing their age, like me.” Everyone chuckled.

We began examining all the blocks up close, but we dared not touch any of them. The poinsettias, bells, and primitive angels were just some of the appliquéd motifs.

“I’m interested in this binding,” Rachael noted. “There’s a very narrow red cording inside the gold fringe border. I’d say this outside border looks to be around three inches, wouldn’t you?”

“Yes, the fabrics used here remind me of the crazy quilts I’ve seen,” Lee agreed.

“Can we see a bit of the backing?” Olivia asked.

Marta folded back a portion of the quilt to reveal satin or a similar fabric that was in various shades of faded green.

“That’s what’s referred to as fugitive green,” Frances informed us. “The green dyes were unreliable, so in time, the vivid green dyes faded to blue and then to yellow. This corner here shows the changing of the colors.”

“What a shame about the dyes,” Greta lamented. “Do you know the quiltmaker’s name, Anna?”

“We think various kinfolk worked on this,” Anna expressed. “There are different hand skills we noticed, right, Aunt Marta?” Marta smiled and nodded.

“We just grew up calling it the Tannenbaum Christmas quilt,” Marta added. “It will now live here in the United States for the next generation to enjoy. Anna will make sure it’s taken care of.” Anna blushed.

“I absolutely love this design,” gushed Cher. “I’ve truly never seen anything like it. Claire and I both love Christmas.

Wouldn't it be grand to have a quilt like this in the family?" I nodded.

"I'd love to try to duplicate this quilt," Rachael noted. "Do you mind if we take a lot of pictures for reference?" Anna shook her head. She was beaming with pride.

"Oh, Rachael, what a grand idea!" I agreed. "It would surely take some time."

"Not if we farmed out the work, which likely happened with this quilt," Rachael countered. "Charlie would've loved to have had a Christmas tree quilt for our tree farm. His family came from Germany, and he was always talking about their traditions."

"I am so, so happy you all love it as much as I do," Anna said modestly.

Chapter 28

The Tannenbaum quilt had caused quite a stir within the group. Marta knew they'd enjoy looking at the intricacies of this old fabric, but she hadn't expected to take up so much meeting time. Greta was looking at her watch, signaling it was time to wrap up.

"Ladies, it's time that we close the meeting," Marta announced as we returned to our seats. "Let's give my niece a round of applause for sharing her quilt with us. We'll have an opportunity at the next meeting to vote on Anna joining our club. I hope you all have a wonderful Thanksgiving. I'll now accept a motion to adjourn."

Greta was quick to make the motion, and Lee seconded it. Rachael and I watched Anna and Marta closely as they folded the quilt with care. Rachael then began telling Anna about having a Christmas tree farm.

"Oh, that sounds wonderful!" she exclaimed. "We could visit, right, Aunt Marta?" Marta smiled and nodded.

"I don't think you've ever been out there, have you?" Rachael asked.

"No, but now we'll have an excuse," she replied. "Billy always cuts our tree down from our woods."

"Anna would love seeing all the barn quilts that Rachael makes," I added. "Marta, do you have a quilt on your barn?"

"No, but perhaps we'll pick one out." Marta grinned.

"Rachael is so talented. I can see why she's interested in this tree quilt."

"I'm happy you like it," Anna said. "There are so many stories that have been passed on through the years."

"Whoever has the quilt before Christmas has to display it twelve days before Christmas," Marta shared. "That's the rule."

"What's the reason for that?" asked Rachael. Marta and Anna smiled.

"Mostly for good luck," Marta answered. "I'm pleased Anna brought the quilt with her. It was at her mother's house, and her mother is in the early stages of Alzheimer's disease."

"Oh, that's terrible." I reacted. "The quilt is sure to bring comfort to the two of you. Now it'll stay in the family and make its new home in America." They beamed at the thought.

"The Quilters of the Door will help you keep it safe," Rachael assured them.

"Danke schoen," Anna said, giving Rachael a surprise hug.

Cher and I walked out of the building knowing we'd fallen in love with Anna and her Tannenbaum quilt. As we waved goodbye, my stomach was growling for lunch.

"How about the Whistling Swan for lunch today?" I suggested to Cher.

"Sure! We haven't been there in quite a while. I love the history of that place, especially the part about it being moved across the bay by horses. Considering it's so close to my house, I don't go there often enough."

"All these buildings on Main Street have quite a history."

As we walked into the restaurant, we commented about its unique décor. Checking out the menu, I noticed that it certainly was a step above the hamburgers we typically ordered at the Bayside Tavern.

"The shrimp and grits sound really good to me," Cher noted.

"I think I'll try their Cobb salad," I decided.

"I loved today's quilt meeting, didn't you?" Cher commented as we handed back our menus.

"Marta's doing a great job. It'll be interesting to see if Greta hangs in there with us as we change. I don't see why we couldn't have approved Anna's membership today."

"Don't forget, my dear: The Quilters of the Door have rules!" Cher said sarcastically. "What if someone in the group objects?"

"One change at a time, Claire. It's better than before, so we have to give them a chance. That quilt today had a lot of people thinking, especially Rachael."

"You can count on her to do something."

Chapter 29

Cher recognized some people from coming into the gallery, so she said hello as they passed by.

"I'm really going to miss the shop when Carl closes for the year after Christmas."

"I knew you would. I didn't tell you how much he liked my White Gull Inn painting. I'm going to work on the Irish shop next. I started some sketches before this morning's meeting, but I haven't gotten too far along. I was so impressed with the way O'Meara's hung that Irish Chain quilt for the show."

"I love the idea of making that your next painting, Claire Bear! I'm sure it'll turn out beautifully!"

"You know, Cher, when I was in the shop to give Carl the White Gull Inn painting, he accidently knocked over a piece of pottery. The pieces scattered everywhere."

"Oh no! I hope it wasn't one of Terri Jordon's pieces. They're quite pricey."

"I couldn't tell you who the artist was, but when Carl started to help me pick up the pieces, I noticed his left hand and arm were reacting strangely. Did he hurt himself recently? He didn't say anything, so I didn't ask about it.

I told him I could handle cleaning up the mess while he hung my painting.

"It's interesting you should say that, Claire, as now and then I've noticed something isn't right as well. I likely wouldn't have said anything if you hadn't."

"Maybe there will come a time when you can ask him about it."

"If not, it won't matter. He's so sweet and kind."

"You're becoming quite fond of him, aren't you?"

"Oh, Claire, I doubt if anything will ever come of it. I have to keep warning myself not to get my hopes up."

"You never know. I don't think he'd have asked you to work there if he hadn't been attracted to you in some way."

"It's nice that he appreciates my knowledge of quilts. I'm learning some things from him, too. I hadn't had dinner alone with a man for ages. It's funny how I keep going over everything he says to me."

"Oh, dear. That's a bad sign," I teased. "I started doing that with Grayson from the very first day we met. I do wish he had more time for me, but I know he's busy between Kelly and his work."

"Just enjoy the moment, Claire. I hope you have a good time at Rachael's for Thanksgiving."

"I will. Harry is deep frying a turkey, which will be a new experience for me. I guess I'll contribute my usual brownies. His granddaughters will love them."

"It's your signature, Claire Bear." We chuckled.

We said our goodbyes, and I went home with the intention of baking.

When I arrived at the cabin, Tom was there putting up the Christmas lights on my small cabin. A rush of excitement came over me as I envisioned the beauty from last year.

"Tom!" I yelled out to him on the ladder.

"Hey, Miss Stewart! Same as last year, right?"

"Yes, of course. I loved it."

"Well, with the prediction of snow and ice on Thanksgiving, I thought I'd better get yours and the Bittners' lights up."

"Snow and ice already? Oh my! I hadn't heard the forecast."

"It's for later in the day. Do you have plans?"

"Yes, and it involves driving."

"You'll be fine with that Subaru. I have another stop after this one, so I'll just send the bill, okay?"

"Okay. Thank you ever so much. Those lights sure cheered up the cabin last year. Happy Thanksgiving, Tom!"

"Anytime the Packers play, which is on Thanksgiving, it's a good day!" I chuckled.

Chapter 30

When I came inside to start the brownies, I wondered if Harry was okay having company on a day the Packers played. Hopefully his son was a fan, too. Thinking about the weather made me nervous, so I decided to call Rachael.

"You're not cancelling on me, are you?" she answered when she saw my name on her phone.

"No, but did you hear the forecast?"

"Yes. Harry's been talking about it. He'd love to be at the game, of course, but I'm glad he decided not to and will be cooking instead. I offered to stay with the girls so they could go, but he said his mind was made up."

"That's real dedication if you're coming before the Packers!" She chuckled.

"I told Harry I was going to encourage you to spend the night. We don't want you driving back in that weather. It's also a win for me: you'll be here at work first thing in the morning, when I'll really need you."

"I never thought of that. If it's not too much trouble, I might take you up on that offer."

"Great! I have two bedrooms for you to choose from."

"I've never been inside your house."

"It's nothing fancy because I'm in the barn all the time. You should see Harry right now. I told him I wanted a big tree inside the shop this year, so he's tackling the lights right now. I'd better go help him."

"Yes, you should. I'll see you tomorrow."

I got my brownies out of the oven and started to plan what I'd need to take for an overnight visit. As it became dark, I went outside to see the lights Tom had strung for me. They were so beautiful! I could've stood there for hours, but it was mighty cold. I couldn't compare to the Bittners' display next door, but from the street, my little place would shine brightly as folks drove by.

When I came back in, I poured myself a glass of wine to take the chill off. I was still getting used to the Door County weather. I was also feeling melancholy, so I decided to sit on the porch and call Mom.

"I hear you're getting some bad weather," Mom didn't hesitate to note.

"That's right. Rachael suggested I spend the night, so I'll be there first thing in the morning on Black Friday to work."

"Good idea. Please wish her a happy Thanksgiving for me."

"I will. Is Michael still coming?"

"Yes, and he told me he may be bringing a guest."

"That would be a first. Are you having turkey and your homemade dressing?"

"Of course. The turkey is thawing right now as we speak. Bill said he may stop by to say hello."

"That sounds like a really nice day for you."

"You have a nice day, too, honey. I sure miss you!"

"I miss you, too! Love you, Mom."

I hung up and wished she were here right now to hug. I turned on the news for a distraction but then heard my cell ring. To my surprise, it was Austen. Should I answer? Maybe I'd just let it go to my voice mail. Why in the world would he be calling? I took a deep breath and went to my voice mail to listen to his message.

"I'm sorry to have missed you," he began. "I just wanted to wish you a happy Thanksgiving. I'll never forget that first turkey you made for us when you cooked it with all the giblets inside. I have more time on my hands these days, so I just wanted to touch base."

I felt weak and bewildered. I really didn't think I'd hear from him again after my last visit. He must not be back at the hospital yet if he had so much time on his hands. I had feelings for him like I would a long-lost friend. I definitely didn't feel the same about him now that I'd had time away and met Grayson. More than anything, I felt sorry for Austen right now. As much as I wanted to be nice, I really felt I shouldn't start a conversation with him.

I sipped some wine and decided to skip dinner since I'd had a big lunch. I took my wine upstairs and started packing for my overnight trip to the farm. I flipped to the classic movie channel to entertain me the rest of the evening. I was pleased to see *Casablanca*, one of my favorites, was playing. There was something so romantic about it, and it reminded me of Grayson since he, too, loved old movies. The ending as always was a tearjerker. I soon fell asleep.

Chapter 31

Thanksgiving morning was a dreary sight. I'd have liked to have slept longer, but Puff was walking all over me.

I was hungry for breakfast since I'd skipped dinner. What could I make that was quick? I decided on frozen waffles. As I was eating, I checked the weather. The evening was calling for snow, and I dreaded what that might mean. My cell rang.

"Happy Thanksgiving," Grayson happily greeted me.

"You, too! We may get our first real snow this evening."

"Are you still going to Rachael's?"

"Yes. I'm planning to spend the night, so I'll be there first thing in the morning."

"Good idea. I'm going to miss you today."

"I'm going to miss you, too, Grayson. I called Mom last night. I hope Michael shows up at her house like he's supposed to."

"Kelly is still in bed, so I had to feed Spot again this morning. Sometimes I wonder if this is my cat or hers."

"I don't think feeding him will hurt you."

"Well, it's the only time he puts up with me. When he's hungry, it doesn't matter who feeds him. I think he knows how I feel about him."

"Now, be nice to him. I wish you could see all my Christmas lights that Tom put up for me yesterday."

"I'd like to. Say, are you free for brunch on Sunday? I'm taking a dear friend to the White Gull Inn around eleven o'clock. I've been wanting you to meet her. Would that work for you?"

"I'll make it work."

"Great. Tell Harry and Rachael Happy Thanksgiving and that I'll be out soon to get a tree."

"I will. Bye, Grayson."

"Bye, sweetie."

I laid out enough food and water for Puff for my time away and gathered my brownies and overnight bag.

"Bye, Puff. Don't get into anything you shouldn't. I'll be back tomorrow."

My drive out to the farm was a good time to reflect on all the many blessings I'd received this year. I prayed that Austen was having a pleasant day. It was odd how he kept creeping into my thoughts when I least expected it.

I was thankful to get to Rachael's before any bad weather started. The farm looked so festive. There were more garlands and lights than last year, making it a real holiday destination. Harry was the first one to see me.

"Hey, Harry! Happy Thanksgiving! What's all that hair I see on your face?"

He chuckled. "Do you like it?"

"I do! It suits you. What does Rachael have to say about it?"

"She likes it, too! What can I help you with?"

"If you'll take these brownies, I'll get my overnight bag. Any word on the weather?"

"Yup, it'll be heading our way this evening."

Once we were inside, the warmth of the potbellied stove was heavenly.

"Oh, Claire! Welcome!" Rachael said with a big hug.

I couldn't believe how beautiful the room looked. A long white tablecloth covered the table in the center of the room. It was adorned with an oblong holly centerpiece that looked so festive with Rachael's holly-themed Christmas china. In the corner was a large cut tree with lights strung around it. This barn sure suited all their entertainment needs as well as Rachael's barn quilt business.

"Wow, Rachael. You've outdone yourself! I love the tree, and it smells wonderful in here!"

"Harry said he's going to keep the girls busy stringing a popcorn garland for it. We've already popped the corn."

"We used to do that when I was a kid. We used cranberries, too."

"I thought of that, but I can just see their red-dyed fingers touching everything!"

Chapter 32

"How about some cider before Harry talks you into something much stronger?"

I chuckled. "Sounds good, Rachael. Are Kent and the girls coming soon?"

"Yes, any minute. They're so excited."

"You make a great grandmother for them." Rachael looked at me oddly then.

As I enjoyed my cider, I poured water in all the goblets.

"Now, before the place goes crazy, I want to share some ideas with you."

"Shoot."

"I can't get Anna's Tannenbaum quilt out of my mind. I've decided to remake that quilt in honor of Charlie, who loved Christmas trees. I don't want to make a fancy one like Anna's, but a more primitive style that fits the farm."

"Ooh! Tell me more!"

"I sketched a design still using the feather tree for the center but surrounding it with other tree blocks from various folks. I don't want the fringe around it like Anna's quilt because that makes it too formal. I'd prefer it to look like a country quilt."

"Oh, that's such a great idea! What can I do to help?" I asked.

"Plenty. I need your advice and help to get blocks made. I think Lee will embroider the center for me. I'll pay her if I have to. I talked to Harry about it, and he thinks we should have a Tannenbaum Christmas party in Charlie's honor. Of course, he has no idea how long this quilt will take to put together. I'd just like to have the top ready to show, I suppose. I can have it quilted later. The tree blocks could include a barn or other things related to the tree farm. What do you think about that?"

"Absolutely! Girl, when you get your mind on something, you go!"

"That's what Harry said," she chuckled.

"I really appreciate your help, Claire. I know you and Cher are both so busy this time of year."

"So what? We'll be happy to muster up a block for you."

"I want to talk with Anna more about the quilt. She said there are many stories that go with it, and I'd love to hear them."

"Agreed! Can you just imagine how different Anna's life will be here in this country?"

"She's lucky to have Marta to help her. Isn't she doing a great job with the club?"

"She is. And I'm happy we're not closed off to new members anymore. I can't wait to get to know Amy better."

"Hey, ladies!" Harry yelled, coming in the door with Kent and the girls. "Look who's here!"

There were hugs and excitement. The party had officially begun.

"Good to see you, Kent," I greeted.

"Well, I guess you'll be seeing more of me," he noted. "Dad has solicited my help for the season, so I'm stuck here."

"It's not a bad place to be stuck. Harry can convince folks to buy most anything, and it's nice he'll have you to help with the heavy lifting, so to speak."

With all the hungry mouths to be fed, I helped Rachael bring out the side dishes of mashed potatoes, creamed onions, sweet potatoes, green bean casserole, cranberry relish, and her grandmother's turkey dressing. We almost forgot the rolls in the oven amidst everything else. Moments later, Harry presented a large platter of his fried turkey. It was big enough to feed an army, and the smell was indescribable.

Chapter 33

"Rachael, how in the world did you get this great-looking gravy without the drippings of a baked turkey?" I asked with envy.

"It's a little secret," she whispered. "Harry, would you do the blessing this year?"

"You bet!" he said proudly. "Let's all join hands. Lord, we're mighty thankful for this year and the feast you've laid before us. We're blessed to have family and friends to share it with. In your name, we give thanks and praise. Amen."

We said amen together, and the girls giggled with excitement as Harry gave them each a turkey leg to start chewing on.

"I'd like to make a toast to our hostess Rachael and the magnificent turkey fryer, my dad," Kent proposed. "Happy Thanksgiving to all!"

"Here, here!" we all said as we clanked our glasses.

In the next hour, we gorged ourselves on all the scrumptious food. The turkey was moist on the inside and crisp on the outside, just as Rachael had said it would be. Now I realized what all the fuss with frying the turkey was about. It was a real treat for me. The chatter was nonstop until we'd each had our fill.

"Claire brought us some brownies today. They're always delicious. We also have pumpkin pie from the Piggly Wiggly," Rachael announced. "You're going to want both, I'll bet." Moans and groans were heard around the table.

"I think a breather of just coffee for me right now," Kent suggested. "I'll have dessert later, but the girls have been waiting anxiously for those brownies of Claire's. I'll lead the charge in cleanup. This was such a great meal, Rachael."

"Thank you, Kent," Rachael responded. "I really appreciate that."

"Claire, let's take our coffee and get back to discussing the Tannenbaum quilt," Rachael suggested.

"Okay, but first let me help Kent clear the table," I insisted. "That's the least I can do to say thanks for this delicious meal."

Harry had promised to take the girls on a wagon ride before the snow started, so he bundled them up, and off they went.

"You do realize that Harry would be taking a nap if he hadn't promised the girls this treat," Rachael revealed.

"I would be, too," I chuckled.

"When Harry enters the room, he fills it with all this energy, and when he leaves, he sucks it all out with him," Rachael joked.

Rachael then laid out the sketches of her quilt ideas and other notes related to the party.

"I'll have to see if I have any tree patterns to use for my block," I noted. "You know I don't enjoy appliqué, so I'm going to think of something unique."

"Honestly, I haven't been this excited about something for a long time," Rachael admitted. "I have to admit that making these bonus quilt blocks for the barn quilts gets monotonous. There are all sorts of possibilities for those blocks, but I want it to look like Charlie's Christmas tree farm."

"Who doesn't love a Christmas tree?" I noted. "I love the first line in the Tannenbaum song that says, "Oh Tannenbaum, oh Tannenbaum; how lovely are thy branches."

"Oh, me, too," Rachael grinned.

"What if you had a block contest to give everyone a little more incentive to make it?" I suggested. "I think you could get Carol at the quilt shop to be the judge."

"I'm not sure I want to go that direction. If anyone took time to make a block, I sure wouldn't want to hurt their feelings."

Chapter 34

After I helped Rachael clean up everything from our feast, it was seven o'clock, and we were exhausted. Kent and the girls had gone home, and Harry was outside doing something related to the trees before the snow came.

Later that evening, we walked up the hill to Rachael's home, which I'd never seen. It was an outdated 1980s ranch house perched on the hill, which likely gave it a great view. The walls were wood paneled, making for easy maintenance. I was certain it was grand in its time. Rachael didn't have much time for housekeeping, but everything was cozy and warm. While Rachael made a fire, I looked out the window and saw the snow coming down quite heavily.

"Oh dear. I'd better check on Harry," Rachael said in her thoughtful way.

She called him, but he was already on his way home. I wondered if he'd be spending the night here with her if it weren't for me.

"Harry said he'd be here around seven o'clock in the morning to clear the road," Rachael reported.

"That's sweet of him."

"You know I couldn't do any of this without him, Claire."

"Well, you could, but you'd have to hire a bit of help."

"But Harry knows how Charlie would've wanted things because he's been here so much."

"Including you?"

"What do you mean?"

"I think Harry knows all about you and wants to please you, too."

She smiled. "He could never replace Charlie, so don't get any ideas."

"I know. He's Harry. It's quite obvious that the two of you have gotten closer, though. As I listened to you at dinner, you practically finished each other's sentences." She laughed.

"Oh, I don't know, Claire," Rachael hesitated.

"I think it's great, whatever the relationship is."

She smiled. "We do comfort each other in down times, and then we have a lot of fun now and then. He sure doesn't need to be working around here. He's well off and could have a leisurely retirement."

"It's you and his friendship to Charlie that keep him here. He seems happy to be hanging around. Many relationships are formed when a person loses someone they love."

"When did you get to be so smart, Miss Stewart? And how come you aren't more aggressive with the handsome Grayson Wills?"

"That would be a big mistake. He's got Kelly to remind him every day of what his first responsibilities are."

"I've seen your maternal instincts come alive around Kelly."

"You have?" I asked. I'd never thought about that. Rachael nodded in answer.

We finally turned in about eleven o'clock as the snow accumulated. The guest room was wall-to-wall photos of life with Charlie and the farm. I pulled back an imported quilt on the bed, which surprised me. Rachael surely had many beautiful quilts she could've used. There was much to look at, but my eyes were ready for sleep. It didn't take me long to give in after the long day I'd had.

The next morning, Rachael knocked at my door.

"Good morning, Claire! It's seven thirty, and I have a nice breakfast ready for you. I hope you slept okay."

Without answering, I reluctantly pulled myself out of bed and shivered at the cold day ahead. I could just picture Harry outside shoveling in this frosty weather.

The smell of crispy bacon and coffee was enough to get me going. I wore my heavy, red cable-knit sweater so I'd be warm in the shop. I'd learned last year what a challenge it was to stay warm in the barn when folks were coming and going so frequently.

Chapter 35

"Well, good morning!" Harry said joyfully. "How did everyone sleep? It looks like I arrived at just the right time. I knew I smelled Rachael's waffles."

"I slept like a log, but the aroma of a country breakfast prompted me to get out of bed and start the day," I claimed.

"When's the last time you had a good waffle, Claire?" Harry asked like he had eaten them before.

"I can't tell you," I confessed. "I think Rachael is trying to load us up with calories because we're going to work very hard today." Everyone chuckled.

We ate quickly, and Rachael said she'd start chili in the crock pot for our lunch today. I jumped up and cleaned the table and loaded the dishwasher. Harry got a text from Kent saying he was on his way and that Harry had better have a fire going in the white house.

"Fill up your coffee cups before you go to the barn. I'll make a fresh pot when I get down there," Rachael announced.

"See you ladies in a bit," Harry said as he left.

By the time Rachael and I arrived, Harry had a good fire going and Christmas music playing.

"Claire, do you remember our system with the bell? We ring it when someone inside needs help." I nodded.

"What would you like me to do first?"

"Seeing there are customers driving in, we need to get the tree watered and the lights on. We'll be busy before we know it."

She was right. In no time, folks started coming in, as did the cold air. Some had children with them who knew about the free candy canes sitting on the counter. I knew part of my job was to get customers to consider purchasing a barn quilt while they were there.

The day flew by, and I finally sat down for some chili around four o'clock. Rachael knew I was beat. By five o'clock, Rachael said if I wanted to go home, she could handle things.

"I forgot what standing on a concrete floor all day felt like."

"I'm sure! We only sold two barn quilts today, but that will pick up," Rachael noted.

"More time for your Tannenbaum quilt, I guess." She grinned.

I reassured Rachael before I left that I'd help spread the word about her needing blocks.

"Thanks again for everything, Claire. The roads should be pretty clear by now, but take your time driving home, and get some rest. I really appreciate your help today."

When I went outside, Harry gave me a hug and thanked me for being there.

I took it slow and easy on my drive to Highway 42, which was a lot clearer than the back roads. My first day at Rachael's shop was fulfilling and put me in the Christmas spirit. Now it was time to start thinking about what I'd like to give everyone for Christmas. Grayson and Mom would be at the top of the list.

When I arrived home, I was pleased to see that the Bittners' plow guy had remembered to clear my drive as well. As I got out of the car, I took a moment to admire my cabin lights even though it was daylight. I still needed to get a tree for the porch to make it complete. Today wasn't the day to bother Harry with that.

Puff was in her chair napping when I came in. She didn't budge. What would this lazy ball of fur do if a mouse ran across the room? I had no desire for dinner because of that filling four o'clock lunch of Rachael's chili and corn bread. A glass of wine would do just fine, though, as I mellowed out for the day. I kicked off my shoes and considered whether to make a fire.

Chapter 36

As I sipped my wine, I decided to call Mom to see how her Thanksgiving went. She sounded tired when I called.

"I hope you had a good Thanksgiving and didn't work too hard," she began.

"I did work hard, but it was a happy place to be. So many folks wanted to kick off the Christmas season by purchasing their tree today."

"Michael actually helped me put up my artificial tree before he left, so that was nice."

"Good! I've been dying to know whether he brought a date."

"No. He said he's given up on women." I chuckled.

"I don't think he's even tried!"

"I don't think he has. He's always been a bit selfish with his time, which is part of his problem. You know he's writing another book, which doesn't leave many hours for wining and dining women."

"I'm happy he's passionate about writing. I just hope he doesn't regret not having someone when he's old and gray."

"That goes for you too, honey."

"Good one, Mom. I guess you brought us up to be a little too independent. I'm sorry there weren't grandchildren for you to enjoy. So, did you and Michael talk about coming here for Christmas?"

"He said it's too soon to decide. We'll let you know."

We chatted a bit more and then hung up.

I was too tired to think about anything else for the day, so I went upstairs to shower. It would've been nice to have heard from Grayson today, but he was likely as exhausted as I was.

Despite my tiredness, I tossed and turned under the covers. I began worrying about so many things, like what to do about Ava. Should I ignore her, which others probably have, or should I approach her as a good friend? At least she was cleared from taking Ericka's rings at Cher's welcome home party. With her reputation of having sticky fingers, Ava was everyone's first suspect.

Mom's words made me wonder if I'd indeed be alone when I was old and gray. I wasn't far off from that age. Dating a devoted widower with a needy teenager might not bode well for companionship in my later years. Would I want more someday?

I wore myself out with unanswered questions until I finally fell asleep.

The next morning was bright and sunny. The snow we received was glistening. Somehow, despite my restless night, I felt revived. It was a good day to go to the Blue Horse for coffee.

I'd learned from experience that Grayson was normally there early, so I was likely to see him this morning. I had to park way down the street, which meant the place was likely packed. I did spot Grayson's SUV and felt a tinge of excitement.

I had to stand in a long line to place my order and saw no sign of Grayson. When I finally ordered their morning brew and a cranberry bagel, I glanced toward the porch for a seat. My heart jumped to my throat when I saw Grayson having coffee with an attractive woman who had a short, dark pixie haircut. The two of them were laughing. I was praying he didn't catch a glimpse of me.

I headed the opposite direction, but all the seats were filled. My coffee was in one of the Blue Horse mugs, or I'd have walked right out the door. I had no choice but to head back their direction. I wove through a crowd and saw a couple leaving their table on the other side of the porch. Now Grayson's back was toward me, and I felt safer. His companion obviously didn't know who I was as she saw me sit down.

Chapter 37

I tried to calm my anxious heart as I nibbled on my bagel. There was no way I could leave until after they were gone. I knew no one else around me, thank goodness. I pulled out my cell phone and kept my head down.

Fifteen minutes later, they finally made a move to leave. It seemed like an eternity. They said goodbye with a friendly smile and light hugs, which could be interpreted in various ways.

Five minutes later, I felt it was safe to leave. I still wanted to get my mail, but shopping was out of the question now.

After my post office run, I decided to stop by Carl's gallery since I knew Cher was working today. She was such a good sounding board. I really wanted a few minutes to talk with her about Grayson.

She was checking someone out at the cash register when I walked in. I said hello to let her know I was there and began looking at the merchandise, which seemed to change frequently. I didn't see Carl anywhere.

"Hello, miss. How can I help you?" Cher asked like a friendly merchant.

"Well, ma'am, I need to start my Christmas shopping and thought I'd look around," I responded.

"I think you came to the right place," Cher nodded.

"Where is Carl?"

"He went to the bank and then to get us some lunch."

"I just came from the Blue Horse and had coffee," I said simply.

"Did you see Grayson?" She knew I ran into him often there. I paused.

"Yes, I saw him, alright. With another woman."

"Are you serious or just joshing?"

"It may have been business for all I know, but it was hard to watch. She was attractive."

"Did you say hello?"

"Of course not. I hid on the other side of the porch until they left."

"Why on earth didn't you just go up to them and say hello?"

"If it had been a man or an old lady, I would have."

"I know you, Claire Bear, and I'm telling you that you're letting your imagination run away with you. Grayson is smitten with you."

"I'm supposed to meet him for brunch tomorrow at the White Gull Inn. He wants to introduce me to someone. I think he said she was an old family friend."

"Well, that doesn't sound like a guy who has another woman on the side. Hey, look around. I have to check on the lady who just walked in."

"I'm sorry. I don't mean to keep you from your work."

I saw a stack of afghans on the shelf, and the one on display was of Door County's popular tourist places. I examined it closer, and it was quite nice. The colors reminded me of Carole and Linda and even Mom. It would be a sweet reminder of their visit here and a perfect Christmas present. I took three of them and placed them on the counter.

"I'd like these, please," I said to Cher, the clerk. Her eyes widened.

"Would you like them gift wrapped, ma'am?"

"You do that?"

"Yes, we do! Carl has some really nice hunter green Christmas paper back there on a roll to use for wrapping."

"Sure! I'd love that! I used to love to gift wrap, but not anymore. If someone comes in, I'll let you know."

"Carl should be back anytime."

"I'm going to check out the nifty hand-painted Christmas cards on this rack. Do you know the artist?"

"No, never met her," Cher said on her way to the back room. "They're quite good, though. You could do that, Claire Bear." I shrugged my shoulders.

While Cher wrapped my gifts, I picked out six of the cards.

When I left the gallery, I ran into Carl. He saw my packages and gave me a big grin.

"You sure have a good saleslady working in there," I joked. He grinned.

"Do you mean the good-looking one?"

"That's the one! Have a good day!"

I went home in a much better mood than I imagined I would after having seen Grayson with his companion. I knew I needed to dismiss my jealous experience in the coffee shop. After all, he was a businessman with many relationships. I certainly didn't know everyone in his world at this point in our relationship.

I hid my packages under the bed, hoping Puff would leave them alone. My phone alerted me to a text from Grayson.

[Grayson]
See you tomorrow at ten o'clock?

[Claire]
I'll be there!

[Grayson]
That's my girl!

My heart melted as if he had just given me that first kiss. Calling me his girl was fine by me. It was just the reassurance I needed after seeing him with that pretty woman at breakfast.

Chapter 38

It was a beautiful Sunday, and I should've gone to an early church service, but my mind was on the morning brunch. I laid out several outfits before deciding which one was appropriate.

I decided to walk, so I left ten minutes early. When I arrived, the hostess seemed to know I was meeting Grayson and took me straight to his table.

"Claire, good to see you!" Grayson greeted. I smiled. "Claire, this is my dear friend, Alice Elizabeth Parker. Alice, this is Claire Stewart, who I told you about."

"It's nice to meet you, Miss Stewart," Alice said in a formal fashion.

"Please call me Claire, and I am most pleased to meet you as well. You look somewhat familiar to me." She pulled her chin up as if she wasn't sure how we'd have met before.

"We just came from church," Grayson noted. "Alice belongs to the Moravian church where I think you said you've visited a time or two."

"Why, yes. That's where I remember seeing you. I think I sat in the same pew as you last Christmas," I recalled.

"I followed you out of the church and you had a driver pick you up."

"I'm sorry. My mind isn't what it used to be, but I'm happy you paid a visit to our beautiful church," she replied with a twinkle in her eyes.

"Alice no longer drives, but she has a wonderful driver, Sam, who takes her anywhere she wants to go."

I was surprised to see Brenda working today on a Sunday. When she looked our way, I gave her a quick wave.

"I feel privileged to join you today," I said politely.

"Well, Alice mentioned to me recently that she hadn't been to the White Gull Inn for some time and that she always loved how they decorated the inn at Christmastime," Grayson revealed. "That made me think of having brunch here, especially since it's practically next door to you."

"I have fond memories of this place and its history," she claimed. "I recently broke my hip, so I don't get out every much."

"Oh, I'm sorry to hear that," I responded.

"She's doing great," Grayson bragged as he held her hand. I was still wondering why he felt I needed to meet her.

We gave our order, which took a bit of time. It was sweet to see the patience and care Grayson was giving her. His tone of voice in speaking to her was so gentle.

"Miss Stewart, I understand you're from Missouri," she commented. "Do you plan to move back one day?" I was caught off guard with her blunt question.

"No, I think I've found a new home here in Door County," I firmly stated. "My mom still travels, so I'm hoping she and my brother will visit for Christmas."

"That would be nice," she responded simply. "Grayson said you have met Kelly."

"I have, and she's quite a nice young lady," I described. "She just acquired a cat recently, so she brought him over to meet my cat Puff." Alice smiled at the thought.

"Alice's family and mine go way back, and we owe her a great deal of gratitude for many things."

"Now, Grayson," she said sweetly, patting his hand.

Our lunch arrived, and I was a bit uncomfortable. I reminded myself of my best manners as I answered the many questions that came my way. I was certain Alice was going to make her best effort to find out who in the world this woman was that Grayson was dating.

Alice was a slow eater, but when she decided she was finished, she indicated to Grayson that it was time to go.

"Alice says she remembers when your cabin was constructed on your property," Grayson informed.

"Oh, how interesting," I replied earnestly. "I'd like to hear more about that." I wasn't sure she heard me, but she was determined to leave right then.

"Have a lovely Christmas, Miss Stewart," she said when Grayson helped her with her coat. "Grayson is lucky to have such a nice friend."

"I couldn't agree more!" Grayson said as he gave me a wink. "Thanks for meeting us here."

"Thank you for the lovely lunch and the opportunity to meet this special lady," I stated as I shook her hand. "I'm going to say goodbye to my friend Brenda over here." Grayson nodded as they left.

As I took my time walking home, I thought about how much of this encounter with Alice and Grayson I didn't understand. Why did he want us to meet? Who was she, really? It was a nice meal, of course, as it always was at the White Gull Inn. I guess I should've felt good about Grayson wanting me to meet her, whatever the reason was.

Chapter 39

The next morning, when I was having my coffee, I checked my emails and read that Rachael was putting out a more extensive plea for Christmas tree blocks. Her description of a party for all involved should be a good incentive.

As I continued to think about Rachael's plans, I mulled over ideas of my own about what kind of block to do for the Tannenbaum quilt. I loved the style of a feather tree and would definitely do something with that design in mind. I emailed her back and reassured her I'd have a block. As I thought more about the dedication to Charlie, I thought a real antique feather tree would be a neat gift to Harry and Rachael. I knew the trees were hard to find, but I could start by checking out the Olde Orchard Antique Mall on 42 that had many booths with unique stuff. I was interrupted by a knock at the door. When I looked out the window, I saw Brenda standing there.

"Hey, girlfriend," I greeted. "Come on in. I'm still in my robe, I'm afraid." She grinned.

"I certainly don't mind. I love all your lights, by the way. Where is your Christmas tree?"

"I'll get that this week. When I worked on Black Friday at Rachael's, we were slammed with people buying their trees, and I didn't want to bother getting one for myself then. How have you been?"

"Good, but there's nothing going on, really. Sorry I wasn't able to talk to you and Grayson at the restaurant Sunday, but we were slammed."

"That's why I didn't bother you. Come on in and have a cup of coffee. What brings you out?"

"Well, I had to go to the inn for something and thought I'd stop by."

"You know, it was about this time last year that we went to the Noble House for their Christmas caroling. We should do that again. Do you still volunteer there?"

"Not since the tourist season died off. I'd love to go, but you're so busy."

"I'll check my calendar."

As I poured her coffee, I told her about Rachael's plans for her Tannenbaum quilt and party. I tried to describe Anna's antique quilt and how Rachael's would be different. I even suggested she make a block, but she didn't respond. Something must be on her mind. She seemed distracted.

"So, Harry and Rachael are a thing now?" Brenda asked.

"You might say so. They certainly need each other, and both are on board doing this Tannenbaum party in memory of Charlie. They sure stay busy just like her and Charlie used to."

"I'm happy for her. I'll think about a block. Let me know when the party will be."

"Do you ever buy a real tree for Christmas, Brenda?" She shook her head sadly.

"Oh, I have an adequate artificial tree I've had for years. Real trees are just too messy."

"They can be, but you should see the excitement on people's faces after they pick out their tree. You should come out Saturday when I'm working, and I'll help you myself. If it's too big, Harry will even deliver it free of charge. They have other things like wreaths, too. It's kind of magical being there, even though I was dead tired from standing on my feet all day the last time I worked."

"I've never been there. I'm fascinated by Rachael's barn quilts, though."

"Oh, they're hung everywhere in the big barn. They have free cider if you get too cold, and if you hit the noon hour, there's free hot chili that Harry makes. It's really good!" For the first time, Brenda smiled.

"Well, I need something to lift my spirits," she said, looking down at the floor. "I'll think about it."

"What's wrong?"

"I just have no interest in anything these days. My daughter's schedule is always full, so I rarely see her. All I do is go to work and then come home. I don't have any interest in hygge since my daughter doesn't go with me anymore." She was reaching out for help, and I wasn't sure what to do.

"I'm sorry to hear that. The holidays can be depressing for many. You're such a pleasant and attractive person to be around. Please don't shut yourself off to those around you. I liked you the minute I met you at the inn."

Chapter 40

"Hey, I just thought of something. You know our quilt group is now accepting new members. Does that interest you at all?"

"No, not really. From what I hear, it's too structured for me."

"I understand. We're working on that. It's a lot more relaxed now that Greta's not leading the meetings anymore. There's a strong feeling of tradition, though, so the changes can't be done overnight."

As we chatted, I could tell her mood was improving.

"I appreciate your thinking of me for quilt club," she said with a smile.

"Not to bring up a sore subject, but does Pete still come in the restaurant?" He seemed like a heartbreaker to avoid, as he'd tried to pick *me* up after she'd clearly been interested in him. I hoped her answer was no.

"Funny you should bring that up because I haven't seen him there for some time. I don't miss him. I was a fool to think he had any interest in me."

"Don't be silly. You're attractive, Brenda, and it's a blessing he hasn't been around lately. He was toxic, really, and you deserve better than him. Someday you're going to meet a really nice guy."

"It's not easy being single in Door County. I'm not one to hang out at the bars. You're lucky you found Grayson. He seems kind."

"I know. I truly am lucky. Cher has told me that many go to Green Bay to meet people. Speaking of which, you're a Packers fan. How about checking out guys at a game?"

She chuckled. "I'm afraid I'll never be lucky enough to get to one of those games. The games are expensive, and I didn't inherit season tickets. You can't get me away from the TV when they're playing, though. I root for them from the living room!"

"I went to a game when Rachael fixed me up with Harry. I'll never forget it in more ways than one. Someday, I'll tell you more." She nodded and laughed.

"Well, I have one rule when it comes to the Packers. I have to watch the game alone. It's just too tense and personal."

I smiled at the thought. "Yeah, you sound like Harry."

"Well, I'll think about coming out Saturday. You've sparked my interest about getting a real tree. "

"That's the spirit! Just don't be surprised if Rachael asks you to make a block for her Tannenbaum quilt. She needs a lot of help for it."

"I don't think I'm good enough, but I don't mind helping her. She's a great gal. Well, I've kept you long enough. Do you have a current painting project? Looks like there's something on your easel."

"Yes, I'm doing a series of Door County buildings with quilts hanging on them. I figure it's a good way to advertise our outdoor quilt show. Right now, I have a painting started of the Irish shop."

"You're something, Claire. So, would you rather paint than quilt?"

"That's like asking if I like chocolate or vanilla ice cream. I love both. I do have to focus on getting a quilt top done for Kelly. She loves the quilt Grayson bid on at the benefit auction for Rachael, but he claimed it for himself. I've wanted to make one just for Kelly. I doubt if I can get a quilter to do it this close to Christmas, though. When Kelly's quilt is done, I have to squeeze in at least one block for Rachael's Tannenbaum quilt."

"You do have a lot on your plate. Maybe I'll see you Saturday."

"Cheer up, my friend. I'll see you later."

With Kelly's quilt on my mind, I went up to my fabric stash and started making some decisions. Some of my red scraps were as small as six-inch squares, so I decided a Four-Patch block would be cute, alternating it with white. Playing with fabric again was comforting. I could envision all sorts of patterns and ideas. I'd need a fun name for the quilt when I presented it to Kelly. I was sure she didn't have a clue about traditional names for quilts.

Two hours went by, and Puff didn't leave my sight. I honestly was beginning to think this cat loved quilts as much as I did. Now I had to make sure she didn't take over my fabric as her own as I was working. When I started chain piecing the few blocks I'd cut, I realized the project might go quicker than I'd thought. Puff was watching like she wanted to see the end result.

My mind drifted, and I started thinking about Brenda being down in the dumps. I'd love to find someone to fix her up with. Who, though? If she showed up at the farm, I was sure her mood would improve. You just couldn't be in a bad mood there. There was too much festivity going on.

Chapter 41

The next day, I started rearranging my porch in anticipation of getting my Christmas tree. Puff monitored my movements the entire time. She didn't like that her favorite chair was in a different spot now.

My domestic chores were done, so I decided to get my mail and stop in to see Cher at the gallery.

When I arrived at the library, I was happy to see Ava in the hallway.

"Oh, hi, Claire! How are you? Isn't it exciting about Rachael's Tannenbaum quilt? I told her I'd make a block for sure!"

"That's great. I need to decide on my block soon. Say, do you have time to get a cup of coffee?" She looked at me in surprise.

"Why, yes, I do. I'm getting hungry. Want to grab something to eat at The Cookery?"

"I'd love to! I'll see you there."

When I returned to my car, I started thinking about what I thought I'd seen at the séance and whether to confront Ava about it or just drop it. I didn't want to lose her as a friend, and I certainly could if I didn't handle this right.

We arrived at the same time and sat in a booth near the door.

"This is a grand idea, Claire. You and I never really get to visit with each other."

"We're both always so busy."

"Well, I'm single now, and I've never been happier. I felt lonelier in my marriage than I do being alone."

"Oh, I know that feeling very well."

"I never really knew why you decided to leave your hometown and come to Door County."

"It's a long story, but when Cher needed to go back home to take care of her mother, I took her up on her offer to move into her cabin."

"I have to say, Claire, you've been such a welcome change for our quilt club. We needed some shaking up."

We ordered our meal, and then I decided to take the plunge and talk about the séance.

"So, Ava, how did you enjoy the séance?" She grinned, and her face lit up.

"Oh, I love stuff like that. And from what I've observed, Frances is just as good at predicting things as the woman she invited to be our medium."

"You may be right. Frances had a vision with something related to me, and it came true."

"Oh, these pancakes are delicious. This was a great idea."

"Ava, I like you so much, but I want to bring up a sensitive subject. Do you mind?" She stopped eating, and her face tightened up.

"Whatever about?"

"I want to ask you a question, and I don't want you to get upset. Okay?"

"I guess it depends," she joked.

"When we were at Frances's house, I thought I saw you put something into your purse that didn't belong to you." She paused and then nodded.

"Are you referring to when I put the Christmas bell into my purse?"

I nodded with surprise.

"Don't worry, I didn't keep it. You may not know me very well, but I've been known to do stupid things like this before. Frances saw me take the bell, too, and gave me a dirty look. I'm not a thief, Claire, but sometimes I take things without even thinking. I think it goes back to my childhood when I'd steal any crumbs I could when I was hungry. We had it pretty rough growing up."

"Aren't you worried you could get in serious trouble?"

She shook her head. "I told you I don't consider myself a thief. My ex-husband has plenty of bad things to say about me, but he never called the police. There was a time when he truly understood me. I'm not sure that's the case anymore. I'm rarely tempted to steal, and it's always little things that trigger my impulses, like when I'd go to the five-and-dime as a kid.

"Can you get some counseling before someone decides to charge you with something?"

"I've been there. It's hard to explain, Claire. I have a clean conscience about it, but I appreciate your concern."

"How many people know about your weakness?"

She took a deep breath as if she were losing patience with me. "Not many. I really appreciate that you approached me directly about this and didn't make a scene in front of everyone."

"I'd never do that to anyone. Thank you for being honest with me."

"I'm fortunate to have everything I'd ever want in life now, but that doesn't mean I'm not tempted to help myself. I thought about writing a book about my childhood. A therapist I had at one time thought it would help me."

"It just might. Maybe you should."

"Thinking about all we did to survive in my family is painful. I'm not sure I want to relive those memories."

"I don't know how spiritual you are, Ava, but I talk to God constantly. If I'm not asking him for help, I'm thanking him for something He's given me. I was raised with those values, so it comes easy for me. He's there for the asking." She looked at me and stared in thought.

Chapter 42

Ava and I hugged each other like good friends when we departed. I was sorry to hear about the rough childhood she'd had that had prompted her to take things that weren't hers. It made me appreciate my own childhood. I knew God had helped me find the right approach to take with Ava today. I was grateful that we left our breakfast visit as even better friends.

When I arrived home, I got back to work on cutting squares for Kelly's quilt. I kept working until my phone alerted me to a text around four o'clock.

[Grayson]
I just left Kelly off at the ice rink. Do you have time for a cocktail?

[Claire]
Sure! Where?

[Grayson]
The rink is in Sister Bay. Is meeting at Husby's too far for you?

[Claire]
Give me twenty minutes. I'll see you there.

My heart fluttered like my high school boyfriend had just called. I did a quick change of clothes and checked my face before I dashed away to meet my knight in shining armor.

"Hey, sweetheart." Grayson greeted me when I walked in the door. "Thanks for coming on such short notice. I wanted to stay close by in case Kelly called to come and get her sooner. She was having bad monthly cramps today, and she wasn't sure she'd feel up to skating. She was determined to try, though."

"I'm sorry to hear she wasn't feeling well. Does she have those bad cramps every month?"

"I'm afraid so, and I'm not much help, unfortunately. Hey, how about some pizza?"

"Sure! I had breakfast with a friend but no lunch, so pizza sounds good. I love their supreme, I think it's called."

"I'm on it," he said with a big grin. "So, Claire, I've been wondering about your impressions of Alice."

"I think there is a real background story there, and I can tell she thinks of you as her own son."

"She does, and I should go see her more often. I'm just too busy to do a lot of things I should."

"I know. It's hard. I feel the same sometimes about my mom. I sense that Alice is very protective of you."

He nodded. "I know she asked you a lot of questions. I was a little embarrassed at some of them, but I hope you didn't mind too much."

"I understand. If she was fond of Marsha, I'm sure she wants to know who you're spending time with."

"I'd talked to Alice about you several times before. She was always asking me questions about you, so I thought the two of you should meet."

"I'm almost afraid to ask, but did she have any comments about me you can share?"

"She said you were certainly nice enough," he said in a teasing manner.

"Thank goodness for that!" We both had a chuckle. "So, tell me, is Kelly a good ice skater?"

"She's been skating since she was five, but she hasn't been driven to get much better over the years. Her friends love to skate, so she wants to be a part of that even when she's not feeling 100 percent."

"Friends are so important at her age, or any age, really. I'm glad she has some good ones. Hey, I work tomorrow at the farm. You should come out and get your tree."

"We'll see what Kelly has planned. She wants a real tree, but now that we have this cat, I think we should put up our artificial one."

"Oh, now. That's no excuse for not getting the real thing this Christmas. Puff got used to mine last year pretty quickly."

I began telling him about Rachael's plans for a Tannenbaum quilt and a party close to Christmas Eve. He knew I was always trying to promote Rachael's business, so he kept nodding as I went on about it.

We'd just finished our pizza when Kelly called.

"I'm sorry, I have to run. You're always so sweet to accommodate my schedule."

"Well, I love being with you. What can I say?" I said grinning.

"I love being with you, too," he said, giving me a light kiss as acknowledgment. "I feel like a lousy partner sometimes. I don't know how you put up with me."

"I know you're doing the best you can. It's all anyone can hope for."

"Hey, let's get out of here so I can give you a proper kiss goodbye."

When we arrived at my car, I got the proper kiss he'd promised.

I drove home feeling half satisfied. It wasn't always easy sharing Grayson with Kelly and his work, but I knew his ties to his daughter and his business from the start.

Sleepy from the two beers that had accompanied our pizza, I was useless and went on to bed. I had a full workday tomorrow.

Once the covers were tucked all around me, I checked my phone for any messages or emails. I was shocked to see a text from Austen.

[Austen]
Thinking of you. Will you be coming home for Christmas?

Oh no. What should I do? Should I give him a simple, cold answer of no, or would that start a dialogue? Why couldn't this text be from Grayson wishing me a sweet good night?

Chapter 43

My sleep was restless, but I managed to drag myself out of bed early to begin my workday. I sat drinking as much caffeine as I could to get myself charged up. I didn't want to think about Grayson or Austen all day if I could help it.

I felt like I was still in a daze as I drove out to the farm. I was glad to arrive and feel the warmth of the wood-burning stove in the barn.

"Good morning!" I called to Rachael behind the counter.

"The same to you, my friend. Grab some coffee and warm yourself. Harry and Kent have been busy with a big order that has an early pickup. Man, am I thankful for Kent's help!"

"Since no one is in here yet, can I go and pick out my tree?"

"Absolutely! It's a good time to do that!"

I had gotten such a pretty tree from here last year, and I wanted something similar this time. I went to tell Harry I was shopping.

"Good morning, young lady!" Harry greeted as he was cutting some twine. "What can I do for you?"

"I think I've found my tree, but I don't want to bother you with it until you have some free time."

"Oh, Kent should be out there and can put it aside for you. Say, you sure have Rachael excited about this Tannenbaum quilt. She agreed that we need to have a party. You know me—I'm always up for that!" He gave his signature hearty laugh.

"Rachael's really passionate about it. It's a great idea, and we all want to help in any way we can. Her idea of honoring Charlie is touching. She has so much energy, and she'll make this a success for sure."

"It's good we have Kent. He's got his hands full with the girls, but he's a hard worker."

"Where are those cute girls today?"

"At their grandparents."

"Ah, I see. Well, I'd better get this done and go find Kent."

"Thanks, Claire!"

I found Kent between the rows of trees. He was always so gentle and quiet compared to Harry. He was handsome in a rugged sort of way, which made me wonder if he had a girlfriend. After I told him to put my tree aside, I went back inside.

Rachael was taking money from someone who had just purchased a tree.

"Now, don't forget to water the tree every day," she instructed. "If you can take the time to boil the water first and let it sit awhile before you water, it's much better. That allows the water to go quickly up the bark of the tree. If you use cold water, the sap gets hard and clogs up. The tree won't absorb as well."

"Gee, thanks! I've never heard that!" the guy responded.

"By the way, we're selling something new this year," Rachael added. "Take a look at this long horn device, and see how helpful it is for watering."

She pointed to something that looked like a long pipe with a cup at the end, where you pour your water.

"I've always hated crawling under the tree branches to try to get the tree watered," Rachael explained. "This way you can stand up while you're watering the tree. It's pretty nifty."

"Well, I'll be darned," the guy responded. "I'll take one of those, too.

After the guy left, I went over to examine the thing for myself.

"This is cool, and it's a perfect add-on sale. I'd also never heard your advice for watering a tree. That was good information."

"Well, he took the time to ask. Most of the time we're so busy that we just take the sale and remind customers to water."

"You sold me! I'll take one of those watering horns myself."

"Great! Would you mind putting another log in that stove for me? It gets cold in here when that door opens."

"Will do!"

My day had begun! Rachael turned up the Christmas music, and the folks started coming in. I couldn't believe how she knew most of their names. One man came to pick up the largest barn quilt I'd ever seen. It had to be at least 36×36. It was an Eight-Point Star in red and green. The man said he was going to surprise his wife by hanging it on the barn and waiting for her to notice.

Chapter 44

"Hey, Miss Brenda!" Rachael yelled out. "It's really good to see you!"

"You too, Rachael," she responded as her eyes glanced about the place. "I finally got here. Your place is fantastic. I'm sorry I've been missing out."

"Hey, welcome!" I added cheerfully. "I hope this means you're going to get a real tree this year." She grinned and nodded.

"Claire is a good salesperson," she teased. "I can't believe I've never come out here."

"I tell her that all the time, and I'm glad you finally made it here." Rachael added. "How about some hot coffee or cocoa before you look around?"

"I'd love some!" Brenda said as she helped herself.

"Come with me. I'll take you out to meet Harry and Kent."

"I've met Harry but not Kent," she recalled.

"Kent is Harry's son who's helping him this season," I explained. "He's so nice and has two sweet little girls."

"Claire, I can see why you like it here so much," Brenda envied. "What smells so good?"

"Rachael always has chili or soup in the crock pot for us when we're working. After you pick out your tree, you come in here to pay. Maybe you'll be hungry for some by then."

"Oh, that's not necessary," she replied.

"Let me put on my coat, and I'll help you find a wonderful tree," I suggested.

As we exited the barn, Kent was just finishing tying a tree on someone's trunk.

"Kent, this is my friend Brenda," I introduced. "She's about to buy her first real tree. Do you have time to help her?"

"I sure can!" he responded cheerfully. "You're in for a real treat." Brenda blushed.

"Well, I'm going to leave you two. I'm cold, and Rachael will be needing me inside."

I rushed back inside and poured myself a cup of hot coffee to warm up.

"Thanks for enticing Brenda to come," Rachael said, making another fresh pot of coffee.

"She's really been down lately. I figured she needed a Christmas picker-upper."

"I don't know her well, but she's sweet."

"She's the best waitress at the White Gull Inn and has been there forever. She's so shy, though. I tried to tell her she needs to help make things happen. Good things don't just come knocking at your door." Rachael nodded and laughed.

After a half hour, Brenda returned to pay for her tree and a wreath for her door.

"You've got to be frozen to the bone, girlfriend," I said as I watched her shiver. "Did you find the right one?"

"I did," she nodded. "It's one of those tall, skinny ones I really like. I have a small corner I think it'll be perfect for.

Kent was a huge help, by the way. We got it attached to my car rather nicely."

"Good! I'll bet a spot of chili would taste really good about now to warm you up," I suggested.

"Well, I have to admit, I'm famished," she admitted.

"Great!" Rachael responded. "You and Claire go in the back room and have some lunch together. "I'll holler if I need some help."

"Sounds good!" I said, heading for the crock pot.

"Oh my, this is so good," Brenda expressed after her first bite. "And I love that you have the Packers game on. I really hated to come out here with a game going on."

"Oh, everyone here is a big Packers fan. Harry and Kent have the game on in the white house, too." Brenda grinned between bites.

"I have to say I'm getting excited about decorating for Christmas now that I have a real tree."

"Me, too. I may even take home one of those little free trees Harry has out there so I can put it in my bedroom this year. The lights would be peaceful."

"Really? Well, I may do the same when I leave. You're going to get me in so much trouble, Claire."

"Hey, ladies. Do you mind if I join you?" Kent asked as held a bowl of chili. "I'm cold and mighty hungry."

"Not at all!" I said as I got up out of my chair. "I don't know how you guys stand it out there all day and night. The game is on, and I know you want to find out the latest." Kent grinned.

"Sorry, Claire, I need your help if you don't mind," Rachael interrupted.

"No problem," I responded. "I just finished."

She did indeed need my help, as the barn was suddenly packed with people. Kids were running everywhere, and some customers were in line to pay.

Chapter 45

I got so busy that I plumb forgot about Brenda and Kent in the back room.

"Thanks for everything, Kent," Brenda said as the two of them came out of the back room together.

"No problem!" Kent replied as he went out into the cold.

"Rachael, that was the best chili I've ever had," Brenda gushed.

"It's my Granny's recipe," she revealed. "I make it a lot during the winter. I'm glad Kent took a little break. I think Harry rides him too hard. I guess when you're the dad, you feel you can get by with it."

"How old is Kent?" I asked.

"I'm not really sure. Maybe mid-forties." Rachael replied.

"I need to get on home," Brenda stated. "I sure didn't intend to stay this long. Oh, and I'll be happy to make a Tannenbaum tree block for you. Thanks again for everything. This is going to be the best Christmas I've had in some time."

"You're welcome, and thanks for agreeing to contribute a block to the quilt." Rachael responded. "I'm going to start on it Monday since it's always a lot slower here on weekdays."

When Brenda left, Rachael started talking about the Tannenbaum party again and said Kent would be grilling bratwursts for it. She kept hinting that she needed to sit down with me to plan all the details.

"Hey, the Packers just pulled ahead, honey bun!" Harry yelled coming in the door.

"That's great!" Rachael cheered. "Brenda is a Packers fan too, so she was pleased to see it on in the back room."

"I'll be darned," Harry said. "I should have known that's why Kent's lunch break was taking so long. Is it my turn to have some of your great chili?"

"Help yourself, big guy!" Rachael said, winking.

"Are you in a big hurry to leave this evening?" Rachael asked me. "I wanted to run some ideas by you before Anna and Marta come out tomorrow. I'm going to talk to Anna about making strudel to sell at the party. What do you think?"

"Yum! Sounds like a winner to me!"

The phone rang just then, but Harry yelled that he had it.

"Well, well. Look at who just walked in the door!" I said as Grayson appeared. "I thought you were too busy today."

"Well, I got to thinking about everything I bought last year for the office," he explained. "I knew I shouldn't put that off too much longer, so here I am. Kent helped me get it all together today, so I need to pay my bill."

"I can do that!" I said, taking his ticket. "What's Kelly up to today?"

"Christmas shopping," Grayson said, shaking his head. "God save my credit card." We laughed.

"Thanks, Grayson," Rachael said with gratitude. "Harry's in the back room watching the game and eating chili if you'd like to join him. It's a pretty good batch."

"Hmm, don't mind if I do," Grayson replied.

He filled a bowl of chili and joined Harry in the back room. It made me happy they were friends.

In a short time, Grayson said he had to be on his way.

"That chili hit the spot!" Grayson said, rubbing his tummy. "Thanks for feeding me. I sure wouldn't mind having that recipe."

"Afraid not," Rachael said, shaking her head. "It's a family secret that keeps folks coming back for more."

"Darn. I understand, though. Merry Christmas to all!" Grayson said as he left.

"You'd better hang on to that guy," Rachael warned.

"I'm trying!"

By five o'clock, the crowd had slowed down. There were a few folks still in the lot, but the barn was mostly empty. We'd had a busy day.

"Have a seat and get your feet off this concrete floor," Rachael advised. "I've got a bottle of cab opened that I think you'll like. This is about the time Harry and Kent get out the malted scotch in the white house and take a nip or two."

I laughed.

Chapter 46

"So, Claire, help me out here," Rachael requested as she poured my wine. "You had all these great ideas for a chili fest for Charlie and me, remember?"

"Well, that's been a while, but yes. When I started working here and saw this place with fresh eyes, I knew it had so much potential. Just this afternoon, a lady wanted to know if we carried poinsettias. If we had them, we'd sell them."

"I heard her, too. I do have a wholesale source, but the price would be higher than what people pay other places."

"I know, but people buy them where they see them. It's just easiest for people to get everything at the same place if they can."

"I thought for other vendors at the party, like Anna, we could use the side yard of the barn."

"Perfect. Just make sure you have lights hanging everywhere so the vendors are viewed as part of the party."

"That's no problem. Good idea."

"Lay everything out like a map on paper. As you plan other vendors, remember that you want to make money at this. If charity is involved, you want to include yourself in a percentage."

"Harry has a niece who sells cherry products. He wants to put her stuff in the shop, but I've been reluctant. This party may be the perfect place to sell those items, though."

"Absolutely. Door County is all about cherries, so why not?" I agreed.

"I saw a make-a-wish tree on TV recently. You paid a small fee that went to charity to hang a bow or something on the tree. You could make as many wishes as you wanted. That's something we could incorporate also. We'd just need someone to handle the money."

"Maybe that would be a good job for someone like Brenda. You should ask our whole quilt club to help in some way besides making a block. It sounds to me like you're creating a Christmas market. You have the perfect place for it, Rachael."

"We really do. I don't think Harry realized what a can of worms he opened when he suggested a party. I can't ask the club for anything more than a quilt block, though. If they attend the party, that's a plus."

"I'm almost done with Kelly's quilt, and then I'll move on to my block."

"You're most generous to make a quilt for Kelly. Of course, you might be Mrs. Wills someday."

"Don't go there, Rachael."

"Well, it's true! So, is that cat they got from here working out okay?"

"Kelly and cat are doing fine. Papa has his moments."

She laughed. "Claire, you look tired. I shouldn't keep you any longer."

"Truthfully, I really am beat, but call me anytime for what you might need for the quilt or the party. I'm going to grab a small tree for my bedroom before I go home."

"Just so you know, your tree this year is free, just like last year. I really don't know what we'd do without you."

I gave her a hug and went out to see what was left in the free tree row. They all looked to be Charlie Brown trees that needed a home. I finally picked one out.

"Do you need help with that?" Kent asked, coming near me.

"I think this size will fit."

"Let me get some newspapers for you to lay it on. I sure enjoyed meeting your friend Brenda today. It's always nice to connect with another Packers fan."

"That she is. Did she tell you she works at the White Gull Inn?"

"Yes, she did. I've only been there once or twice. It's not a place I'd normally grab a bite to eat by myself."

I nodded and smiled. I thanked Kent for putting the tree in my car, and off I went. I couldn't wait to kick off my shoes and rest for the evening.

Chapter 47

After a long, deep sleep, I climbed out of bed remembering I still had the bedroom tree in the back of my car. Before I headed downstairs to breakfast, I made a spot right in front of the bedroom window for my small tree. It would look pretty from the outside, even if it looked like a Charlie Brown tree inside. I was certain I had plenty of lights left from last year I could use.

After I dressed, I carefully retrieved my tree from the back of my Subaru. As I was about to take it in the cabin, Kent drove up, but my big tree was not on his truck.

"I'm in the neighborhood making another tree delivery now, but since you were outside, I decided to stop. I'll bring yours shortly. I'm the only one making deliveries."

"That's fine. No hurry. Brenda sure had nice things to say about you yesterday."

"She did? I'm so awkward around women. I guess since I had a nasty divorce, I'm pretty leery of women in general. I figured she had to be a good egg, being a Packers fan and all. I really don't date, mostly because of my girls. Dad's been great about helping with them. Can you handle carrying in the little tree by yourself, or do you want some help?"

"I can do it myself. I have just the spot for it upstairs in front of the window. I hope I have enough lights. I wonder if that's one more thing Rachael should be selling. There are so many add-on sales she's missing."

He nodded. "It's not a bad idea. Why don't you ask her?"

"I'm good about spending other people's money. When I work there, I get all sorts of ideas. So, are girls excited about Christmas?"

"Oh, lands, yes. They have lists that go on and on. Oh, shucks, look at the time. I need to get going. I don't want Dad to fire me!"

I waved him on and sat my tree on the porch as I watched Puff sniff all around it. I was getting hungry and thought I'd better have a bite to eat before getting involved decorating the tree upstairs. I quickly threw a small pizza in the oven and made a fresh pitcher of iced tea.

After I ate, I drug the tree upstairs, and Puff followed like she was going to miss something. I leaned it against the wall while I went into the office to search for more lights. I also pulled out the red-and-white quilt that I planned to use to wrap around my tree on the porch. I laid the quilt on the bed and placed Puff on top so she wouldn't disturb me as I was stringing the lights. The tree stood nice and straight, and there were plenty of lights to go around. I quickly turned off the bedroom light to witness the magical transformation of my bedroom. Puff wasn't impressed with the tree, but she did love the new quilt I'd set out for her.

Chapter 48

As darkness set in, I rushed outside to see the lights twinkling from my bedroom window. The cold air and my cell phone ringing brought me in rather quickly.

"It's your Perryville sister," announced Carole. "Linda and I are at Mary Jane's having a drink, so we have you on speaker phone. Be careful what you say!" They both giggled.

"Oh dear! What are you girls up to?" I cautiously asked.

"We've been Christmas shopping and decided we needed something stronger than hot chocolate," Linda added.

I chuckled. "Did you buy my present?" I teased.

"Well, I can make you something that sparkles," Linda responded.

"And I can send you another cookbook," Carole joked. "So, what would you really like for Christmas?"

"Well, since you asked, here it goes," I began. "Carole, I'd like a box of your Christmas cookies, and go heavy on those chocolate mint ones. Linda, I'd love a special ornament you make with all your shiny trinkets."

"Done!" Carole yelled into the phone.

"I don't make ornaments, Miss Claire," Linda argued. "I make jewelry!"

"I know, so let me be the first," I suggested. "You can do this."

"Well, we'll see," Linda fussed.

"You guys are behind. I already have your gifts purchased." I revealed.

"I'll take your mother some cookies, too," Carole offered.

"She'll love that. Thank you," I replied. "I miss you both. I just put up a little tree in my bedroom. I don't have my big one for the porch yet, but it should be here later today. How about you guys?"

"Yup, last week. That's the earliest I've ever had a tree." replied Linda. "I don't think I need one in my bedroom."

"I'm doing a lot of small trees this year instead of one big one, just to have something different," Carole shared.

"I like that idea!" I said. "Have a drink for me, okay? I love you!"

"We love you, too!" Linda followed. "Cheers!"

I hung up, hearing the two laughing like I had for so many years. They were from the Claire Bear and Cher Bear days of long ago. I should've reminded them about coming here for the summer quilt show again.

I went upstairs to retire for the night. The thought of my longtime buddies at Mary Jane's, a favorite hangout in Perryville, put a smile on my face. I undressed, gave Puff an unexpected hug, and crawled under the covers to get some sleep.

Chapter 49

The next morning, I lay in bed thinking about Kelly's quilt. I needed to buy white fabric to go with the red patches, and the sooner the better so I could start piecing things together. I hadn't been to the quilt shop in Sturgeon Bay for some time and looked forward to the visit a little later. I assessed what I did and didn't have in my office/sewing room and made a mental note. Then I played around with the pieces on my design wall area and decided I'd call the pattern Hopscotch. It was a playful name for what I envisioned. Kelly may not even know what the game is, but I played it a lot as a kid.

The morning was cold but sunny. As I drove, I noticed the many Christmas decorations on homes and businesses. I wasn't the only one getting into the festive spirit!

Before going to the quilt store, my plan was to stop at the Olde Orchard Antique Mall, a treasure trove of antiques and collectibles just outside of Egg Harbor. My first trip there had been such a fun experience. With all those dealers, I was hoping to find a feather tree for Rachael. Wouldn't she be surprised if I did!

As I approached the mall, I was disappointed to see that it was already closed for the season. So much for walking away with a feather tree today. I might as well find something to eat or drink. Door County Coffee & Tea Company called my name. I pulled in the parking lot anticipating the wonderful aromas that awaited me. Once inside, I picked up packages of amaretto and cherry blend to enjoy at home later. The jars of Montmorency cherries for baking pie stared at me, so I set two of them on the counter. Then I turned around and saw the cutest sweatshirts. One said Dog Mom and the other said Cat Mom. I grabbed the one for cats as a gift for Kelly. My arms were full by then, but I couldn't resist the cutest vintage bib apron adorned with cherries. My mother would love it, and so would Carole and Linda. They had loved the Door County cherries when they visited the last time. After all that shopping, I went back and got my cup of hot coffee and a cherry yogurt muffin at the counter.

My shopping delayed the trip, but that was okay. I'd made a nice start to my Christmas gift shopping.

About fifteen minutes later, I arrived at the nifty city of Sturgeon Bay, the county seat. Its shops, restaurants, and outdoor offerings always reminded me that I needed to come here more often. It was one more reason to love Door County. The stars were aligned for me today, as I was lucky enough to grab a parking spot right in front of the quilt shop as someone was leaving.

When I entered Barn Door Quilts, I noticed Olivia in the next aisle over from me. What a fun surprise to see her!

"Olivia! Nice to see you! I'll bet you visit this shop often since it's so close to your apartment."

"You probably don't know, but I fill in now and then for Carol when she needs someone. I'm handy for a last-minute notice."

"What a dream job!"

"Now, how can I help you today?" Olivia asked, sounding quite professional.

"Well, I need a nice 100% cotton fabric," I stated. "Do you carry Kona Cotton? I'm fond of that brand."

"We do!" She nodded and showed me where it was.

"I'd like nine yards of that, please," I requested at the counter.

Just then, Carol, the owner, joined Olivia. Would she remember me from the quilt show?

"Hello, Carol. Good to see you. Remember, I talked to you about our outdoor quilt show."

"Oh my, yes! I'd like to be one of your sponsors next year, and if you decide to have vendors, I might participate in that."

"Oh, that's wonderful! Thank you!" I noted. "I haven't tried to get permission for vendors yet."

"You just missed Anna and Marta," Olivia said as she cut the fabric. "Anna was in heaven here with all the fabric choices. They purchased quite a bit."

"Oh, I can't wait until she's in the club," I said with hope.

"Me, too!" followed Olivia.

Chapter 50

"Olivia, is there a good shop here in town where I might find an antique feather tree?"

"I don't know about finding an antique feather tree, but I like the shop across the street," she suggested. "I think it's called DC Traders. You can't miss its bright blue storefront. I go there every now and then, and I always find something I didn't know I needed."

"Thanks, I'll check it out," I nodded. "Goodbye, Carol. I'll be in touch about the show."

"Good to see you, Claire," Olivia said as she handed me my bag. "If you see Rachael before I do, tell her I have a block for her quilt."

"She'll be pleased," I noted. "She's really excited about it."

As I left, I immediately noticed the blue shop across the street. As I entered Door County Traders, I spotted all kinds of goodies of interest. I could only find one employee working, and she was busy at the moment, so I kept browsing.

When I reached the rear of the store, I saw a decorated Christmas tree on the counter that was part of a Christmas display. Sure enough, it was a feather tree! It was showing its age, but the green feathers were still intact on the wire limbs.

I couldn't find a price tag on it anywhere, so I'd have to ask the woman working about the cost.

"Can you tell me what you're asking for the feather tree in the back?" I asked with interest.

"Oh, I'm sorry, but the tree isn't for sale," she said politely.

"You're sure? It's just what I've been looking for."

"Well, they're hard to find. I've had this one for many years, and I just get it out to do a display every year."

"So, you won't consider selling it?" I pleaded. "I have a really good home for it."

"No, I'm sorry. I don't know if you realize it, but they've become quite pricey."

"I do realize that," I nodded with a smile. "What amount would you consider letting it go for?" She shook her head.

"I don't think I could ever let it go for less than $400. Besides, I really don't want to get rid of it."

I took a deep breath. "I'll pay you $500," I committed.

She looked at me in disbelief. "You would?"

"Yes, I would," I confirmed. "I have a friend who's making a Tannenbaum quilt with a feather tree design in the center. She's honoring her late husband. They ran a Christmas tree farm together. She'd love this so much."

"That's a lot of money to pass up," she said with hesitation. "You do realize you could likely find one cheaper if you really looked around."

"I don't know where to start. The one place I thought might have one is closed for the season. I think I was supposed to walk in here and find this one," I said with a chuckle.

"Well, I'd want to keep those ornaments," she noted. "Most of them have been in my family for years."

"Of course," I happily agreed. "I think my friend would be likely to leave it without ornaments."

"So, do you know the history of the feather tree?" the woman asked.

"I do!" I nodded. "I recently met a girl from Germany who shared information about it."

"Well, okay then," she said with reluctance. "I'll just charge you $450. I can't in good faith take your offer."

"Thank you! Thank you ever so much!" I gushed.

"Now, you have to realize how delicate this is," she began to explain as she was removing the ornaments. "These wire branches are fragile. When the trees were new, they were designed so that you could bend these branches up for storage, but if you did that now, after over a hundred years, they could break off. Did you notice that the tips have a small metal candle holder? Some have them, and some don't. Now and then, you'll see a red berry attached on the end as well. Tell your friend that she can still find the narrow candles if she wants them. Do you have room in your vehicle for this, so it won't get damaged?"

"Yes, I think I do," I said with hope. "I sure appreciate everything you've told me."

"Now, if she's not happy with this tree, tell her I'll buy it back from her."

"That's very generous of you," I said with a smile. "But I don't think she'll be disappointed. I think it'll be happy living on a Christmas tree farm." She smiled at the thought.

I walked out of the shop feeling like I'd accomplished my mission. I laid the tree down carefully on its side in the back of my Subaru. It just fit. Now it was time to head home. I had an unexpected Christmas surprise to deliver. I didn't want to think about the money I'd just spent.

Chapter 51

On the way home, I stopped for fast food so I'd have something to munch on the way home. It had been a while since I'd eaten that cherry yogurt muffin. As I waited in line, my cell showed a call from Brenda.

"Hey, Brenda! What's up?" I answered.

"Can you talk?"

"I'm on my way home from Sturgeon Bay, so I'll call you tonight if that's okay?"

"Sure. It's not that important."

"Okay. Talk soon!"

I headed home wondering what she wanted to talk about. I was pleasantly surprised to see more Christmas lights as the dusk was turning to darkness. I was getting sleepy. The sooner I got home, the better.

I turned on the radio to help pass the time and learned there would be a big snowstorm heading our way. Perhaps it would melt by the time we had quilt club. I hadn't known the group to cancel unless the library decided to close.

My mind wandered on all I had to do before Christmas. My tree for Rachael was a real accomplishment. I sure hope she wouldn't mind my idea.

When I arrived home, I pondered where to hide the feather tree so Puff wouldn't bother it. She was sound asleep, so I went upstairs to place it on my desk. I'd just have to keep the door closed all the time. I was growing fond of this tree and even considered keeping it for myself.

I was ready for an early night, so the call to Brenda would have to wait until tomorrow. I put on my pajamas and turned on the classic movie channel. I was pleased to see that *It's a Wonderful Life* with Jimmy Stewart was playing. I always wondered if we could possibly be related. The movie held my interest for a while, and then I fell fast asleep.

The next morning, the TV was still on. I then recalled that part of the movie ended up in my dream. I couldn't remember the details, though.

Puff and I went downstairs for our breakfast. There sat all my packages from yesterday's shopping experience. I pulled out a package of the cherry crème coffee and waited for the delightful smell and taste. I sat at the kitchen table with some toast and started making my plans on Kelly's quilt. Brenda called before I could make any progress on the quilt. I felt bad that she had to call me again.

"Oh, Brenda, I'm so sorry I didn't get back to you. I had quite a day yesterday, and I was dead tired when I got home."

"That's okay. I just wanted to share a bit of news with you."

"I hope it's good news."

She chuckled. "Well, let me begin by saying that I was at the Pig yesterday. When I was checking out, Kent was in line ahead of me. He recognized me immediately and became rather friendly. I know he's shy, so it made me feel good."

"Oh!"

"So, then he wanted me to follow him out to the parking lot. We were making small talk, but then he asked if I had any interest in getting a cup of coffee at Carroll House."

"I'm liking this call more and more! I hope you went."

"I thought about making an excuse, but then I said, 'Sure!'"

"And how did it go?"

She paused. "I'm not sure. I was pretty nervous. I felt odd sitting there with a younger man. Believe it or not, we found plenty to talk about, especially when we were chatting about the Packers. I felt like he really needed someone to talk to."

"Maybe so."

"We sat there with our coffee for over an hour. Then he walked me to the car and asked if he could call me sometime. I felt so stupid that I don't recall what I said."

"This is good! He must be attracted to you. Take that as a compliment."

"He's almost young enough to be my son. His oldest girl is about nine, I think. My daughter is now over twenty!"

"I'm not sure you should be thinking of age here. You're in your fifties, right?"

"Yes, fifty-two."

"Well, he's in his forties, so that's not too much of an age gap. He just wants to be good friends with you, not marry you!"

She burst into laughter. "You're right, I guess. When I talk to him, I don't sense the age gap."

"Brenda, I don't think you realize how attractive and sweet you are. Even Pete wouldn't have flirted with you if you weren't. Remember that. If Kent calls you to go out, do it. I'll bet both of you could use a friend right now. He had a bitter divorce from what I hear."

"Yeah, he briefly touched on that, but I didn't comment."

"Well, I hope you go."

"Oh, he probably won't call. He's likely regretting that coffee invitation."

"Brenda, I don't think your age matters to him. You obviously made a positive impression when you were at Rachael's. Kent's a down-to-earth guy who isn't going to worry about how things look to other people. Your love for the Packers gives you both something happy to talk about."

"Yeah, he was quite surprised, I think, about how much I knew about them."

"Well, Harry has season tickets, so that's another reason to stay in touch with Kent," I teased.

"You're terrible, Claire!" she joked.

"Look, you called me for reassurance, and I'm giving it to you."

"You have, and you're a good friend."

I was happy for Brenda in this moment and hoped that something would develop for her and Kent. I couldn't help but wonder what I'd do if I were the older woman being asked out by a younger man. I'd probably just laugh. I suppose there will always be that double standard of a man needing to be older. What an outdated concept. Anyway, her spirits were lifted, and that made me smile.

Chapter 52

My morning time was shot, but I was still determined to make time for Kelly's quilt. So, without hesitation, I did just that. The feel of fabric comforted me. When I painted or quilted, it was easy to lose my thoughts or concerns and just zone out. I also liked watching something develop right before my eyes.

As I continued, I was reminded how much I dislike the cutting part of quiltmaking. I needed to stay focused on the goal: getting Kelly's top completed, doing whatever it took. I don't think I'll ever want to see a Four-Patch block again. By six o'clock, I had everything done except the border.

I needed a break, so I came downstairs and decided that spaghetti would taste good for dinner. I poured myself a glass of wine and threw together a simple salad.

I looked out the window and blinked twice. I couldn't believe it, but Grayson was getting out of his car! I quickly checked my phone wondering if I'd missed a call or text.

"Hey, beautiful!" he greeted as he came in the door. "I hope you don't mind that I'm just popping in."

"Please come in!" I said, wanting to squeeze him tight but resisting.

"What smells so good?"

"You're a typical man, alright," I said laughing. "I'm making spaghetti. Would you like to join me? I have to admit it won't be as good as the kind you and Kelly make with the homemade sauce, but I like it."

"It's tempting, but I'll at least join you in having some wine."

"Good, have a seat here at the table. I have to slow things down a bit."

"I won't stay long," he stated sadly.

"And why is that? I'd love for you to share my store-bought spaghetti and meager salad and then retire in front of the fire with our wine while you tell me about your day."

"You're serious, aren't you?" he said, coming close to kiss me.

"I am!" I said, touching his lips with my finger of spaghetti sauce. He knew I was enticing him.

"Okay, you win. Let me give Kelly a quick call. You're irresistible, Claire Stewart."

Grayson went out to the porch to make his call while I added more noodles to the spaghetti pot.

"Is everything okay?" I asked when he came back into the kitchen.

"Everything's just peachy. Kelly has already eaten and has an agenda in her bedroom on her computer."

Grayson reached out just then without saying another word. I heard the pot of spaghetti boiling in the background as I enjoyed his passionate kiss and embrace.

Chapter 53

After Grayson's display of affection, it was hard to concentrate on putting a meal together. He insisted we eat right there at the kitchen table.

We were drinking more than we were eating, which enhanced our playful mood. At one point, we were feeding each other spaghetti and losing our appetites. At times, the sensual motions were most provocative.

"I say we leave this table and take our wine in front of the fire," I suggested sweetly.

"If you insist, but I make a pretty good bottle washer."

"Don't tempt me!"

We took our glasses and the bottle of wine to the fireplace. While Grayson put another log on the fire, I arranged my floor pillows right in front of the blazing fire.

"This is just perfect, Claire. Why is it that when I'm with you, I never want to leave?"

"Let me count the reasons," I teased, clinking his glass of wine. "It's nice to see you relaxed. You're always in a rush to come and go."

He nodded in agreement. "I'll be even more relaxed if you let me hold you close," he whispered as we both laid back.

"It's nice to hear nothing but you and the crackle of the fire," I said as I felt his breath close to mine.

This was a rare opportunity to be alone with each other, and we were taking advantage of it.

Few words were spoken after that as we discovered each other's desires. I had mixed feelings, but my emotions won out. We'd waited well over a year to get to where we were physically this evening. The fire and the wine had helped us relax and put our inhibitions aside. I felt safe with Grayson—more than with any other man I'd ever known.

We fell asleep in each other's arms, covered by the quilt I typically had on my couch. I didn't want to wake up. At one point, I detected a slight snoring sound that convinced me Grayson was completely happy and relaxed.

Hours later, I felt Grayson moving around in the darkness, lit only by a slight glimmer from the fireplace.

"It's four o'clock, sweetheart, and I need to leave," he whispered in my ear. "Continue to sleep. I love you."

"I love you, too," I whispered back as I pulled more of the cover around me.

I didn't even hear Grayson go out the door since I was in such a pleasant state. Several hours later, I felt Puff brushing against my face and knew that morning had arrived.

"Oh, Puff, get your own breakfast," I called out. Her fierce meow told me what she thought of that.

I got up slowly, feeling the effects of too much wine. The messy kitchen wasn't a welcome sight, but the memories of what had transpired made me smile. I actually laughed aloud when I saw spaghetti in places where it shouldn't have been. I could almost taste the kisses with sauce on our lips.

I made my coffee and moved slowly to clean things up. It was quilt club day, so my focus needed to be on getting a shower.

Leaving a dirty kitchen was not an option with Puff roaming around, so I did what I could before leaving for club.

The brisk air contrasted with the slight headache I was feeling. I tried to put it aside by remembering Grayson's words of "I love you." Ah, life was good.

I practically skipped into the library room, where most of the members were getting their coffee. I couldn't wait to have that second cup. I kept smelling something wonderful.

Chapter 54

"Good morning, Amy," I greeted our newest member.

"Good morning, Claire. I'm happy to be here."

"Not as happy as we are," I added. "If I can answer any questions about anything, just let me know."

"Thank you," she said, looking relieved.

"Ladies, ladies, let's take a seat and get started," Marta said aloud. "The first order of business is to welcome Amy Burris this morning." We all clapped as she blushed. "We also have a guest, Anna Marie Meyer, who we'll be voting on later in the meeting. Welcome back, Anna."

They both looked happy to be there, but nervous.

"Now ladies, it's close to Christmas, but you still have time to make small gifts," Marta reminded. "Anna has brought a few things with her that she used to sell, so I'll let her explain. After she's finished, Rachael requested to have the floor."

"Ladies, here are some of my simpler trinkets, as I call them," Anna began. "I never waste cloth, so I call these 'schnibbles.' " We all chuckled because we knew exactly what she meant. "I also brought some of my kitchen quilts, small goblet quilts, and small pretties for the tree."

Her items were lovely, even if we did have different names for them. We admired what we knew as pot holders, coasters, and various Christmas tree ornaments, which included a hexie-pieced tree garland.

"I sew these by hand, as you say. I get quicker when I do so many," she said with a chuckle. "I'll pass them around for you to see."

Her work was incredibly well done. The garland was alternating green and red calico hexies carefully connected by hand stitching.

Five minutes later, Marta got our attention once again.

"Ladies, I didn't get word about Ava not being here," she noted. "Anyone heard from her?"

Everyone shook their head. Of course, I didn't want to share with the others that the last time I'd seen her was when I confronted her about her sticky fingers. I hoped her absence today wasn't because she thought I'd told the other club members about our conversation.

"Well, I hope she's alright. Rachael, you now have the floor," Marta announced.

"Thanks, Marta," Rachael began as she looked at her notes. "As all of you know by now, I was quite taken with Anna's Tannenbaum quilt. I knew right away I wanted to re-create one. Since I have a Christmas tree farm, I want to dedicate the quilt to my deceased husband, Charlie, who loved Christmas trees. My design will include your Christmas tree blocks, which will surround a feather tree in the center, like Anna's quilt does. It'll be much more primitive than hers to suit our Christmas tree farm. Thanks to Lee, who has agreed to embroider the medallion tree for me. I'm so excited to announce also that there will be a

Tannenbaum Christmas party at our place, where I hope to show the quilt."

Everyone applauded, and Anna went over to Rachael to give her a hug of support. Greta smiled, but in her heart, I knew she was probably thinking that this idea was completely inappropriate.

"Thank you, Rachael," Marta graciously said. "Now, who has show-and-tell today?"

"I brought a whole cloth that I just finished for my sister-in-law in Minnesota," Greta stated. "It's the first large whole cloth I've done, and I learned a lot in the process."

All of us responded overwhelmingly to show our support for her. She'd done a magnificent job.

"Greta, you're amazing," I said as she sat down next to me.

"Thank you, Claire," she responded modestly.

Olivia was the only other one to have show-and-tell. First, she announced that she had a tell, which was that she was helping out at Barn Door Quilts down the street from her. She then pulled out of a bag a pineapple design lap quilt made with bright solid fabrics. It was so Olivia, and so striking.

"If no one else has any announcements, we'll proceed to vote on Anna's membership. If you've all been wondering what you've been smelling this entire meeting, it's Anna's wonderful apple strudel. Now, don't let her goodies affect your vote!" Everyone laughed. "Thank you, Anna!"

Everyone rushed to the table for a piece of strudel as soon as they submitted their secret ballot. It was obvious Anna was going to be our second new member. No one was in a hurry to leave that morning, which I could tell made Greta nervous. She kept checking her watch, likely worried the library police would be knocking on our door at any minute. We rarely had refreshments when Greta was in charge.

Chapter 55

"So, Claire, can you lunch?" Cher asked as she approached me.

"I was wondering the same thing," Rachael asked.

"Well, sure. Where shall we go?" I asked with excitement.

"I love Gibraltar Grill, and it's close," suggested Rachael.

"Sounds good, but this strudel was plenty for my lunch," I added.

Cher and I left before Rachael because she wanted to chat some more with Anna about the Tannenbaum party.

When Cher and I arrived, we requested one of the tables near the fireplace.

"What's with this happy face today, Claire Bear?" Cher teased. "Do you have something juicy to tell me?"

"Perhaps, but wait until Rachael gets here, or I'll have to repeat myself. Is there anything new with you and Carl?"

"He's a challenge to figure out. I think he's torn as to when he can and can't flirt with me." I chuckled. "Since I'm an employee, maybe he thinks I'll file sexual harassment charges or something."

Surely, that wasn't on his mind, was it? "I think he just has to get to know you better so he feels comfortable with his words."

"Maybe. I sold a quilt yesterday, and he gets especially nice when that happens."

"Well, it's because our reputation is on the line with him regarding his expansion. I think it'll really pay off for him to sell quilts. No one in the county is doing that to my knowledge."

"Hey! We're over here," Cher yelled across the room to Rachael.

"Did you accomplish much with Anna?" I asked with interest. The expression on her face said it all.

"Anna is so excited," she began. "She just wants to sell her strudel because that's her specialty. And I think it'll sell quicker than she can make it since it's so good! Everything's happening rather nicely for her."

After we all ordered our favorite chicken quesadilla, we asked Rachael to tell us more about Anna.

"Marta chimed in to say they're trying to find the right building for Anna to buy rather than rent," Rachael continued. "She's determined to get that bakery going so she has an income."

"In Baileys Harbor?" I asked.

"Yes. I think she's going to need Marta's family to help," Rachael shared.

"Right before you came, Claire was about to share something with me, but she wanted to wait until you got here," Cher revealed.

"You got engaged!" Rachael said rather loudly.

"No, no, not that," I quickly stated. "I have to admit, though, that I'm totally in love with this man. He came to dinner last night unexpectedly and didn't leave until the wee hours of the morning. It was the best night of my life!" Rachael and Cher looked at each other. They knew exactly what I was trying to tell them.

"It's about time!" Cher finally said.

"You two are meant for each other," Rachael added. "You guys are taking way too long to tie this thing up."

"Hey!" I scolded. "I don't want to make another mistake. To be honest, it's the first time ever I've felt safe with a man. Does that make sense?" They both nodded like they were about to cry.

"It hasn't been easy for Grayson to tell me he loves me," I shared. "He's always been in a rush to be somewhere else, or he's been worried about Kelly."

"I'm so happy for you, Claire Bear," Cher said touching my hand. "I'd give anything for that feeling."

"I'll never have again what I had with Charlie," Rachael admitted sadly.

"Of course not, but the feeling can return. It's obvious Harry's really warming up to you, Rachael," I consoled.

As we ate our lunch, I was reminded of what it's like to have close girlfriends, no matter the age. Even in our fifties, friendships like ours were life giving. We were still sharing the details of our lives that were important, like that first kiss or getting our first menstrual period as teenagers. After talk of the men in our lives, we jumped to other topics.

"So, Rachael, if I do a painted block for the quilt, it'll be okay?" I asked with some reservation.

"It'll be fine," Rachael noted. "Charlie will like whatever you add. Remember, it's all for him."

Chapter 56

I didn't get back home until four o'clock. There was a lot to like about my day. An hour later, Grayson called, much to my delight.

"I just wondered if you were having spaghetti for dinner tonight," he joked. "I sure enjoyed it, as well as the dessert." I chuckled at his dry humor.

"I could make it again if you like," I teased back. "The kitchen is just as we left it. I just don't understand how noodles managed to get everywhere they did." Grayson joined me in laughter.

"My memory has no regrets," he sweetly noted.

"So, seriously, Grayson, how were things when you returned home?"

"Very quiet. I snuck upstairs like a tardy teenager and got a few more hours of sleep."

"She never said anything?"

"Not so far. Did you eventually move off the floor?"

"Not until Puff walked across my face!"

He chuckled. "Are you coming to the chamber breakfast meeting tomorrow at the Waterfront Grill?"

"Oh, I haven't thought about it. Are you going?"

"Yes. I'd love to see you."

"Will you save me a seat?"

"I'll try. I really have a lot to do, but I feel I need to be there. I'm hoping they have spaghetti."

I chuckled. I hung up with the comfort I'd see him again in twenty-four hours. I wasn't hungry since I'd had lunch and too much strudel. I made a fire to enjoy, and then my phone rang. I looked and saw it was Carole.

"What a nice surprise!" I responded. "How is everything?"

"Good. How about you?"

"Pretty good. I just made a fire."

"I just felt I needed to tell you what Jill has been sharing with me."

"Oh. Is this about Austen?"

"Yes. He's really depressed and seldom comes into the office according to her sources. I don't think he's recovering as he had hoped."

"Well, his kind of recovery takes time. He's never been a very patient person."

"I just thought if he heard from you, it might cheer him up a bit."

I paused. "I'll give it some thought. Who knows what's going on in his mind?"

"On a happier note, I got a call from the kitchen shop on the top of the hill, and they ordered more cookbooks. They told me they're selling well as Christmas gifts. I'm thrilled people are buying them!"

"I'm happy for you, Carole. That shop does pretty well. How's Linda?"

"She's good. Her granddaughters keep her busy. She, too, has had an order or two of her jewelry."

"Tell her hello for me."

I hung up with a sad feeling in my gut. If I responded to Austen, he'd know it was pity on my part. Will he always be in my life in one way or another?" My cell rang again almost immediately after I'd hung up. I wondered it if was Carole calling back to tell me something she'd forgotten. It ended up being Ericka.

"Hi, Claire. I'm sorry it's been so long since we've talked, but I've been preoccupied. Hey, what do you know about Cher and her boss? She seems quite taken with him. Do you know him? Is she getting herself in trouble?"

I had to chuckle to myself about her line of questioning. "To my knowledge, he's a wonderful guy and a great boss. I got to know him a bit when we did our quilt show this past summer. Cher and I were there when he talked about his new addition and needing some extra help. That's when Cher jumped in and offered to work for him."

"I just don't want her getting hurt."

"Neither do I. They're both adults, and it may not go anywhere."

"Alright. I'll stop worrying."

So, what's going on with you lately?" I asked.

Chapter 57

"Nothing good, I'm afraid." She paused. "I'm afraid I've joined a club I never wanted to be part of: women with breast cancer."

"Oh no, Ericka! That's awful. Did you just find out?"

"About a week ago. I had to let myself absorb the news first, and I wasn't sure I wanted anyone at all to know about it. The last thing I want is to be pitied and have people ask me all the time how I feel, like I may die at any moment."

"Ericka, you're young and strong. You're not going to die. Women survive this beast every day, and you're going to survive it, too. What's your diagnosis and treatment?"

"It's the pits, I'm afraid, because I'm stage 4. First, they want to do some surgery, then radiation, then chemo. The rest of my life is doomed, even if I live."

"Ericka, we need to keep a positive attitude about this. You're a dear friend to so many. I know how strong you are. You can survive most anything if you take one day at a time and accept all the prayers from those of us who care for you."

"I'm afraid I know too much about my diagnosis from being in the medical field. My chances of survival are slim."

"Please don't talk like this. Cher and I will be there for you, and I promise not to tell a soul if that's the way you want it."

"George is taking this really hard. Our mother died from cancer, so that's been on our minds. He promised to help me when I need to be driven for treatment. I have to go into Green Bay for radiation and chemo. I do have a cousin who lives there, so I may be spending some nights with her if I have to."

"Please take advantage of every kind of help you can, Ericka. People want to help and just need to know how. This isn't the time to be some sort of hero. Please keep us posted. We love you."

"Thanks, Claire," she said before hanging up. I knew she was starting to cry.

I immediately called her best friend and mine.

"Oh, Claire, I'll bet I know why you're calling," Cher quickly answered.

"I feel so, so sorry for her," I said in dismay. "I didn't realize her mother had died from cancer."

"I know how scared she is," Cher said, breaking into tears. "I hate that this is happening to her. It's stage 4, for God's sake. I wonder if she had a clue and just tried to ignore it."

"I know, I know. But I believe in miracles and prayer."

"We have to keep this a secret for her as long as we can. It means a lot to her."

"Absolutely. I'll do whatever it takes to be helpful to her."

"Truthfully, I'm angry with her for putting this off."

"I've heard that folks in the medical field are sometimes the worst patients. They self-sabotage. I truly hope she didn't wait too long to beat this. On a more pleasant note,

I heard from Carole. She said that The Main Course kitchen shop ordered more of her cookbooks. They're a big hit this Christmas, I guess."

"How wonderful for her! She just needed to get the books in the right stores."

"On a sour note, she encouraged me to think about calling Austen. He's getting more depressed and not wanting to come into the office. I don't know what to do."

"So, no progress, is that it?"

"I'm afraid so. I can't tell you how bad I feel, but I'm at a loss now for what I should be doing."

"I'm no help. Austen and Ericka truly need our prayers, that's for sure."

We said our sad goodbyes, unable to console each other. My head was hurting from all the bad news. Take it to God, I kept reminding myself. Then I remembered that God said he helps those who help themselves. I was going to have to figure this out for myself.

I lay there for what seemed hours, going back and forth from concerns about Ericka to concerns about Austen. This had to be so hard for both of them because they were used to being so strong. We never know what lies ahead. Tears finally put me to sleep.

Chapter 58

The noise of sleet hitting my window got my attention early in the morning. I could also hear the roar of thunder in the background. Puff was acting somewhat nervous, so I went ahead and got up. I couldn't imagine going to the meeting in this weather. I was wishing I hadn't told Grayson I'd be there.

When I got downstairs, I could see nothing but icicles hanging in front of my kitchen window. I bravely texted Grayson.

[Claire]
Is the chamber meeting still on?

It took a while for him to respond, so I poured some more coffee.

[Grayson]
You're in Door County now, not Missouri!

Well, apparently, I'm a wuss. My poor Subaru had to be completely covered in ice. Oh, what I wouldn't give for a garage. Many don't have garages around here since they fly the coop to warmer locales in the winter. When I checked the forecast on my phone, I discovered we wouldn't be having sunshine until late tomorrow. The ice was going to stick around awhile.

I went upstairs to get dressed and give myself a pep talk. I should at least go out and check on my car even if I didn't go to the meeting. Wearing heavy wool, I went to start my vehicle and chip away the ice on the windshield. The ice tingled against my face. As soon as I cleared a spot on the glass, it was immediately covered again with ice. I was done. I went inside knowing I had no business being out in this mess. I took off my coat and sent Grayson a text.

[Claire]
This Missourian tried and failed. I surrender. You've got to show me how to do this.

[Grayson]
Would you like for me to come and get you?

[Claire]
No! I'm staying put. If you insist on going, please be careful!

[Grayson]
Are you sure?

[Claire]
I'm sure. Have a good meeting.

I got into comfortable clothes for the day. I now had free time to do something more productive. I could finish the border on Kelly's quilt. Then I could call the quilt shop to get on their list for quilting. As I began to restructure my thoughts for the day, the phone rang. Brenda was on the other line.

"I figured I'd find you home," she teased.

"I did have plans, but I'm frozen in here."

"I have a couple of things on my mind," she began. "If you don't mind a really simple quilting design for Kelly's quilt, I'd be happy to get that done for you before Christmas."

"Oh, really? You could?"

"I'm no professional. I only quilt my own work with simple designs."

"Well, it sounds wonderful to me. I'm sure Kelly would be happy with anything you came up with."

"I do have other news you'll find interesting. I heard from Kent again."

"Ooh! That *is* interesting!"

"He arranged with his dad to get some of his tickets to see a Packers game on Sunday. I'm in shock!"

"Girl, that must be the gift of a lifetime for you," I teased.

"It is!"

"He must really like you, Brenda. I'm happy for you."

"Oh, he just knows I'm a great Packers fan. It'll be such fun!"

"It will. You'll have to let me know how it goes."

"Well, I'll pick up your quilt top when I work again. It won't take me long."

"Great! I'll see you then."

The news I'd received from Brenda was much better than what I'd have heard at a stiff chamber meeting that would have forced me out in the cold. I wanted to get some Packers clothing for Brenda for her Christmas present. Maybe I could find something for her soon and then give it to her when she picked up Kelly's quilt top. The On Deck store down the street is where I purchased some Packers clothes for myself when I attended the game with Rachael, Charlie, and Harry. Brenda would love a team shirt. I could only hope that this friendship between Brenda and Kent would develop into more than just a shared love of the Packers.

Chapter 59

The next day, I was tempted to call Grayson and ask about the chamber breakfast, but I changed my mind. Cher called while I was pressing Kelly's quilt top in preparation for Brenda.

"I have an idea!" she said with excitement.

"I want to give Ericka something special for Christmas, and I think I've decided on something."

"I'm listening."

"I want to go out to Amy's quilt shop and get her an Amish quilt. I know she likes them. It would be a nice show of our members supporting her as well. I just hope I can find one I can afford."

"Great idea, and don't worry about the price. We could go in together on the gift."

"Swell! That would help."

"I've been thinking about her, too. My guess is she's dreading Christmas and likely won't put up a tree this year. I might try to find a nice tree at Rachael's and take it to her house and string the lights for her. It could lift her spirits a little."

"That's a sweet idea, but it sounds like teamwork might work best. We can bring the tree and her quilt the same day and make a little party out of it."

"Great! Maybe I'll get a wreath, too!"

"I know we'd be spending a lot on her, but she sure needs the support right now. I work tomorrow. Could you go later this afternoon?"

"Sure. I could go right now. I'm getting Kelly's quilt top ready for Brenda. She offered to quilt it for me."

"I didn't know she machine quilted for people."

"She doesn't, but she knows I'm in a pinch to get it done before Christmas and offered to do it for me. I'll fill you in on her latest news when I see you. Around two o'clock?"

"Great! See you soon!"

I went back to the office where I was ironing and saw Rachael's feather tree sitting there. So far, I had been able to keep Puff out of the room. When I leave today, I'll make sure the door is shut and Puff is put in her chair.

The sun was out, and a lot of the snow and ice had melted. It was actually nice to get out in the fresh air and do something fun. My hibernation yesterday had left me well rested and ready to step out. I made Cher and me a hot tea in to-go cups. She was right on time and was pleased as punch to see the hot tea in my hand.

"So, Claire Bear, did you make it to that chamber meeting yesterday?" she asked in a joking manner.

"No way! Grayson offered to come and get me, but he should have known better. I'm a wuss. I guess he went, but I'm not sure."

"I'm looking forward to our outing today. I never get to Jacksonport much to see what it has to offer," Cher admitted. "Amy will be tickled to see us since she's now a member of the Quilters of the Door!"

"She's such a great addition."

"Oh, my goodness!" Amy said in surprise when we walked in the door. "It's a delight to see you! And I can't thank you enough for letting me be part of your quilt group. I was so nervous."

"Our pleasure, and we should've done it sooner," Cher noted. "Your place looks great as always, but we're actually here to spend some money!" Amy's face lit up. "We're here to buy a quilt for a friend who is going through a rough time. We need a queen size, and I'm guessing something in blues if I'm remembering correctly. It seems like that was the color of her bedroom the last time I saw it. Claire and I want to buy this together for her."

"Now, you're the kind of friends to have!" she joked.

"Are all the quilts you have in stock stacked on this bed?" I asked.

"Oh, no. I have some in the back room as well," she revealed. "There are some blue ones in this stack, so let's take a look here first."

"Do you have a lot of Amish ladies contribute to your supply?" Cher asked as she helped Amy lift one.

"Yes, many, but not surprisingly, there are a few Amish quilters who sell more than others. Once someone likes a certain quilter's work, they usually request another quilt from that same quiltmaker. Ethel Yoder is my top-selling quilter. In fact, this Broken Star we're looking at now is one she made. Do you prefer a pieced quilt over an appliqué quilt?" Cher and I looked at each other. We hadn't talked about that.

"I think pieced," Cher said with a nod. "Ericka has simple, clean tastes. Right, Cher?" I nodded.

"Yes. She's not the girly-girly type," I said with a chuckle.

Amy smiled and nodded. "I have a blue-and white Jacob's Ladder quilt. It's a much simpler design and a little cheaper than a lot of these others. Actually, it was made by one of Ethel's nieces. There are three generations who have made quilts for resale."

"I'd like to see that one," I instructed.

When Amy pulled it out to show us, the pieces were smaller than usual, which made it look fancier. I paused.

"Now, I do have a blue whole cloth quilt in the back room that would give you a lot of flexibility," Amy said. I don't put the whole cloths on the floor because when people handle them, everything shows."

Chapter 60

"Okay, let's check out that one," I said with interest. Cher nodded.

As soon as she unfolded the beauty, I fell in love. The entwined rows of feathers were really impressive.

"It's gorgeous!" Cher praised.

"I know this is a bit formal for Ericka, but she'd truly admire this work. And the solid color will be helpful in whatever room she uses it in."

Cher picked up the price tag to show me, and I nodded as I calculated what half the price would be.

"It's perfect. Let's do it. She's worth it."

"I have a nice gift box I can put the quilt in," Amy noted. "All you'll need is a bow."

"Thanks, Amy. That sounds perfect," I said approvingly.

"Cher, look at all Amy's other cute items here. I'm going to have to remember this."

"I know, but I'd feel guilty not buying my Christmas gifts at Carl's gallery."

"I understand," I nodded. "I love the things in Carl's shop, too. Hint, hint." She burst into laughter.

"Here you go, ladies! I gave you a little discount." Amy added. "Tell her it's labeled by Martha Yoder, who lives in Ohio."

"Thanks, Amy. We'll be back," I promised.

Off we went, feeling quite happy. We hoped the gift of giving would make up for the expenditure.

"Claire, if you bring Ericka's tree home, let me know as soon as possible so I can arrange to go with you to set it up."

"It's a deal."

I was exhausted when I got home. I knew we had done the right thing, and it certainly would make Ericka feel better. While she was on my mind, I pulled out extra lights for her Christmas tree. I couldn't think of how we should decorate it, but someday, I may try to make a hexie garland like Anna did for her tree. That would be a project for a tree in the future.

I gave Puff a little attention before going upstairs for the evening. I wondered if she ever got lonely or whether she was perfectly happy to have peace and quiet.

I turned on my favorite TV channel, Turner Classic Movies, and *Rear Window* with James Stewart and Grace Kelly was playing. I've always liked that movie, but I hoped it didn't make me paranoid about who might be looking in my window. It kept my attention for a while before I fell into a deep sleep.

The next morning, the TV was still showing its regular scheduled programming. It might be nice to stay in bed all day and gorge on movies.

Abandoning the idea of being a total slug, I got dressed and headed downstairs. After breakfast, I wanted to hit the

On Deck store to find Brenda some Packers fan wear. Puff followed me around the cabin.

Puff finally got her food, and I left the cabin precisely at nine o'clock to drive down Main Street. There were few people out this early, so I was able to find a place to park right in front of their store. Inside, I went directly to the corner where I found the Green Bay Packers outerwear I'd purchased sometime back.

I loved seeing their other clothing merchandise, but right now, I had no special event or a reason to buy anything other than a gift for Brenda. I found a couple things I thought she'd love that should fit her well. While I was close, I also stopped in the Fish Creek Market to purchase a few groceries and get one of their famous deli sandwiches to last me a few days.

I was back home by ten thirty. Not bad! As I was unpacking my groceries, Brenda pulled up. I asked her to come inside.

I went upstairs to get Kelly's quilt and took the price tags off the Packers wear I was about to give her. I kept them in the store's bag, however.

When I came back down, I opened Kelly's quilt top for her to see. She was gracious and said she liked it.

"This will be no problem for me to handle," she said, sizing it up. "It won't take me long. I'll be done by Christmas!"

I smiled in appreciation.

Chapter 61

I was pleased to hear how Brenda thought she might quilt it in geometric lines.

"Oh, Claire! Look who just pulled in your drive! It's Kent! This might be awkward. There's a big tree on the back of his pickup. Is that for you?"

I nodded. I went out to greet Kent with great anticipation.

"Is this a bad time? I see you have company."

"That's Brenda's car. She came by to pick up a quilt top that she's going to quilt for me. Let me give you a hand."

I grabbed one end of the tree, and we managed to get it inside as Brenda held open the porch door.

"Hey, Brenda!" Kent greeted her.

"That's a gorgeous tree you're bringing!" Brenda complimented.

"I love it! It's perfect!" I cheered when Kent stood it up.

"It's great you have the height on this porch to accommodate it," Kent noted.

"Can I get you something to drink?" I asked Kent, watching his eyes on Brenda.

"No, no," he said quickly. "I have too much to do. Brenda, I guess I'll be seeing you soon."

"Yes," she giggled. "I'm excited."

"Thanks again, Kent," I said as he left.

"Speaking of your big game coming up, I have an early Christmas present for you."

Brenda looked at me strangely. I handed her the bag from the On Deck store, and she said she couldn't imagine what it was.

"No way!" she reacted loudly when she pulled out the clothing. "This is too much, Claire!"

"You made it easy for me. I had this in mind for you anyway, but when you told me the game was coming up, I rushed to get it for you."

She gave me a big hug, and I knew I had scored. We visited for another half hour as she swooned over my choices of clothing. It was a good morning, as I got Kelly's quilt out the door and gave Brenda her Christmas gift.

After Brenda left, I pulled out my ladder and didn't waste any time putting the lights on my Christmas tree. I placed Puff in her chair so she wouldn't be in my way. As I got close to the end of my decorating, I wished I had someone to share it with. As I started to put my ladder away, my cell was ringing. I picked it up and saw it was Rachael. I stayed close to the tree so Puff wouldn't get any ideas.

"Hey, it's Rachael. I tried to reach Ava again without any luck. Have you heard from her?"

"Not since I ran into her at the post office."

"She was supposed to come out and bring me her block. I was planning on using it, but it's been two days now, and she's a no-show."

"Frances would be the only one who may know something. I might not get mine to you in time, either. Kent just delivered my tree while Brenda was here. It sounds like they have an exciting date coming up."

"Yeah. What do you make of that?"

"I'm not sure, but it appears they have really hit it off."

"They're both terrific people. I also wanted to tell you that the Tannenbaum Christmas party is up on our website now, plus I did some flyers to put around town."

"When in the world do you have time for all this extra stuff?"

"At night when I'm here alone. I feel Charlie is with me when I'm planning this. It sounds crazy, but it comforts me. I miss him so much."

"I know you do. I think this whole idea is just awesome, Rachael. Let me know if you hear from Ava."

Chapter 62

If I had anything to do with Ava's disappearance, I'll never forgive myself. I stared at my beautiful tree to get my mind off of her. I grabbed the red-and-white quilt I had gotten out to use under the tree. Puff was watching in hopes it could be her landing spot like it was last Christmas. She stood there wondering if it was safe to inhabit.

I got down on my knees to arrange the quilt. Then I took ahold of Puff and placed her on top. She looked up at me as if she couldn't believe my generosity. I smiled. This cat I had initially protested was really growing on me.

"This is permissible, but don't think for a minute you can get into this tree," I warned, like she'd listen.

Last year I did a little painting of Puff under the tree, which I gave to Cher for Christmas. Puff got comfy, hoping I'd just go away. The warmth of the lights must be comforting to her.

When evening came, I ran outside to see what my big tree on the porch looked like with its lights. I'll bet people could see my cabin from across town, I thought. It was magical. Cher said my cabin sparkled from back in the woods last year.

Happy with the way the tree looked from afar, I came back inside, shivering. My cell was ringing. It was Grayson, so I sat in front of the fire on one of my floor pillows.

"How goes it, Miss Stewart?" Grayson asked politely.

"It's going swell. I'm sitting in front of the fire admiring my Christmas tree and wishing you were here."

"Oh, you're making me feel bad. I wish I were there, too."

"Are you at home or at work?"

"I'm actually calling from Sturgeon Bay. I'm at a dinner meeting and hoping to leave before the speakers start, but that may not happen. I brought someone with me who seems to be interested in staying until it's all over.

"I hope your food is delicious at least."

"The main menu certainly appears to be so."

"Does Kelly mind when you don't come home for dinner?"

"She's spending the night with a friend, so I don't have to worry. Do you remember meeting some of my friends at least year's New Year's Eve party? Well, they may be doing that again and wondered if I was still seeing you."

I chuckled. "And what did you say?"

"I said, 'Yes, she's a keeper.'"

"Oh, that's an excellent answer. Thank you!"

"I hope we can see each other more this Christmas. I remember meeting your mother last year when she visited for Christmas. Will she be coming again?"

"I don't have a good feeling about that, so I haven't brought it up recently. I know this may not be the time, but do you have a second for me to ask you for some advice?"

"I have ten more minutes. What's up?"

"It's about Austen. I haven't heard from him lately, but I'm hearing he has no improvement on his condition and is extremely depressed. My friend Carole thinks a phone call from me would help him a lot. He sent me a text a while back asking if I was coming home for Christmas, but I just ignored it. I didn't want to start a dialogue but felt rude ignoring it completely. I know he doesn't want my pity. So not feeling partial to the situation, what do you think I should do?"

Grayson paused. "Claire, just listening to this scenario is sad. I can only imagine how it makes you feel since you were so close for many years. If you think for one moment that a call from you would help him keep his spirits up, I'd call. This guy has one heck of a challenge ahead of him, and everyone should help him wherever they can."

I took a deep breath. "He may not take my call."

"But you don't know that, do you?"

"No, not for sure. Thanks, Grayson. It really helps to have another perspective."

"My time is up, honey. Enjoy your fire and your new tree. I hope to see you soon!"

"I hope so, too."

I was hoping for an "I love you" before he hung up, but maybe he wasn't in a situation where it would've been comfortable. I lay back on the floor pillow thinking about how kind and thoughtful Grayson was. I'm always nervous to bring up Austen with him, but I don't think he has a jealous bone in his body.

Chapter 63

It was seven o'clock. Was there a good or bad time to call Austen? I quietly asked God to guide me on my words and judgments. I clicked on his number, which was still on my phone.

It rang and rang. I wondered if something had changed since an outgoing message from him didn't come up. Finally, a voice.

"Austen here," his low, soft voice answered.

"Austen, it's Claire. How are you?"

He cleared his throat. "Fine."

"I'm sorry I didn't return your call regarding my Christmas plans, but I really wasn't sure about them until just recently." No response. "I just decided to stay put here in Door County in hopes of Michael bringing Mom with him. He keeps saying he'll visit, so my fingers are crossed." Still silent. "So how are you? Have you been going to the office?"

"I have."

"That's good. Are you making some progress on walking?" I regretted that question immediately.

"No."

"None?"

"No."

"I'm so sorry, Austen. You don't deserve this." More silence.

"I appreciate your call, Claire."

"Austen, this breaks my heart. You must believe that you can walk again. Don't give up. You have a whole new year ahead of you. I happen to know you're a fighter for everything you want. I do care what happens to you, despite our differences."

"Like always, a grand cheerleader," he said sarcastically without emotion.

"I hope I haven't lost my touch," I said with a chuckle in my voice.

"Good to hear your voice, Claire. Goodbye."

Just like that, he was gone. Tears filled my eyes. It was as if Austen were dying or already dead. My head leaned over on the floor pillow, and I cried deeply, thinking he'd never recover and I had a role in it.

I must have cried myself to sleep because I woke up the next morning in the same place with my clothes still on. Puff was nowhere around, so I assumed she was on my bed.

I went into the kitchen to start my coffee and noticed the cat under the Christmas tree. Maybe if she hears me in the kitchen, she'll come and get her food. I needed to remove her to water the tree.

I took the long pipe-looking water can and filled it with warm tap water instead of doing the water-boil treatment Rachael had suggested. The can was a clever gadget for sure. Puff jumped and ran to the kitchen as I predicted. She and water didn't mix.

I went up to shower and dress for the day. I hoped to finish my tree block and take it to Rachael's. I also wanted to get Ericka's Christmas tree as soon as possible to cheer her up. I called Cher to see if she was working.

"Yes, I'm about to leave for work. Why?"

"I intend to get Ericka's tree today, so would you be free after work to visit her?"

"Sure! She gets off at five o'clock, and I'll make sure she'll be there around six o'clock, okay?"

"Great. I'll pick you up since I'll have the tree. I'll bring the extra lights I have, too."

"I think I'll stop at Nelson's and buy her a poinsettia when I go by there this morning."

"Sounds good. I'll see you a little before six o'clock unless I hear from you."

I went downstairs and dabbled on paper a watercolor design I had in mind for my quilt square. It was simple, but I rather liked it. I sure hoped Rachael would approve. Feeling pleased, I painted my quilt square and then gave Rachael a call to tell her I was coming. The phone rang and rang.

"Girl, I wish I had hired you full time. We've been so busy!"

"Good! I'm coming out today to bring you my block and get a small tree for Ericka."

"Okay, but why are you getting a tree for Ericka?"

"I can't say. She's in the dumps and doesn't want to do Christmas at all, so Cher and I are going to change that."

"Well, what are friends for? I'll see you later then."

Chapter 64

After I fixed a grilled cheese sandwich for lunch, I went out on the porch to see if my block had dried. It appeared to be, so I laid it flat on a box to take to Rachael's.

Before I left, I put Puff in her chair and placed a box in the middle of the floor for her to play with away from the tree. Hopefully she'd be entertained until I returned.

The day was sunny, but like all winter days in Door County, there was always snow lying around. In Missouri, if we had a snow, the likelihood of its being around a couple of days later was slim. Driving through Egg Harbor on my way to Rachael's was always a pleasure. There seemed to be changes all the time. I was told that years ago there was an egg museum here. I'd have loved to have seen it. I'd read about the lady's collection of eggs from all over the world.

When I arrived at the farm, Harry was tying another tree on top of someone's car.

"Hey, lady," Harry yelled out. "Do you have your days and nights mixed up?" I laughed.

"No, I came to deliver something and to purchase a tree for a friend."

"Well, go see your buddy, and then if you need help out here, come in the white house to get me."

"Thanks, Harry."

I walked in the barn and smelled something wonderful, as always.

"What's cookin' today, girlfriend?" I yelled out to Rachael coming from the back room.

"Seafood gumbo, a favorite of Harry's. Help yourself!"

"Thanks, but I just had lunch. Here's my block. Please be honest if it doesn't fit the look of your quilt."

"You're amazing, Claire," she said with her hands on her hips. "This is almost too beautiful. It really should be framed. I'll use it in some way for sure. Charlie would want you to be a part of his quilt." I smiled.

"So, back to this tree you're buying. What's going on?"

"Ericka asked me to keep it confidential, so I can't say much more than that she needs cheering up."

"Well, I don't want you paying one penny for it. It's my way of helping, too."

"That's not necessary, friend. You always give away too much. How are the party plans coming?"

"Oh, I don't think I told you! Harry has a German friend who belongs to a small German band that plays professionally. When Harry told him we were having a Tannenbaum party, he offered to play for nothing!"

"Oh my! Anna will love that for sure."

"I know! He said they speak German among themselves when others aren't around. Of course, they can sing 'O Tannenbaum.'"

"This is really coming together, Rachael. Wow. German music at a German Tannenbaum Christmas party. I think in Germany, they call it a *Christkindlmarkt.* I can't wait!"

A man came in to pay for his tree, so I told Rachael I needed to pick out a tree and get going.

I went to the pine trees leaning near the fence that had just come in. They were on the slim side, which seemed like it would work in case Ericka had only a small place for a tree. Harry came over, and I showed him the one I wanted.

"Free of charge, little lady," he said.

"I just can't, Harry. Just take this twenty-dollar bill and say you found it on the ground. Please?" He grinned and nodded.

Off I went, hoping I had enough time to stop at Main Street Market in Egg Harbor. Besides grabbing a few things for myself, I'd have them make one of their pizzas from scratch to take with me. I was hungry, and most likely Cher and Ericka would need to eat something, too.

I texted Cher that I was on my way to her house.

"Thanks for picking me up, Claire Bear. I sure hope Ericka takes this in the right spirit."

"I hope so, too, Cher Bear. I stopped at the market and got us a pizza to bake. I'm starving, and you most likely are, too."

Chapter 65

"So, did you have a busy day at the shop today?"

"We did!"

"I get so frustrated that I can't get more quilts for him to sell. I don't know where my time goes. By the way, Cher, before we get to Ericka's, I want to confess something to you." She turned her head with concern.

"I returned a phone call to Austen."

"Why now?"

"I told you about the growing concern for his depression. I couldn't get it off my mind, so I asked Grayson's advice. I know it seems odd, but he was sympathetic to the situation and thought I should call Austen if there was any chance of it helping him feel better."

"That was incredible of Grayson. So, what did Austen have to say?"

"I did all the talking. He barely responded to my questions. His last words to me were, 'Good to hear your voice, Claire. Goodbye.' So, he just hung up. That was it."

"How sad. That's just not like him. He must not be getting any hope for a recovery."

"That's what I'm thinking."

"Okay, now that we've arrived at Ericka's, I'm going to text her to open the front door."

Cher grabbed one end of the tree and I grabbed the other, and we headed toward Ericka's front door.

"Surprise!" Cher and I greeted Ericka as she opened the door.

"What in the world?" she responded. "I can't believe you guys!"

"We're bringing Christmas to you, so hold the door open, please," Cher requested. "Where would you like this?"

"I guess in front of that window. That's where I've had one before."

"I brought the lights!" I added cheerfully.

"Well, we aren't going to decorate the tree until we have something to eat," Cher announced. "We brought a pizza from the market to put in the oven."

"Eat?" Ericka said, overwhelmed.

"You haven't eaten, have you?" I asked. She shook her head. "I'll bet you have a bottle of wine open from our last visit, don't you?" She smiled and shook her head in disbelief.

"I have never had a real tree in my life!" Ericka admitted. "It smells wonderful. Does it get messy?"

"Not if you water it every day with warm water," I informed her. "If you aren't here some days, have George or someone do it for you."

"Poor George," Ericka said as she sat down. "He isn't handling my situation very well at all. I was always the strong, healthy one in the family."

"Well, tell him to suck it up," Cher firmly stated.

Cher took over putting the pizza in the oven and got out the wine to pour for each of us.

"So, Ericka, has Cher told you about all the excitement regarding a Tannenbaum Christmas quilt that was brought by our new quilt club member, Anna?" I asked, changing the subject.

Cher and I started talking at once about Anna's family quilt and how Rachael got carried away in making one herself. Then I described what the Tannenbaum party would be like. I couldn't tell if Ericka was really listening or not.

"She's doing the quilt and party in Charlie's honor, which is nice."

"I see," Ericka said in a listless tone.

I was sure Ericka would feel the excitement as we told her more details, but she just listened and nodded.

When the pizza was ready, Cher and I quickly gobbled it up. Ericka only had one piece and a sip or two of wine.

"Okay, this tree needs some lights to brighten up this party," I said, pulling them out of the bag.

Chapter 66

When we finally wrapped the last sting of lights around the tree, it glowed like no other.

"Look at this! It's gorgeous!" Cher said, standing back to admire it. "What do you think, Ericka?"

"I'm speechless!" she said, shaking her head. "Who does this for someone?"

"Good friends do!" I confirmed. "We knew you would be avoiding Christmas, and we weren't having it."

"Oh, and we have another surprise for you in the car," Cher announced. "Hold on a minute while I get it."

Ericka looked puzzled, and I just grinned until Cher quickly returned with the quilt under her arm.

"This is a quilt for you from Amy's shop," Cher said as she unfolded the quilt.

Oh, this is too much!" Ericka responded. "It's beautiful!" Ericka broke into tears.

"I hope those are tears of joy, because we're not giving up on you," Cher scolded. "Folks recover every day from this nasty cancer, and you, Ericka, are strong enough to handle this." I thought of Austen and wondered if he had anyone to cheer him on.

"I'm sorry, I'm sorry," Ericka said, trying to get a grip on herself.

"Don't worry about it," I comforted. "Breaking down with your friends is therapeutic. Just remember, we're here for you."

"You haven't told anyone, have you?" she asked as she stared at both of us.

"No, and we won't if you don't want us to," Cher answered.

"I guess when I become bald, I won't be able to keep it much of a secret," Ericka said as her nose sniffled.

"Some find comfort in talking to others going through the same thing. Maybe there will come a time you won't want to keep it a secret," I noted.

"Not me!" she firmly said. "Not me!"

"And that's okay, too," Cher nodded.

"Speaking of secrets, I'm going to share something with you that just happened with me," I revealed. "Now, I was not sworn to secrecy, but since you both know about Ava, I think you'll find this interesting."

"Speaking of Ava!" Ericka said with relief, "thank goodness I didn't accuse her of taking my rings since I found them in the drain. I should've never mentioned her name."

"Well, Ava does have a problem," I stated as they both looked at me in wonder.

"Oh, dear. What did you do, Claire Bear?" Cher asked in fear.

"We ran into each other at the post office recently and I asked her to lunch," I began to explain. "I delicately brought up the fact that I saw her take something at the séance."

"You did what?" Cher asked with disbelief.

"Oh, Claire! You didn't!" Ericka followed.

"She actually was very open about it," I stated. "She explained how when she was growing up, they were very poor, and there were times she had to steal food."

"Well, she sure doesn't need to anymore," Cher added bluntly.

"She said she doesn't realize that she's doing it at times," I went on to explain. "She knows it's wrong and tries to correct it when she can."

"Oh, boy." Cher reacted. "Does she really think she can get by with it?"

"She must really trust you as a friend," Ericka observed.

"I have no intention of reporting her," I said sincerely. "I want her to get help. She said she's already been to counseling. Frankly, I feel sorry for her."

"I'm not sure I do," Cher voiced.

"I guess it's more complicated than that for her. I'm not sorry I brought it up, though. She took it really well, and we hugged when we left each other. Well, friends, it's getting late, and I need to get home." I looked at my watch. "Ericka, we love you and hope this little bit of cheer tonight will help you. Don't forget the true meaning of Christmas. Appreciate what you have! We love you!"

Ericka smiled with affection as we put on our coats.

"We need a group hug," Cher suggested. "Merry Christmas, everyone."

It was a good way to end the evening. Ericka would have to figure out how she was going to handle her health crisis, but as friends, we did our part. Cher and I were quiet on our way home. I felt it was good to bring up the struggles Ava was having to get Ericka's mind off of her own problems.

I could only wonder how Ava would handle her problem. Likewise for Austen.

Chapter 67

The next day, I needed to put my worries aside and finish my painting of O'Meara's Irish House. I wanted to get it to the gallery before Carl closed for the season.

I sipped my coffee as I dabbled paint on the Irish Quilt Chain quilt. I wondered which building I'd paint next. I was leaning toward wanting to do something with the Blue Horse Beach Cafe since I spent so much time there. Surely, I could find a suitable quilt design to paint in blue colors.

I was having a good time thinking creatively until Rachael disrupted my thoughts with a phone call.

"Don't worry, I'll be there tomorrow," I quickly responded. She laughed.

"I just called to tell you my blocks are ready to attach to the center. Lee is coming out this afternoon to bring me the center. I can't wait to see it!"

"Neither can I!"

"Lee is also quite taken with Anna's quilt and has been cooking up some of her own ideas. She talked to Anna this week, and they think they may have found a building for sale that would suit Anna's need for a place to live as well as a bakery."

"In Baileys Harbor?"

"Yes. From what she described, it must be just down the road from Chives restaurant."

"I hope it works out."

"I still haven't heard from Ava. Harry asked if I had reason to think there might be foul play involved."

"Really? I think I may give Frances a call. The two of them seem to be close."

"Great idea. Let me know if you learn anything."

When I hung up, I sure hoped we'd find Ava before someone called the police to check on her. That could open a whole can of worms. I put my brush in the water and called Frances.

"Frances, it's Claire. I hope you're well. I'm calling to see if you have any word from Ava lately. Some of us have been trying to reach her without success."

"I'm not surprised, but I'm sure she's fine."

"Why do you say that?"

"I know her pretty well." I paused, trying to think what she meant. "It's not the first time she has vanished."

"Vanished?"

"You know what a free spirit she is. Please don't worry about her. To my knowledge, she's probably fine."

"Do you think we should do more to find her?"

"No. She's an adult with an unusual life. We should respect her privacy."

I hung up and wondered why Frances could be so sure of Ava being fine. Did she have one of her premonitions about her? Perhaps I was overreacting.

I got back to my painting and continued until five o'clock. I decided to take another look at it tomorrow to see if enough had been done. My mother always said, "If in doubt, do without." I stood back to observe it and somehow knew it was complete. It's like making a quilt; you know when you've achieved what you set out to do. I opened the front door to take a deep breath of the cold air. It felt refreshing after being holed up in the cabin. Now that darkness was setting in, my lights would brighten the neighborhood.

I went back inside to the sound of nothing at all. I was alone, with the exception of my precious Puff, who walked on padded, silent feet. For a second, I wondered what Grayson was doing.

I wasn't hungry, so I poured myself a glass of wine and built a fire to settle into the evening. Puff stayed under the tree, so I had the fire all to myself. I lay back and asked God to give guidance to Ava, Ericka, and Austen. I hoped the unsolicited advice I'd shared with each of them was sound. Mom had always been one to give good advice, so I began thinking of her. It was nine o'clock, and I wondered if she'd still be up.

Chapter 68

"Mom, did I wake you?" I asked quickly.

"No. I'm watching the news and doing a little crocheting."

"Oh, what are you working on?"

"I can't tell you. It's a surprise. What's on your mind, dear?

"Austen, for one thing," I said with a sigh.

"Yes, I heard he's really struggling, but honey, you shouldn't blame yourself for anything. I'm sure he's getting the best healthcare possible."

"I care about him, Mom. I can't help it."

"Of course, you do. That's the kind of girl I raised."

"Thanks. You always remind me about the Stewart values, Mom." She chuckled. "Now, on a brighter subject, have you and Michael made a decision about Christmas?"

There was a pause. "Honey, I hate to depress you even further, but I told Michael I wanted to stay home for Christmas this year."

"Oh, is there something wrong?"

"No, but I want to listen to my own body and heart. Thinking about the trip was becoming stressful to me. I talked to Bill about it last week, and he's in the same boat. His daughter is becoming insistent about him coming to see her, and he said he finally put his foot down and said no. He told her he wanted to stay put, Christmas or no Christmas."

"It's okay, Mom. I understand. I was hoping you'd come, but I sure wouldn't want the trip to be stressful for you."

"Thank you for understanding, honey. I told Bill I'd cook him Christmas dinner on Christmas Eve, and I wish you could've seen how delighted he was." I had to smile to myself.

"It sounds like a perfect arrangement for both of you. So, how about Michael?"

"I can't tell you. I want you to know he was leaving the trip up to me, so don't be hard on him about this decision."

"I hope he'll be with you if he doesn't make it to Door County."

"Try not to worry so, Claire. I'm afraid you inherited that trait from me. By the way, Carole came by yesterday with a lovely box of Christmas cookies. My goodness, she has quite a talent there and has such a good heart."

"Yes, she does. Now, you'd better share those cookies with Bill, don't you think?"

"I intend to!"

Our conversation wrapped up, and I felt downhearted. Should I change my plans and go see her? I had to admit she was being quite the grown-up about making her own decision to be there with Bill for Christmas. I couldn't help but admire a decision that followed her heart. I hoped I'd never have to boss my mother around.

I put out the fire and went to bed. I had to convince myself that Mom, Ava, Ericka, and Austen would all be just fine.

I turned on the TV as I got into bed, and one of my favorite movies was playing. *To Kill a Mockingbird* was on the classic movie channel, and in no time, it had my complete attention.

Morning came with a booming thunder that had me quickly sitting up. I looked out the window and witnessed a mix of rain and sleet. Would this cold, wet weather ever end? I had to make it to quilt club today. It was our last meeting before Christmas, and I didn't want to miss it. It would also be Anna's first meeting as a member.

I went down to the kitchen, but Puff didn't follow. It was earlier than usual and very dark, so maybe she had decided to sleep in. I made my coffee and looked out the window to see my ice-covered Subaru. I sat down to read the *Pulse* newspaper and saw that the library was going to be showing afternoon movies this winter in the room where our quilt group met.

I finished eating and climbed the stairs to check on Puff. She was awake and just lying there.

"What's wrong, Puff?" I asked sweetly. "It's not like you to miss a meal. I picked her up and took her downstairs, placing her in front of her food bowl. To my amazement, she walked away. Now what? I wondered. I'll see Cher at club and I'll ask her what to do. I didn't have a vet to call. This is what happens when you inherit something you know nothing about.

I got dressed for club, and my phone rang. I wondered why Rachael was calling since I'd be seeing her soon.

"Girl, I gotta tell you, I won't be coming in for club. Harry said the roads are treacherous. Plus, I'm so behind on the barn quilt orders."

"That's probably a good idea. I don't know if I'll get very far either."

"Would you please tell everyone thank you for the quilt blocks? Also, tell them Lee did a fantastic job on the center."

"I sure will!"

"Be careful, you hear?"

"I don't have to go far. I'll be fine."

I put on my coat and put Puff in her chair. What in the world was wrong with her? I carefully scattered salt on my steps and on some of the stepping-stones that lead to my car.

The ice on my windshield took nearly half an hour to melt so I could see out to drive. I kept telling myself it was worth the time it took. My car was nice and toasty once I was in the driver's seat. I made my way to the library.

Chapter 69

I was glad to see Anna and Marta when I arrived at our meeting room. Marta was concerned the meeting might not happen since the likelihood of having a quorum was slim. There were not too many present, but it was still early, and the weather was bad.

"Oh, Anna, I hear you may have found a place to live and work!" I noted cheerfully.

"Yeah, yeah, so far so good!" she said. "There is red tape, as you say." She giggled. "My uncle brought us this morning since the roads are so bad. I was looking forward to seeing Rachael's Tannenbaum quilt, but I hear she won't be coming."

"Yes, that's right," I nodded. "I'm pleased you'll be selling your strudel at her party. Rachael's thrilled about that!"

"Yes, at the Christkindlmarkt," she grinned. "It'll be so fun!"

As I looked around the room, I saw no signs of Amy, Ava, Lee, Frances, Greta, or Olivia. I saw Cher coming in from the hallway.

"Lordy, I'm glad to be inside right now. My car took a spin coming into the parking lot," Cher claimed, rather shaken.

"The roads are terrible, and that parking lot still has a lot of ice. Where is everyone?"

"So far it's just Marta, Anna, you, and me," I noted. "Relax and have some coffee. I'm glad you made it safely."

"Ladies, please take a seat," Marta asked politely. "I'm sorry to say, we won't be able to have a meeting this morning. I just heard from Greta, and because of her driveway conditions, she can't come. I'll have you know, this is the first meeting she's ever missed. Olivia and Frances made it as far as Carlsville and had to turn around. It's just a mess out there right now. Anna, I'm sorry your very first meeting as a member has been affected by this winter weather."

"Did anyone hear from Ava?" There was silence.

"Now, I suggest you all just stay here and enjoy your coffee and give the roads a little time to clear," Marta suggested. "We may be able to arrange another time to meet before Christmas, but we'll have to check with the library."

"If I may," I interrupted with a louder voice. "Rachael wanted me to thank everyone who made blocks for her Tannenbaum quilt. She also noted that Lee did a marvelous job on the center of the quilt. You'll all be getting more details on the big Tannenbaum party and market she and Harry are planning."

"Ladies," Anna said shyly. "Thank you for letting me be a member of this group. I wanted to bring you some cherry kuchen this morning, but there was a lot of ruckus to deal with." Everyone chuckled. "Another time. You see, I hope that by the first of the year, I'll be out of my auntie's hair and into my own place." Everyone clapped.

"You all have a very Merry Christmas!" Marta said in closing.

"You do the same," I called out to her.

When I went to get a little more coffee, Anna was near the pot.

"Anna, when you showed us your Tannenbaum quilt, you said there were many stories handed down with the quilt through the years," I reminded. "Can you share any of them?" She blushed.

"Each family had their own stories to share as the quilt moved around," she began before being interrupted.

"Yes, and some of those stories should only be taken with a grain of salt, if you ask me," claimed Marta, with her hands on her hips.

"I don't think anyone ever slept under the quilt because it was supposed to bring bad luck," Anna said in all seriousness. "That's what mama always told us, anyhow. I'm not so sure Aunt Marta wants me to share too much." Marta shook her head and walked away.

"Claire, do you live alone?" Anna asked out of the blue. I nodded.

I briefly told her about Cher moving to Missouri and how I took over her little log cabin.

"I'd like to visit sometime," she suggested. "It must be so cozy—like living in a real cabin, huh?" She once again giggled in her shy manner.

Cher then joined us and asked Anna if Marta had told her about our outdoor quilt show. Cher was sure to give credit to Anna's aunt, for Marta had been in charge of distribution of the quilts that day.

"Yeah, she's good like that!" Anna nodded.

"Maybe next year if we can have vendors, you can sell your baked goods during the show," I suggested. Her face lit up.

"Oh, I'd love to!"

"Cher, before you leave, I need to ask you about Puff's recent behavior," I said with concern.

"Is she okay?" Cher asked.

"Puff is a cat?" Anna asked. I nodded and smiled.

"She's not eating and is very listless," I described. "What could it be?"

"Well, it could be various things, but most likely it's a hair ball," she noted.

"A hair ball?" I said a little too loudly.

"Not to worry, she'll eventually throw it up, but if she doesn't get any better, take her to Northern Door Pet Clinic."

I wanted to ask more questions, but Marta interrupted to say we had to move out of the meeting room now. Cher then checked her watch and announced she needed to stop by the gallery and help Carl with something. Our non-meeting was over.

Chapter 70

While I was this close to the Blue Horse, I decided to get lunch and take it home. This place was a definite favorite of mine. There were so few people here today, which I assumed was because of the bad weather. I ordered a tuna sandwich to go and got on my way home. As close as I lived, I couldn't believe how long it took me to get safely back home.

I made it back to the cabin and took off my coat, relieved to be home again. It didn't take me long to notice that Puff had thrown up on the porch floor. It wasn't a pretty sight, but there was no doubt that it was a hair ball. There she was, sleeping innocently on her chair. I'm glad she didn't throw up on the quilt. After I cleaned up the mess, I sent Cher a text.

[Claire]
Puff did throw up a hair ball. Now what?

She quickly responded.

[Cher]
See what happens. She should be fine.

[Claire]
Thanks! It was nasty!

[Cher]
You're such a wuss!

I smiled.

I went in the kitchen to eat my lunch. I wasn't there long before Puff came in the kitchen. She looked at her untouched bowl and ate a tiny bit of it.

As I sat there and thought about our meeting, I decided to try calling Ava again. This time, I couldn't leave a voice mail. It was probably full. It was all so odd. Why weren't more folks upset about her absence?

I heard a knock at the door. Looking out the window, I saw Cotsy from next door. She was all bundled up with a fur hood on her head.

"Come on in, neighbor!"

"Oh, brr, brr," she said, pulling her hood down so I could see her better. "I just got home and thought I'd come over to invite you to our little Christmas party again. You seemed to enjoy it last year."

"I sure did."

"Well, this year, it'll be significantly smaller, so I didn't send out invitations. It'll mostly be folks along the row here who will soon be going south for the winter. It's next weekend. You're welcome to bring a guest if you like."

"I'll ask Grayson Wills. He and I have been dating," I said, blushing.

"I thought I saw him over here a time or two. That's great."

"Can I bring anything?"

"Oh, that's not necessary. Dan would be offended, as you well know," she chuckled.

"Well, I'd love to stay, but I have to unload the car. I'm glad you can make it."

"So, you'll be leaving right after Christmas?"

"Yes. I can't wait to get away from all this snow!"

"I'll keep an eye out while you're gone. Thanks for the invite, Cotsy."

As soon as she left, I texted Grayson to save the date. He texted back a heart, which I thought was pretty sweet. Then a text came in from Brenda.

[Brenda]
Quilt is done! I'll drop it off tomorrow.

[Claire]
Great! No hurry. Be safe.

I looked out and noticed more snow was coming down. Could this be the year we shovel snow off the roof like Cher said she had to do one year?

It was too late to start a fire, so I grabbed Puff, and we retired upstairs for the rest of the evening. I had a water bowl there for her, and she did take a drink. She must be feeling better. As I undressed and looked at my closet, I wondered what I'd wear to the Bittners' party. I wanted to look festive for it. I took another look out the window, and my Subaru disappeared into whiteness.

Chapter 71

I woke up to a loud noise from the Bittners' snow removal guy's truck. My drive was being cleared! There was no question I'd be snowed in for some time. I wanted to roll over and go back to sleep, but Puff wouldn't have it. Her insistence to be fed was another good sign.

I wrapped up in my heavier house coat and descended the stairs. As far as I was concerned, I'd remain in this garb for the rest of the day.

After I fed Puff, I built a nice fire to keep us both cozy and warm. Next, I made coffee, and it couldn't have tasted better. The phone rang after I'd had a couple sips. It was Grayson.

"How's my snow baby this morning?" he joked.

"She's bundled up nice and warm. Are you still home?"

"Yes. It's a snow day for Mr. Wills today, as I can do quite a bit in my office here at home."

"Yes, the same for me. Is Kelly home as well?"

"Oh yes, but she's still asleep. By the way, she soon will have her seventeenth birthday."

"She was a Christmas baby!"

"Yes, she was quite a gift that year. She finally got her driver's license, so I'm buying her a car for her birthday."

"Why did she wait until now?"

"She had been reluctant to learn to drive, so I didn't push her."

"Will there be a party for her birthday?"

"No. She wants to go skiing at the Wisconsin Dells with her girlfriend Sadie."

"Well, I have a quilt I made for her for Christmas, so I suppose it'll be her birthday present, too."

"Oh, Claire, she'll love that. If I think of some occasion where you could give it to her, I'll let you know. I've also been meaning to tell you that our work Christmas party is coming up, and I'd love you to be my guest. It's at the Kress Pavilion, which is quite nice. If you haven't been there, you'll be impressed."

"Are you sure you want to bring me as your date?"

"Do I have reason for concern?"

"You aren't concerned with gossip?"

He laughed. "I'll let you know more details later."

"Sounds great, Grayson. How many employees typically attend?"

"Over a hundred, at least. It's gotten more casual over the years. In my dad's time, everything was much more of a gala affair."

"I remember those days. Dr. Page drug me to many such affairs."

"I'll bet. It's more business casual now. Well, we should both get back to work."

"Yes, I suppose we should."

I smiled at the thought that Grayson was willing to bring me to his work party.

I went out to the porch, where the windows were covered in white. I uncovered my painting on the easel and decided that the featured green-and-white quilt needed a few more touches. My cell phone rang. It was Cher.

"Carl didn't bother opening the gallery on this snow day, did he?"

"No, but he said he'd be there for a couple of folks to pick up their special orders for Christmas. What are you doing?"

"I'm about to complete the Irish shop painting, so I'm putting the final touches on that."

"Better get it done before Christmas."

"I'm not worried about that. I'm thinking these paintings will sell well when we have the quilt show this summer."

"Ooh, they would! Speaking of the show, when do you think we should schedule our appointment with the board to get our permit?"

"Soon. I know many want to hear if they'll be able to vend there this year."

"Did you get any word on Ava?"

"No, and it's bothersome to me because I likely had something to do with her disappearance. How's Ericka doing?"

"Her surgery is scheduled for tomorrow. I told George to let me know if he needs me. He said she has a pretty good attitude about it all lately."

"I think we had a little something to do with that, don't you?"

Chapter 72

The whole next day I was occupied with thoughts of Ericka and what she was going through with her breast cancer surgery. I prayed she'd have a good outcome.

Tomorrow was the Bittner party, which was something to look forward to. The first thing I did after I got dressed was to look at what winter dresses I had to wear. I had several I'd never uncovered that I brought with me. I had to wonder if I would even fit into them. Since I'd moved to Door County, my dress was usually casual, and I was eating more than usual.

Most of the dresses were brighter colors than I wanted to wear in the middle of winter, but the black-and-white beaded jacket was one of my favorites. I wanted to decide today what I'd be wearing since I would be working all day tomorrow at Rachael's. I'd either go with the black-and-white jacket with dress slacks or my red velvet dress. At least I'd narrowed it down.

I finished my painting and decided to walk it to the gallery since my car was still snowed under. It would be good to have fresh air, but I needed to salt my front steps.

Once I applied the salt, I drudged along in the heavy snow and made it to the gallery. Carl was quite surprised to see me. I unwrapped my painting and held it up.

"Claire, I don't how you do it. This is quite lovely. By the way, I have a pretty strong nibble on the first one you did."

"Oh, Carl, that would be great if it sold."

"I also have an order for one of your Quilted Snow pieces. Of the four seasons, this by far, gets the most attention."

"You know I can't get this done before Christmas."

"Yes, I told her that."

"So, it sounds like business has been good. I don't suppose Cher is working today?"

"No. It's been slow. This snow in particular has brought everything to a halt for a while."

"I'm so happy you hired Cher. She really loves working here."

"She's a great asset for sure. I can't talk the quilt talk like she does."

"Carl, I've never asked, but have you ever been married?"

"Close," he said, looking to the floor. "I thought I was going to have a wife for a bit, but she walked out on me when I had my accident."

"Accident?"

"Oh, it's a long story, and perhaps it was a blessing in disguise."

"So, do you ever think you'd like to marry one day?"

"Why in the world would you be asking such a thing? Do you have someone in mind?"

I chuckled. "Well, I might!"

He waved his hand like it was nonsense. "Do your friends try to marry you off, too?"

"Yes, they certainly do."

"So, are you and Grayson a possibility?"

"I don't know about that, but we do have a really good relationship."

"That's all that's important in my opinion. Well, it's time to turn the sign to Closed. If you want to stick around, I can pull out the vacuum cleaner."

I chuckled. "Okay, okay, I'm out of here," I said, giving him a little hug.

I went out into the cold and covered my face from the wind. I thought about Carl and Cher and what a great couple they would make. It's odd that Carl never told Cher about the accident, but maybe he was afraid to because he'd already had one woman walk out on him because of it. The accident did explain the issue I'd noticed with his arm.

When I arrived at the cabin, I saw Tom clearing the Bittners' sidewalks.

"Well done!" I yelled to him across the yard.

"Did you see the big limb that fell across your little shed?" he yelled back.

"What?"

I went to the backyard, and sure enough, a sizable limb had fallen onto my poor little shed that still had the strength to remain standing. I'd have to have Tom address this once he was finished helping the Bittners prepare for their party.

Puff was comfy under the tree, so I started my usual evening fire. I began preparing a salad for my dinner until Cher interrupted me with a call.

"Hi, Claire. I knew you'd want to know that all went well with Ericka's surgery," she said quickly. "The doctor told George that things went as expected, and he thinks he got all the cancer. She won't know her exact treatment until she has her next doctor's visit."

"That's such good news, Cher. She's been on my mind."

"I'm drained just thinking about what all she has ahead of her."

"I know, but she has all of us to help her through it. Thanks for filling me in. I appreciate that."

Chapter 73

At six o'clock in the morning, I looked out the window to check on the weather. Nothing had changed, which told me the roads would likely be clear for me to go to Rachael's.

I lay back for a few minutes to plan my day. I wanted to take Rachael her feather tree so she could use it for the Christmas season and especially have it for the Tannenbaum party. I figured I might as well get up. I went to the office to take the tree down with me to breakfast. Puff followed and wondered what it would mean for her as she saw me place it on the kitchen table. Of course, I gave her stern instructions.

Before I left for Rachael's that morning, I stripped my bed and threw a load of clothes in the washer. Then I watered my beautiful Christmas tree, which still smelled so good and fresh. I hoped the one Cher and I bought for Ericka was bringing her joy. I took Puff upstairs with me when I dressed for work so she wouldn't get any ideas about the tree on the kitchen counter.

It was the coldest day I could remember ever experiencing. Surprisingly, my Subaru started right up. Too bad it didn't have a little coffee maker inside I could turn on. Driving out to the farm, I saw plenty of snow remaining. Would it ever disappear?

Harry was in his truck still pushing snow in the parking lot when I arrived. I waved as I carefully pulled the feather tree from the back of the Subaru.

"What on earth?" Rachael said when I walked in the barn.

"Merry Christmas!" I cheered. "I think it's the year of the feather tree, am I right?"

"Where in the world did you ever find this?"

"At a shop in Sturgeon Bay that's close to the quilt shop. I could just see it on your counter. I'm not sure you even need to decorate it."

"Claire, you've really outdone yourself this time. I can't get over it. I'm sure you paid way too much, but I'll cherish this forever."

"I can't wait until Anna sees it. It's fragile, so don't try to bend the metal limbs."

I moved closer to the wood stove and poured myself that hot cup of coffee I'd been thinking about on the way here.

"Harry and I had some cinnamon buns this morning. There are still some in the back room if you'd like one."

"Do I ever pass up anything you cook? Of course, I want one! So, what's on the agenda today?"

"It's hard to say. This last storm set us back a bit. I think there will still be some pickups today. I haven't watered the tree, so you can start there, I suppose."

"You know, Rachael, coming here to the barn is like coming home. It has the warm smell of the cedar tree and a roasted fire. That's not to mention the smell of coffee and whatever magic you're cooking in that crock pot."

She smiled and nodded in agreement. "It's chicken and dumplings today. I was a little late getting it all together because Harry wanted me to trim his beard a bit this morning." I grinned, knowing he probably spent the night.

"You two are just like a husband and wife. You know that?"

She looked at me and paused. "We are, aren't we? Honestly, Claire, I don't know how this happened."

"It's a good thing. Charlie would want you and Harry to be happy."

"But how can this be? I loved Charlie with all my heart and still do. He's always on my mind."

"It's natural, Rachael. You and Charlie built all this. Harry wouldn't want you to put Charlie out of your mind. He thought the world of him, too."

"Claire, are folks talking about us?"

I chuckled. "I'm not sure what you mean, but the last time I checked, you and Harry were not being whispered about."

"Oh, thank goodness."

The phone rang, and Rachael jumped to answer. I took off my coat and headed to the back room for a cinnamon bun.

I finished eating one and came out front when a man arrived to pay for his tree.

"Hey, are you Claire?" he asked.

"Yes, I am. How can I help you?"

"Grayson Wills is a friend of mine, and he told me you worked here. He's been servicing my boat every year for quite some time. I told him I was coming out to buy a Christmas tree today, and he mentioned you."

"Well, you came to the right place. Grayson is a good guy," I said as I took his charge card.

"Yeah, I'll never forget when his wife was killed in that boat accident. It really changed him. Those two sure were crazy about each other. Now it's all about his work and his daughter."

My gut was beginning to ache.

To change the subject, I advised him about watering his tree every day and then showed him the water pipe, which he ended up buying.

Chapter 74

When he left, I looked down at the counter, trying to forget what he said about Grayson and his wife.

"Claire, I overheard that guy," Rachael admitted as she came closer to me. "I'm sure he didn't realize the two of you were dating."

"It is what it is, Rachael. I can either accept the relationship as it is or run from it."

"Grayson is running closer to you, not away, but he needs time. You're smart to let him have that."

"Hey, ladies!" Kent yelled, coming in the door. I hear chicken and dumplings are cookin' today. That sounds like just what I need to warm my belly."

"I don't know if it's warm enough yet, but have at it," Rachael offered.

"How was the Packers game, Kent?" I asked while he filled his bowl.

"We had a swell time," he grinned. "I don't know if I had more fun watching Brenda react to it all or actually watching the game myself."

"She'll never forget the experience. I know I haven't." He chuckled.

When Kent went into the back room to eat and the shop was empty, Rachael came up to me with a serious look on her face.

"I tried calling Ava again, and now her landline is disconnected. What do you make of that?"

"Well, it's not good. She could've just gone out of town, but disconnecting her phone is a bit odd."

"She's always been an odd one if you ask me."

"Well, when I called Frances to see what she knew, she assured me she was fine, like she had a premonition or something."

"She'd surely notify Greta or Marta if she was going to quit the club, wouldn't she?"

"You would think so, but who knows with Ava."

"Hey, did I tell you that Harry secured some tents for our Christmas market? We figured the food and merchandise needed to be protected a bit from the weather as well. He told me the idea of the wish tree has to go. There just isn't room, and besides, it doesn't fit the German theme."

"He's probably right. You may want to put the German band under a tent, too, with their instruments and all. You never know what the weather might do.

"Good idea. Anna said she'd be in costume, so I teased Harry that he'd have to find some lederhosen to wear."

I laughed trying to imagine Harry in those. "Well, they'd keep him warmer. Now what shall we wear?"

"I don't know, but we'll be working inside where it's warm, so that's good. I'll ask Anna if she has any suggestions. I wish I had more time to build up my merchandise, but this quilt has taken priority and has been eating up all my extra time."

"Why don't you ask Brenda if she can squeeze in the quilting for you?" Her face lit up, but we were interrupted by screaming.

A lady came in with a little boy wailing at the top of his lungs as she tried to contain him in her arms.

"What's the matter here?" I asked, looking directly at his little red face.

"Oh, he thought he was going to see Santa today when I told him we were going to buy our Christmas tree."

"Oh, I'm sorry, but Santa did leave some yummy candy canes on the counter over here if you'd like one," I offered over his loud screaming.

"Oh, look, Randy," she said to the little boy, who didn't have any interest in looking at the red-and-white peppermint sticks.

Chapter 75

"Ho, ho, ho!" came a loud voice in the doorway. Harry was all decked out in a Santa suit. "I'm here to see if you've been naughty or nice!" Randy's head popped up from his mother's shoulders.

Rachael and I looked at each other in shock as we noticed the boy had stopped crying. Harry walked over to a chair to sit down as he stroked his beard and looked at the little boy.

"Now, I'll bet there's someone here who would like to tell Santa what they want for Christmas," Harry chuckled.

The mother got closer to Harry, but the little boy turned away in embarrassment.

"Randy, honey, Santa wants you to talk to him," the mother encouraged.

"Now, Randy, you be a good little boy, and I'll see you on Christmas Eve," Harry said handing him a candy cane.

Randy swiped the candy cane right out of Harry's hand and then hid in his mother's arms.

"Thank you, Santa," the mother said, smiling.

"You ladies be good now, too, you hear? Santa is always watching. Merry Christmas!" Harry yelled on his way into the back room.

"Bye, Santa!" I yelled.

Finally, the mother was able to sit the boy down and sign for her credit card.

"Sometimes miracles happen around here," Rachael joked as the lady and little boy went out the door.

"All clear, Santa," Rachael yelled.

When Harry joined us, he explained that he had witnessed the temper tantrum and decided to put on the Santa suit that was hanging in the white house.

"You're just an old softie," Rachael said, pinching his cheek.

"That was a call beyond duty," Harry admitted with a wink. "I'll bet he'll remember me." We nodded and laughed.

I went in the back room to have some of Rachael's delicious dumplings but heard a familiar voice come into the shop.

"Amy! I thought that voice sounded like yours! What are you doing here?" I called out.

"Well, I have a new quilt sister who has a barn quilt business and a tree farm, so I thought I'd better check it out."

"How sweet of you to come, Amy," Rachael responded. "I haven't been to your shop for a long time, but I'll get there."

"I can't believe all this merchandise!" Amy noted, looking around. "I might be able to help sell some of your smaller pieces in my shop if you like."

"Good idea, Rachael," I added.

"Maybe after Christmas," Rachael replied. "Right now, I'm behind producing what I need."

"How do you find time to do all this?" Amy wondered.

"Sometimes I make two of something if I like what I'm painting," Rachael noted.

"This tree is really something else. So unusual. Before I forget, here's my ticket for the one I just bought," Amy said.

"Thanks. I'll give you a discount, too. I really appreciate the quilt block you made," Rachael acknowledged.

"Well, I'm not going to miss that Tannenbaum party for anything," Amy said with excitement. "I'm telling everyone about it. Some of my Amish friends speak German, and they would love an event like this."

"I think you might end up with a real parking problem, Rachael," I warned. "You may want to have people parking down at the Hacker farm and bring them here to the farm on a golf cart."

"I think Harry and Kent have already cooked up something like that," Rachael nodded.

"If you need a cart driver, Billy, Marta's grandson, would love to do something like that."

"Another great idea, PR person," Rachael teased. "Amy, if you ever need a great promoter, Claire is the best!"

"I'll remember that," Amy grinned.

Chapter 76

By five o'clock that evening, I was drained from talking so much and standing on my feet. I don't know how Rachael did it every day. We weren't spring chickens.

I went outside to say goodbye to Harry, and he looked as drained as I felt.

"Harry, are you as tired as I am right now?"

"I don't take time to think about it, but I'll tell you what. Tomorrow is the Sabbath, and Kent and I are going ice fishing at Kangaroo Lake. That's the best stress relief there is."

"I believe it. I wish Rachael would do the same."

"She never stops. I hope you know how much she appreciates you, Claire. You're a tremendous help."

"I loved her from the minute I met her," I said with a smile.

On the drive home, I tried to get excited about tonight's Bittner party. I was pleased Grayson wasn't arriving until eight o'clock so I'd have time to freshen up.

Puff came running to me for some attention when I walked through the door. I scooped her up for a few minutes of cuddles and then hopped in the shower.

On the bed was the outfit I'd chosen to wear. I'd decided on the jacket and pants ensemble knowing it would be too cold for me to wear the red velvet dress. I hadn't worn this jacket since I'd gone to a medical conference in Jefferson City with Austen.

I took my time getting dressed and sipped a glass of wine until Grayson arrived at the door.

When I opened the door to let him in, he grinned from ear to ear as he looked me up and down.

"You are one beautiful woman!" he said after a kiss on the cheek.

"I'm not overdressed, am I?"

"Not for me! It's Christmas! Do you want to leave now or wait a bit?"

"No, I'm ready. I noticed there are just a few cars out there, so it must be a small party, as Cotsy said."

"By the way, we got our tree up, and Kelly is anxious for you to see it."

"I'd love to! It'll be a good time for me to give her my Christmas present."

"She's anxious about her ski trip. I hope she comes home in one piece."

We left for the party, trying to find a path in the snow to walk the few steps to Cotsy and Dan's next door.

"Welcome!" Cotsy greeted. "How nice to see a couple of our favorite people come together this year!"

Their place looked absolutely gorgeous for the Christmas season. It made me wonder if they'd had it professionally decorated. Dan took our coats and guided us to the bar. Several couples were enjoying beverages, and when we were introduced to one of the older couples, they asked me to repeat my name. It was obvious that most of the couples knew each other. And judging from their appearances, they were dripping with money.

We walked by the buffet table to see that Dan had outdone himself again. There was a beautiful ice-carved Christmas wreath in the center of the table.

Grayson identified a client he knew. He was repairing one of his boats, so he wanted to give him a brief update on the progress. I made my way toward the devilish buffet of delicacies to see what I'd like to try. The older couple approached me directly.

"Miss Stewart, Carter and I felt we recognized you, but we couldn't remember from where," the lady noted. "Were you by chance married to Dr. Austen Page?"

The question threw me. "No, I never married Dr. Page, but we were together for five years," I explained.

"Oh, I'm sorry," the lady tried to correct.

"I knew Austen quite well before I retired from the practice I had in Cape Girardeau, Missouri. We'd frequently run into each other at Southeast Missouri Hospital."

"I see. It's a small world," I said politely.

"Yes, we ran into both of you together somewhere, but we can't remember where," the lady added. "By the way, I'm Nancy Porter, and this is my husband, Carter."

Chapter 77

"I'm sorry that I don't remember meeting you," I said with sincerity.

"Oh, we understand," Carter replied. "How is the old chap anyway? You know we spend most of our time here now that I'm retired. We always visited Door County a lot, but now we live here, and in the summer, we head to Sarasota, Florida, where we have a place."

"How nice," I nodded. "In regard to your question about Austen, were you aware of his accident?"

"Accident!" Nancy responded in shock. "What happened to him?" I prayed for guidance in answering properly.

"He was in a car accident some time ago, and his recovery has been a challenge."

"Oh my. How so?" Carter asked.

"He's in a wheelchair while he's trying to regain strength in his legs so he can walk again."

"Oh, my goodness," Nancy said, shaking her head. "How awful!" Carter looked shocked.

Grayson now joined us, looking perplexed.

"Am I interrupting?" he finally asked.

"Grayson, this is Nancy and Dr. Carter Porter," I introduced.

"Nice to meet you," he said, extending his handshake.

"If I may ask, Miss Stewart, how did you end up here in Fish Creek?" Carter asked. "Cotsy said you live in that little cabin next door."

"Yes, I do," I nodded. "When my best friend had to move back to Missouri to take care of her mother, she asked if I'd take over her cabin, so I did."

"Oh, I see," Nancy nodded. "Our place is just down the row near the first curve you come to."

"Well, I'm glad we ran into to you," Carter said with obviously mixed feelings. "I'll make contact with Austen. Nice to meet you, Grayson."

"You as well," Grayson responded.

Grayson and I looked at each other not knowing what to say.

"Wanna get away?" Grayson joked.

"I'd love nothing more," I said with a grin.

We helped ourselves to some fancy food that we couldn't identify by sight and found two white velvet chairs by the fire.

"This is an interesting group, isn't it?" he said as he looked about. "I'm afraid I couldn't quite fit in with all the international travel everyone was talking about. When I told them about my business, they wanted to tell me about a damn plumbing problem they had on one of their boats."

I burst into laughter. "Oh, Grayson. You're wonderful," I praised. "At least you aren't living in the servant's quarters next door in a cabin."

He leaned back and chuckled. "Well, Cotsy and Dan are gems and I'm glad we came, but I'm ready to leave if you are. I think I'd prefer your fire over this one," Grayson noted with a grin.

We graciously said our goodbyes, and I don't think one person there cared that we left.

We tromped back to my cabin, and when we got to my front steps, I stopped.

"What is it?" Grayson asked.

"I need to do something. Hold on."

"What is it?"

I turned around and fell straight backward so I could make a snow angel. Grayson's face looked horrified.

"Are you crazy?" Grayson asked as he backed away from me. Meanwhile, I waved my arms making my angel wings.

"I dare you, Mr. Wills. Let's see who makes the best angel.

Grayson shook his head and paused. "Okay, Miss Stewart. You're on!"

With that, Grayson leaned back and spread his wings. It would've been hysterical if any of the guests next door were watching. If they were, I'm sure their mouths were agape!

We pulled each other up and dusted off the dry snow. Laughing, we examined our angels. There was no doubt I'd made the better angel. Grayson's overcoat gave a distorted shape.

Once inside, we shook the snow from our coats. Grayson said hello to Puff under the tree and then began building a fire. Without saying a word, I retrieved two wine glasses and my opened bottle of merlot.

Chapter 78

Grayson and I were relieved to be alone as we sat on the couch sharing our stories of the evening. We both agreed it was more fun sharing the stories than actually being there. We both felt the biggest treat of the evening was Dan's delicious food.

"I happen to know that your floor pillows are a lot more comfortable than this couch," Grayson teased.

"I'd better not repeat that to Cher, who has had this couch for many years." He chuckled.

We grabbed our wine glasses and got comfortable on the floor.

"You have a way of making me feel so relaxed," Grayson said with a sigh. "Who else would I trust enough to just throw my body back into the snow to impress them?" We both laughed.

"I hope more snowflakes don't cover up our angels. They'd bring a smile every time I went out to my car."

He threw another log on the fire and then leaned back into my arms. I felt that sense of being safe with him that I'd experienced the last time we were here like this. His masculine tenderness was something I'd never experienced with a man before. I also took great pleasure in pushing his emotions where he'd never been before.

Late into the night, we continued where we'd left off with our last encounter. We both needed the reassurance of our feelings. I didn't want to think of the past or the future right now. It was enough to just enjoy the present moment of being in his arms, safe and warm.

When I awoke the next morning, Grayson was gone. I grinned with delight at the sight of his red scarf on the floor pillow next to me. I grabbed it and buried my face in it. It smelled just like I remembered.

Puff was waiting patiently in the kitchen, thinking she was going to be fed. I gave her an extra spoonful of food just because I was so happy.

I sat at my kitchen table with my coffee and checked my phone. There was a text from Grayson.

[Grayson]

Early morning meeting. Sorry. My scarf will have to do.

I grinned. There was a lot to remember from our evening, but now I had to get back to my daily world, which involved checking on Ericka. I called Cher.

"I'm glad you called. George is bringing her home today. She has some discomfort, but all in all she was in good spirits when I talked to her last night."

"Good. Will you be working anytime soon?"

"No. It makes me sad because I always so look forward to it. Carl's just not busy enough for another person right now."

"That's too bad, Cher Bear. I'm sorry. I finished another painting, so I dropped it off to him. He had a special order for one of my Quilted Snow pieces, so I'd better start on that today."

"I have one for the shop as well that I've been working on. That makes me miss the shop even more."

"And the owner, right?"

"I suppose."

"Well, there's no law that says you can't contact him or ask him to dinner."

There was a pause. "You're serious, aren't you?"

"Of course, my friend. What does he do with his time? He's single and doesn't live with family, so what's stopping you? My advice is to stay in touch with him, or he could easily not make contact until spring when he opens the store again."

"Oh, I never thought of that."

"That's what friends are for. The next time you see him, tell him how much this job has meant to you and how much you've learned from him. Who doesn't want to hear that?"

"Why do you always have to outsmart me, Claire Bear?"

I laughed. "I'm just sayin'!"

Before we hung up, I touched on my evening with the Bittners. When I told her to come by and see the snow angels Grayson and I made, I thought she was going to lose it with her hysterics.

Chapter 79

I traced all the snowflake designs on my fabric and started quilting from the center out. My mind was on Ava once again, and an idea came to me about how to reach her. I called Cher to see what she thought.

"Let's go to her house. Why didn't we think of this before?"

"Whose house?"

"Ava's."

"I mentioned that before when I suggested we call the police to check the place out, and you said not to do that, or it could open a can of worms."

"Well, that's different. I'm not talking about involving the police. We could just casually stop by. Doesn't she live near you in Egg Harbor?"

"Yes, it's a darling Victorian house. At least, I think she's still living there after her divorce."

"We can't rule out foul play, you know."

"Now, Claire Bear, I'm not interested in playing detective here. And what's that noise I'm hearing?"

"Oh, it's Tom and his chain saw removing that big limb that fell on my shed out back. So how about it? We could go see Ginger's shop since she's missed two meetings in a row, and then I'll treat you to some Joe Jo's Pizza nearby."

"How am I supposed to get any work done with your ideas always taking off like wildfire?"

"You have time for this, missy. So, have you taken my suggestion and called Carl yet?"

"No, I haven't. What if he declines? It could break my heart, and I'm not anxious for that to happen."

"It's your call, but I think you should go for it. What time can you pick me up later?"

"After lunch. I want to finish this block I'm working on. Just so you know, I'm not changing clothes!"

"Me either, so see you soon."

I made a grilled cheese sandwich and continued quilting until Cher picked me up.

Getting into the car with my bestie was always an adventure. I'm so glad she'd decided to come back to the area after her mom passed away. Talking to her on the phone was nice, of course, but seeing her often was another thing entirely and something I'd missed when we'd been in different states for a while.

I was happy to see Ginger's shop was still open for the season. When Cher and I walked in, we caught her by surprise.

"I don't believe it!" she cried out. "It's so good to see you both!"

"We thought we'd better check on you since you haven't been to club for a while."

"How sweet of you," she said with sadness in her voice. "I just can't leave my shop in the middle of Christmas season. I need every penny I can get since the divorce. It's also hard to make conversation with folks when things are so bad in your personal life."

"We totally understand, Ginger. We like you both and hate that this happened."

"Well, I see something I'm going to buy," I said, going across the room to a scary old Santa Claus. "We used to have one like this at home, and many folks were scared of it because his eyes appeared to follow you everywhere you went."

"Yeah, it's freaked some folks out," Ginger added. "I hated putting such a high price on him, but he's rare."

"Well, I'm willing to pay your price," I nodded. Ginger grinned.

"So, tell me about what I'm missing at club," Ginger asked as she wrapped up my Santa.

"Well, last month we didn't have a quorum for the first time ever," I informed her. "Anna is now a new member, which is good."

"That's all the news? When I asked Ava, she didn't know anything either." Ginger noted innocently.

"Ava? You saw Ava?" I asked with surprise.

"Yes, about three weeks ago, I guess," Ginger assessed. "Why?"

"We've been trying to reach her," I stated. "Did she say anything about anything?" Ginger laughed and shook her head.

Chapter 80

"Did she buy anything?" I asked. Ginger paused.

"Hmm. I don't think so. Not that I can remember anyway. We mostly talked about our divorces. My experience was considerably different from hers. I think she just wanted to vent."

"Did she say where she was going from here?" Cher asked.

"No. Do you think something's wrong?" Ginger asked with sincerity.

"We don't know. We just discovered that she discontinued her landline."

"Well, I did as well, so don't go by that."

Before we left, Ginger promised she'd make it to the Tannenbaum party as well as our next quilt club meeting. It was certainly understandable that her business had to come first.

Keeping my promise, we went to Joe Jo's pizza to have lunch. I had a secondary reason for wanting to go there. Kathy and Dick Luther, the owners, were both quilters and displayed quilts on the wall in their restaurant. Kathy sold raffle tickets for her guild at our quilt show.

The place was nearly empty, and Kathy waved to me as we walked in. We went ahead and ordered pizza and a salad. Kathy herself brought us our lunch and sat down with us.

"It's so good to see you both," Kathy noted.

"How's your quilt guild doing?"

"We're staying busy. When we have bad weather, like we've had of late, we do Zoom meetings."

Cher and I chuckled. "Can you just see our little club doing that?" Cher joked.

"So is Dick still quilting, too?"

"Oh, yes," she nodded, pointing to the front wall. "He just finished that one, and he's really more productive than I am."

"Is he here?" I asked, looking around.

"No, he's running errands," she claimed. "He'll regret not being here to see you."

"You know, Kathy, you and Dick could have your own quilt exhibit at our outdoor show next year," I suggested. "It would be in Noble Park, if you remember."

"Oh, that's so nice of you to offer, but I don't know how Dick would feel about having our quilts outdoors and all."

"I understand completely," I nodded. "Your guild is always welcome to sell their raffle tickets again if you have another quilt."

"Thanks, Claire," Kathy smiled. "You've been more than generous."

Kathy got called to the kitchen, and we enjoyed every bite of the Italian cuisine. When we rose to leave, Kathy approached us with some of her handmade cherry preserves. There was a jar for each of us.

"Do you sell this?" Cher asked.

"Oh, no. It's for special folks," she said with a grin.

We each thanked her and gave her a hug.

On the way to Ava's house in Egg Harbor, we chatted about what good publicity it would be for the show to have a husband-and-wife exhibit.

"This is a perfect story to tell the town board when we go there. We need to make sure that it's about promoting the local folks of Door County."

"I still don't think they'll let us have vendors," Cher claimed.

"Well, it's another opportunity to help their citizens and business owners."

When we pulled up in front of Ava's house, I wasn't surprised to see the style. In her quilting and in her clothing style, she liked fancy adornments. Her home was just as embellished, with lots of Victorian gingerbread. The entire house and driveway were covered in snow, as if no one had been there for days.

"I don't see a garage, and I don't see her car," I observed. "I don't even see footprints of a mailman going up to her door."

"Claire, if you think I'm going to knock on her door, you're crazy. She's not home."

"At least she's been out and about according to Ginger. I still feel like I'm responsible for her disappearance. I should've left well enough alone and not confronted her."

"Let's head home, Claire. I don't like stalking people," Cher said as she drove away.

Chapter 81

The next morning, I was focused on getting my Christmas packages mailed. I was about to leave for the post office when Carole's number showed up on my phone.

"Good morning!" I greeted her cheerfully.

"Do you have time to talk for minute?"

"Why, sure. What's wrong? Is Mom okay?"

"It's not your mom. It's Austen." There was a pause. "Linda is on this call with me."

"Evidently, he tried to take his own life yesterday," Carole reported sadly.

"Good heavens. Is he alive?"

"Yes, he'll likely be fine, but it was from an overdose. No one knows if it was an accident or on purpose," Carole informed me.

"I think a doctor knows exactly what he's doing, so my guess is that it was on purpose," Linda chimed in.

"From what Jill said, he was nearly gone when he was found," Carole added.

"I ... I ... don't know what to say." I claimed. "Do you think all the drugs he was taking altered his thinking? He's a smart man."

"Perhaps we'll know more later," Linda thought.

"I'm sorry we had to call and tell you this, Claire, but we felt you needed to know right away," Carole expressed.

"I'm sure as everyone tries to figure out why he did this, my name will come up," I said. "Did Jill say whether they think he'll be okay?"

"I think he will, or she'd have told me," Carole noted. "We need to pray for this lost soul."

"Well, thanks for telling me," I said. "I'm sure I'll be getting a call from Mom and Michael very soon. I need to digest this news."

With my coat still on, I kept moving toward my car to leave. I found it hard to believe that Austen thought so little of himself to do this. I drove to the post office wondering if Austen had any kind of relationship with God. I sure didn't see signs of it when I lived with him. What if he had been successful in his suicide attempt? I didn't want to think about that, so I got out of my car and went to my mailbox.

I stood in line waiting to mail my boxes. I should've told Carole and Linda that their Christmas presents were on their way, but I got distracted by their news. Meanwhile, Austen again occupied and controlled my mind, just as he had done over the five years that I was with him.

I nodded and said hello to a few familiar faces before getting back in my car. The Blue Horse was right next door, and for a second, I thought about whether I could hold myself together to get some coffee and a sandwich for lunch. Instead, I began looking through my mail. My tear-glazed eyes wouldn't let me focus on what I was supposed to be reading. Without warning, my tears turned into overwhelming sadness, causing me to put my head down on my arms covering the steering wheel. This was crazy. I had to get a hold of myself before someone saw me like this. The tears turned into sobs and my heart ached, causing me to wonder if I was still in love with Austen. The thought of him dying ripped my heart out. I couldn't quite get a grip on where all this emotion was coming from.

I looked around and tried to breathe. Grabbing some tissue, I tried to focus on just inhaling and exhaling to calm myself. I needed to get out of there and head home.

Chapter 82

Feeling listless when I returned home, I had no desire to paint or quilt. I mindlessly built a fire, which helped me calm down. I sat on the floor staring at the logs catching fire one by one. I then moved to the couch, and minutes later, Puff joined me. A text made me jump. It was Grayson.

[Grayson]
Pick you up at six o'clock tomorrow?

I paused. I had to remind myself that life was going on with or without me. I had to put thoughts of Austen out of my mind.

[Claire]
Fine. See you then.

The thought of going to Grayson's party wasn't sitting well with me. Should I cancel? How could I pretend to be merry when someone close to me had just tried to die?

I quickly picked up my quilting to get my mind off this train of thought. I eased my stress through working my quilting needle faster and faster on Quilted Snow. My cell phone rang. Just as I thought, it was Mom calling. I couldn't talk to her about any of this yet. I could predict all the things she'd tell me. I didn't even want to listen to her voice mail.

An hour later, a call from Cher came in. Most likely Carole and Linda had called her as well. I just couldn't handle what others had to say about Austen right now. None of their opinions would change what was going through my mind.

At dusk, I got up from the couch and poured myself a glass of wine. This time tomorrow I'd be with Grayson, pretending that none of the news about Austen mattered. How would I do it? Would I tell Grayson and ruin his big evening? That would be a horrible thing to do. This was my burden, not his.

I hadn't eaten all day, so I put a frozen pasta dinner in the microwave. After that first swallow of wine, I knew I had to get something in my stomach.

I sat down at the table to eat and wondered what everyone else expected me to do. Worrying about others' expectations of me was something I did often. I picked up my phone to scroll through my pictures because I wanted to see Austen's face. When I found him, I tried to remember a happy time for us. Why couldn't I remember how we met? Everything was wonderful until I moved in with him. It was like he achieved his goal and I became his at that point.

I quickly remembered the sense of freedom I felt when I drove out of town and away from that life with him. The pressure was off to be who he wanted me to be, and I was out to find myself again. Having a place like Cher's cabin to go to made it easy for me. Door County's artistic community was waiting for me.

I was starting to feel better again once I started thinking about how much happier I was here than at his side in Perryville. I knew God had a plan. I got another text. Cher was not giving up.

[Cher]
It's not your fault! He'll be fine. Love you, Claire Bear.

Her message helped, but I still didn't feel like talking. Puff somehow knew I was struggling and gave me the silent support I needed. If Cher were to tell me she wanted Puff back, I'd have to refuse.

Chapter 83

Surprisingly, I slept well, and I woke up feeling refreshed. I knew I had to think of a way to wrap Kelly's quilt today. As I looked at one of my own homemade pillowcases, an idea came to mind. I had plenty of leftover fabric from Kelly's quilt, so why not give it to her in a pillowcase that she could actually use? As soon as I had coffee, I'd come back and attempt to make a pillowcase.

Mom called again around nine o'clock. I knew I couldn't put her off much longer, or she'd really worry about me.

"Are you okay, honey?" she asked with concern.

"Yes, I'm fine. Is there any late word on Austen?"

"Not that I'm aware of. Carole called and told me about it all. It's such a sad scenario."

"Mom, I know it is, but I really don't want to talk about it."

"Sure," she replied softly.

"Grayson's work party is tonight, so I'm pretty excited about that."

"How nice for you both."

"He told me to bring Kelly's quilt to give to her, so I'm going to sew a matching pillowcase to put it in."

"Great idea! Let me know how she likes it."

"I will. She has hinted about a quilt for some time, so I think she'll love it."

"You're sweet to do that, dear. Well, I'll let you go back to sewing. I just had to call and see how you were doing."

"If you hear an update on Austen, please let me know."

After we hung up, I wasn't sure I really meant that. Why should I have to bear the pain that he inflected on himself?

I began sewing the pillowcase to get Austen off my mind. I would love to sew something for Grayson, but the man had everything. He hinted at wanting to see my paintings, but I also knew he had plenty of nice artwork at his house.

I finished the pillowcase and rolled up the quilt to put it inside. I turned the quilt so she could see my simple label that said, "Merry Christmas! Love, Claire."

Now I needed to decide once and for all what I'd wear this evening. My cocktail dresses were too formal. I did want to wear some of the many strands of pearls I'd collected over the years, including a lovely one from Grandmother Stewart. I'd have to wear black to do them justice. I found the perfect black dress, but I needed to remove the glitzy belt it came with for it to work. Once I did that, I jumped in the shower.

As I let the warm water pour over me, I felt I needed to wash away any negative and worrisome thoughts before I saw Grayson this evening. I didn't want to be thinking of Austen tonight.

I paid extra attention to my makeup and hair, as I knew I'd be judged from head to toe. When I added the pearls, I thought it all went together nicely.

Staying calm until Grayson arrived was difficult. I couldn't hold Puff to pet her now that I was dressed. She's a sweet cat, but I didn't want to be covered in her hair.

In no time, Grayson arrived.

"Hello, gorgeous!" he greeted as he helped me with my coat.

"You're pretty gorgeous yourself! I don't suppose you'd like that red scarf back, would you?" He grinned. "I think you should take it so I'll recognize you."

"Good idea. We have an hour before cocktails start, so let's go by the house so you can see our tree and give Kelly her quilt. Her friend Sadie is spending the night."

"Did you tell her I was bringing her a quilt?"

"Oh, no, of course not. She'll be very surprised."

I wrapped my fur coat around me close to keep warm. Even the coat had memories of Austen to haunt me. I pushed them away as Grayson reminded me that cocktails were at seven o'clock. He'd greet as many people as he could during cocktail hour. Then he'd have to make some remarks during dinner, which started at eight o'clock.

Chapter 84

Grayson's house had very few outdoor Christmas lights, but they were very tastefully placed. I recognized the large, beautiful wreath on the front door as one from Rachael's tree farm.

The girls heard us enter the hall and came running downstairs. After a quick introduction to her friend, Sadie, Kelly noticed my gifts.

"Merry Christmas, Kelly," I said, handing her what I'd brought.

"For me?" she smiled.

When she opened the Cat Mom sweatshirt, she laughed and put it on, right then and there, and twirled around for Sadie and Grayson to see. I could tell she approved. Next, she moved to the homemade pillowcase.

"I kept my promise!" I reminded her.

She pulled the quilt out of the case and looked at me in wonder.

"Claire, you really made this?"

"Just for you!" I nodded. "Since you liked the red-and-white quilt that your dad had won, I decided to make the same colors for yours."

Sadie helped Kelly hold up the quilt to examine. Then Kelly dropped her end of the quilt and came over to give me a huge hug.

"Thank you so much, Claire," she gushed. "These are the best presents ever. Dad, is it okay if I give her my gift now?"

"Why, sure! It's Christmastime," he cheered.

She handed me a small package, which I quickly unwrapped. It was a bracelet with a cat charm attached. How appropriate, I thought.

"I love it, and Puff will too. I guess we were both thinking of each other's cats this year, weren't we?" I joked. "Thank you!"

Sadie smiled when she saw my new bracelet.

"When I was sewing all those squares, Kelly, I gave this quilt a name. But you can name it whatever you want."

"Quilts have names?" Sadie asked.

"They do indeed. This one I named Hopscotch," I revealed. "Do you even know what the game hopscotch is?"

"Oh, my older sister used to play hopscotch on our sidewalk," Sadie noted.

"That's right!" I nodded. "So did I. Oh, I love your tree, Grayson!" I said as I walked closer toward it to examine the ornaments.

"My mother saved all my ornaments I've ever made, so they're all over the tree," Kelly shared.

"Some look pretty clever," I complimented. "You were always an artist, weren't you?" She smiled.

"We've had this tree for a long time," added Grayson. "We have tall ceilings, so it's perfect in here."

"I still want a real one," pouted Kelly.

"Maybe next year. Well, Claire, we'd better get going," Grayson said, looking at his watch.

The girls were anxious to see the quilt on Kelly's bed, and we left for the party.

When we got in the car, I told Grayson I was pleased with Kelly's reaction. He smiled.

"So, tell me a little more about this place we're going."

"Well, it's a versatile venue for many things, from a library to a banquet center. It's a pretty new building, finished in 2018, and is officially called the Donald and Carol Kress Pavilion. It has dozens of floor-to-ceiling windows that offer gorgeous views of the bay and surrounding orchard. My work party is in the Great Hall on the second floor. They consistently have great food, but I leave most of the planning for the party up to my staff. I've never been disappointed."

Chapter 85

Grayson was right. The entrance to our banquet dinner was a long, beautiful canopy of white lights shining over us. Even though we were there before cocktail hour officially began, the room was full of gaiety.

The greeters at the entrance to the banquet room made sure we received a bag of goodies to take home with us. We were then given our table number. To my relief, there wasn't a head table.

As our table filled, Grayson graciously introduced everyone, which included his personal assistant, Jeanne. She didn't arrive with a male partner but came with Phyllis from their accounting department. Jeanne was conservatively attractive and a tad on the cold side when she met me. As I looked about the room, Grayson reminded me that most of his employees were men and were here with their spouses.

As I tried to make conversation with Jeanne through the cocktail hour and dinner, she didn't ask me one question. Maybe Grayson had already told her everything she wanted to know. I preferred that over thinking she didn't care to know anything about me.

Her attention was on Grayson as she continued to ask if there was anything she could do to help. The food was spectacular and plentiful. When our dessert arrived, Grayson got everyone's attention and thanked them for coming. He also bragged about a successful year and looked forward to having another one in the year ahead. He kept it brief and concluded by wishing everyone a Merry Christmas and a Happy New Year.

"Well done," I said, gently tapping his hand on the table. He grinned.

"Now, for better or worse, let's attempt some moves on the dance floor," he said with a grin.

I could feel the eagle eyes of Jeanne follow me to the dance floor. Grayson held me tight, and he did indeed have those romantic moves that a girl only dreams about. He gave me a kiss on the cheek as if he were truly enjoying the moment. When the tempo changed to faster music, we headed back to the table.

"So, how are you holding up?" he whispered in my ear when we were seated.

"I'm good and so proud of you," I said with sincerity.

Grayson needed to have a word with an employee who was heading out, so he left me at the table with Jeanne.

"So, Jeanne, how long have you been working at Sails Again?" I asked to start a conversation. She paused.

"Many years," she replied. "I started in accounting with Grayson's father, Mr. Wills. Grayson is dedicated to the business just like his father was. The only other thing that matters to him is Kelly." I knew she was sending me a message loud and clear.

"I just saw Kelly before coming here," I revealed. "I made her a quilt for Christmas, and she really liked it."

Jeanne didn't know what to say. "She's a sweetheart. No one will ever replace her mother, Marsha," she added with a stern look in my direction.

"Understandably," I nodded. "Do you have children, Jeanne?" She looked shocked at my question, like I should already know the answer.

"No," she stated. "How about you?"

I shook my head. "I have a cat, and sometimes I can't even deal with her," I joked.

"Well, sweetie," Grayson said as he joined me, "it looks like everyone is happy, so what about one more dance before we cut out of here?"

"Great!" I said, as he took me in his arms. I could feel Jeanne's jealousy fill up the room.

Chapter 86

All in all, it was a pleasant evening. I truly was impressed with how much Grayson's employees thought of him. I also understood how Jeanne had protected and helped Grayson through the years and was most likely in love with him.

"Hey, let's have a nightcap at Alexander's!" Grayson suggested out of the blue. "I want to extend this great night with my best girl."

I leaned over and kissed his cheek. "Good idea since I really didn't get to visit much with you tonight. I didn't mind sharing you one bit, though, because they love you so."

He chuckled. "I feel lucky, but I'll never be able to measure up to my dad. I think they all realize I'm trying, though."

"Let me ask you more about Jeanne. She's very protective of you." He nodded. "Do you sense that she's actually in love with you?" He paused as if he didn't know how to answer.

"Yeah, about Jeanne. She's got a heart of gold, and there are times I want to caution her about her feelings toward me, but it would crush her. She really loves her job."

"That's tough," I sympathized.

"I purposefully wanted her to sit next to you this evening so you could get to know each other better. I also wanted her to understand and see for herself that we were a couple."

"Well, I tried, but I'm not sure she learned anything."

"You know, I'm not sure Alexander's is going to appreciate my holding you and kissing you the way I want to right now. Do you have any objection to us heading back to that little cabin in the woods?" I chuckled and snuggled into his neck to kiss him.

With his sweet suggestion, we arrived back at the little cabin where we'd shared tender moments in the past.

Two hours later, and with half of the wine bottled emptied, Grayson reminded me that he had a guest staying at his house. I agreed that the two teenagers would indeed be playing close attention to what time he returned home. I didn't mind. We'd had a great evening.

The next morning, despite resistance from Puff, I slept two hours later than normal. I had too many wonderful memories to replay in my mind.

Leave it to Rachael to call this early.

"Don't you ever sleep in?" I joked.

"Don't you remember what time of the year this is? I have a Christmas tree business. I wanted to tell you thank you for recommending Brenda to finish the quilt. I can't believe she said she could have it done in time for the party. That's amazing."

"If she says she will, she will. She's someone who can be counted on, and she's simply a wonderful human being."

"Well, I think she was disappointed when I told her we discontinued the wish tree idea. I did ask her to help us inside the shop that day, and she seemed to be happy to do so."

"Great idea. I think we'll need her."

"The tents will be going up this week. I think I want the quilt to hang in the main tent behind where the band will be playing."

"That sounds like a perfect spot, especially if the weather gets goofy."

"Harry assures me we'll be fine. He watches that weather like a hawk."

"Did you decide what we should wear?"

"Yes. I was going to suggest you wear that red cable sweater you have. I have one that's very similar. We have to dress warmly. I'll tell Brenda the same thing."

"Great!"

"Harry said that for the party, you should park on the side of the white house where he keeps his Hummer."

"No problem. My goodness, Rachael. You and Harry have thought of everything."

I was looking forward to the Tannenbaum party. I picked up the *Pulse* newspaper and checked out their calendar of events. It showed that the town board would be meeting next week. It was never too early to start thinking about our next outdoor quilt show.

I called the number that was listed. A different lady answered than I'd spoken to before. She called herself Miss Bennet. I thought of *Pride and Prejudice.*

"Oh, yes, Miss Stewart, we can schedule you next week. It's our last meeting of the year, so with the holidays and all, we don't have much scheduled."

"That's great. What time?"

"Seven o'clock sharp, like last time."

"Okay. We'll see you then."

As soon as I hung up, I called Cher to tell her the news.

"Lordy. My stomach is churning just thinking about it."

"You did much better than I did the last time," I reminded. "I think this year you should be the one to make our presentation instead of me."

"I can't promise you that. We'd better figure out how many vendors might be interested. I know they'll want to know that."

"We'll be ready. Not to worry, Cher Bear."

Chapter 87

The next morning, Brenda called to see if she could stop by to show me the Tannenbaum quilt she'd just finished for Rachael. I was delighted to see it before the party.

I straightened up the cabin for her visit and put some packaged cinnamon buns in the oven so I'd have something to offer her.

At ten o'clock she arrived with the quilt under her arms.

I welcomed her in and offered to get her some coffee and a hot roll out of the oven.

"Oh, Claire, that would be great. My shift starts at eleven o'clock, and I didn't take time for breakfast at home. Please take a look at this quilt and be honest with me. I want to remind you and Rachael both that I'm not a professional at this."

"I was happy with Kelly's quilt, so I'm sure it's fine."

She unfolded the quilt, and I looked at what designs she had used and where.

"Did I do enough quilting? I felt diagonal lines were best in that tree background so I wouldn't distort the embroidery. Do you see your block in the corner?"

"It looks really good, Rachael. Thank you. There are some nice tree blocks here. I really prefer this simpler version over Anna's quilt. I think Rachael will be pleased, too." She smiled.

"The Christmas caroling is going on tonight at the Noble House. I was going to ask you to go, but I have to work now."

"Oh, that was so much fun last year. I was so touched that you asked me to go. It's supposed to start snowing again, so it's just as well that we skip it this year. By the way, how are things going with you and Kent?"

"He came to the inn for lunch yesterday, which I found interesting."

"Well, because of you, I'm sure."

"We were pretty busy, but I got to visit with him a little bit. I was able to give him a complimentary piece of pie, so he really liked that."

"I'll bet he did. Any plans to see him again?"

"Now, Claire, we're not a couple. He did ask me if I'd be at the farm all day when I help out for the party."

"We'll have fun, but they'll be super busy, just so you know. Hey, did Rachael ask you if you had a nice warm, red sweater?"

"No, but it just so happens, I've been eyeing one at the On Deck store. It would be a great Christmas present to myself."

"Some people at the party will be in German attire, and you'll get to see Harry in lederhosen, which should be quite the sight." She laughed and nodded.

"Claire, I can't help but notice that this Santa you have standing by your tree follows you around with his eyes."

I chuckled and nodded. "Yes, it sure does! I just bought him at Ginger's place. We used to have one like him at home, and it would freak out all the children. I'm surprised Puff doesn't feel threatened by him."

"Well, I'd better head to work. I'll see you at the big party."

"Sounds good. Yes, I need to get back to work so I can get this piece to the gallery."

Chapter 88

Late in the afternoon, Mom called.

"How's my favorite mom?" I teased.

"I'm doing well, but since I hadn't heard from you since we talked about Austen, I just wanted to check on you."

"Oh, not to worry, Mom. Have you been getting any news on him?"

"No, not much. It's a small town, so there are all sorts of rumors."

"Yes, it's a small town for sure. I haven't heard anything from Michael, so I suppose he's not going to come for Christmas either."

"Well, have you invited him or encouraged him? You need to communicate with him more directly, Claire."

"It works both ways," I complained.

"You two never change. You act like you did when you were ten years old. By the way, I got your packages today."

"Oh, good. Don't peek."

"I promise. I already have them under the tree. This year I just put up that tabletop tree that fits in the corner. If you were coming home, I could've been talked into getting a big one."

"I'm sorry I'm not coming home, Mom."

"It works out fine. Say, you sure have been getting a lot of snow up there."

"That's for sure. It's a lot compared to last year, anyway."

"Oh, it's almost time for my soap opera, honey," she hinted.

"I can't believe you're still watching *Days of Our Lives.*"

She laughed. "Goodbye, sweetie," she said, hanging up.

As I got back to my quilting, I was pleased to hear that news about Austen was pretty quiet. I had to wonder if he had any regrets or would try another time. An hour later, I got a call that surprised me.

"Michael! How are you?"

"I just talked to Mom."

"Oh, say no more. Did she do a guilty number on you like she did me?"

He chuckled. "Well, about Christmas. I had agreed to come to Door County to bring Mom if she really wanted to go, but then when she decided not to, I chose another direction myself."

"Michael!"

"Don't take it personally. I do want to experience that world you live in one day, but not necessarily in the dead of winter. With all the water and outdoor opportunities, I'd like to come in the warmer weather."

"Have you ever heard of ice fishing?" I said sarcastically.

"Okay, I get your point, but I'll visit later. So, when do you plan to come back?"

"Well, I came the last time in hopes of cheering up Austen, but we know how that turned out."

"Yeah, that was crazy for him to do. That had to be a bit hard on you as well."

"It was. It's sad to think of anyone wanting to die, especially someone you were close to for five years. So, are you still working on your next book?"

"Yeah, I'm about halfway, but time's an issue right now. Are you still seeing Grayson?"

"Yes, I believe I am," I said with a chuckle.

"Mom says he has a teenage daughter. How are you dealing with that?"

"I'm holding my own. Michael, I really appreciate that you called."

"Time is ticking away, sis. I have some gray hair now, by the way."

"I didn't know. You'd better email me a photo." He chuckled. "Please check on Mom, okay?"

"I'm sure I can see her on Christmas Day. She said she'd be with Bill on Christmas Eve."

"Please do that for me. Thanks for calling. I love you."

"I love you too, sis."

Chapter 89

With the big Tannenbaum party tomorrow, I decided to check in with Rachael to see if she needed any last-minute help.

"So, how's it going out there?"

"Pretty good. I'm just kind of watching it all happen. Harry and Kent put up the tents and lights yesterday, and it all looks quite festive. You won't recognize the place."

"Do you need my help with anything today?"

"No, but I'd love for you to be here by seven o'clock tomorrow morning if you can swing it. You're welcome to come out tonight if you don't want to get up so early."

"I'll think about it."

"Anna and Marta are coming out today to bring Anna's things she'll be selling. She'll be baking her strudel tonight. I can't wait."

"Were you pleased with how Brenda sewed your quilt?"

"Oh, yes! It looked great! She's also excited about helping us tomorrow."

"Now I have to worry about her taking my place," I laughed.

"Not a chance, sister. See you tomorrow!"

I hung up feeling like things were in control. The weather was supposed to be good, so if I set the alarm early, I'd drive out in the morning.

My mind was on Grayson and when I would possibly see him at the party. He had suggested bringing Kelly and Sadie when I'd talked to him about the party a few days ago. I didn't like calling him since he was so busy, so I'd just have to wait and see what happened.

With nervous energy I ran the vacuum, which Puff hated. Her reaction was usually to hide under the bed or couch during the process. Still feeling energized, I decided to make brownies to contribute for tomorrow's helpers.

I looked out the kitchen window, and to my surprise I saw Grayson pull up the drive.

"Well, hello! What a nice surprise!"

"I could smell those brownies all the way down the street!"

I burst into laughter. "Do you have time for some?"

"Not really. I'm meeting some salesmen for lunch at the White Gull Inn, so I'd thought I'd stop and discuss tomorrow with you."

"You're coming out, aren't you?"

"Most likely, but I can't commit to a specific time. Christmas is at our doorstep, and I have tons to do. Kelly said she thought it would be fun."

"I'm happy she'll be coming with you."

"You're going to be a busy lady tomorrow, so I'd better give you a kiss right now away from the crowd." I blushed as he pulled me close. "Now, this will have to do because I need to be on my way."

I smiled with affection as I watched him leave.

I added a few more stitches on the binding of Quilted Snow and then decided to call Carl to see if he was still at the gallery.

"Hey, Claire," he answered happily. "What's up?"

"I finished the special order on the Quilted Snow and wondered if I could bring it by."

"Well, if you come soon. It's been quiet today, so I thought I might close early."

"I'll see you in fifteen minutes."

I bundled up for the short walk to the gallery.

Carl was vacuuming the floor when I walked in.

"I guess you're missing that wonderful help that you usually have here," I teased.

"I just have to stay busy," he said, grinning.

"Well, I know when I work for Rachael, there's always something that has to be done."

"Hey, this is a long shot, but when I finish up here, do you have any interest in getting a hamburger at the Bayside? I haven't eaten all day, and I'm starving."

I paused. "Sure. Why not? I'm pretty casual today, though."

"I don't think the Bayside is going to care what you're wearing." I nodded and smiled.

After I gave him my quilt, we went on our way. Oh, what Cher wouldn't give to be in my place right now.

We decided to sit at the bar, and I couldn't help but think of Rachael when she helped out here on Saturday nights. We ordered beers and their famous hamburgers. Trying to make small talk, I told him the latest with the Tannenbaum party that was the next day.

"Is Cher planning to go?" he asked with curiosity.

"Yes, she said she wouldn't miss it. It's going to be quite something. It's too bad you're working."

Chapter 90

"Can I be frank with you, Claire?"

"Of course. What's on your mind?"

"You probably know Cher better than anyone. She's pretty private about her life, I've noticed." I nodded. "I'm just not sure how to read her sometimes."

I smiled. "What would you like to know? Do you want me to be frank as well?"

"Please!"

"Cher and I always say, 'What happens at the Bayside, stays at the Bayside.' He leaned back in laughter. "I'll bet you want to know if Cher has feelings for you."

His face perked up in surprise. "Okay. Let's start there."

"Yes, she does have feelings for you, besides thinking you're a terrific boss."

He was speechless. "I'm not sure how to respond."

"Why don't you try by saying how you feel about her?"

"I find her friendly and attractive. I always have. But as her employer, I have to be careful how I proceed, if you know what I mean."

"I figured as such. The two of you remind me of being in high school. I told her that she needs to invite you to dinner, but she's shy about being that forward. She said she'd be mortified if you turned her down."

"Oh, this is most helpful and a source of great relief!"

"She loved that dinner with you at Alexander's. I think she'd be more comfortable if you were the one to ask her to dinner."

"I guess we need to keep this at the Bayside, right?"

"It's probably a good idea."

"Another beer?"

"One more can't hurt," I nodded with a grin.

When we finally parted at nine o'clock, I hoped no one had seen us and thought we were a couple. I felt I did Cher and Carl a big favor.

I sure picked the wrong night to have a few beers with needing to get up so early. I set my alarm, laid out my red sweater, and put my brownies by the door so I wouldn't forget them in the morning.

Before I finally went to sleep, I thought about the budding relationship of Cher and Carl. I'd done my part, so the rest would be up to them.

Much to my discomfort, the alarm went off at six o'clock as planned, and I was not ready to face the world. I reluctantly stumbled out of bed, and Puff followed me to the kitchen as always. I picked her up and explained I'd be gone all day and into the evening, but she jumped out of my arms to eat instead of paying attention to me.

On my drive to the farm, I tried to get excited about the party. The sun was doing its part and coming up with the promise of a new and glorious day. I parked where Rachael asked me to and had a look around. I couldn't believe how the farm had been transformed. Where was I? I loved the

O TANNENBAUM sign on the main tent. Now I knew where I was.

Chapter 91

"Am I in the right place?" I joked as I walked through the doorway. Harry and Rachael laughed.

"It looks like Christmas is happening here, doesn't it," Harry bragged.

"I love every last bit of it!" I praised. "As soon as I down this second cup of coffee, I'm ready to go to work."

"Help yourself," Rachael said. "All of the food will be out in the tent today. Kent is grilling bratwurst, and it should be delicious."

"Hey, Miss Claire. You didn't even notice my lederhosen!"

I chuckled. "Oh, but I did!" I noted. "You were made for that outfit."

"I know a little German, by the way," Harry bragged.

"Well, you'll get your opportunity to use it today," I reminded.

"Okay, Rachael. You come with me to make sure we hang the quilt in the right place," Harry instructed.

"Guten Morgen," Anna greeted as she and Marta came inside.

"Look at you, fräulein!" I complimented her. "You and Marta look great!"

"Danke," she said as she curtseyed.

"After I show Harry where to put the quilt, I'll come to your tent to help you set up," Rachael instructed.

They all went about their business, and I was left alone. I figured no one had had time to water the Christmas tree yet today, so I started there. Brenda arrived shivering from the cold.

"Good morning! Hey, you treated yourself to the red sweater you'd talked about! It's pretty!"

She nodded and smiled. "I did, and thanks, Claire. I'm all ready to work. Cars are starting to arrive. Let me just grab a cup of coffee before I do anything else."

"Did they have the quilt up yet?"

"Yes, and it looks perfect there. I love the sign, too. I just hope all the smoke from grilling doesn't get into the quilt. By the way, what's in that little white house?"

I snickered. "It started out as a little man cave for Charlie. They used to take all the sales from the trees over there, but it got too busy. The barn is better for add-on sales due to the traffic."

"That house must have a fireplace, judging by the smoke coming out of the chimney."

"No, there's just a woodburning stove in there, and boy, does it get warm. Kent and Harry find various reasons to use the white house. It's actually quite charming from the outside."

"Brenda, Claire, this is my niece, Clara," Harry introduced. "She'll be the one selling cherry merchandise in the tent with Anna."

"Nice to meet you, Clara," I responded. "I'll be out to buy some things when I have a chance to leave here. I can't wait to see what you have."

"Help yourself to some coffee while you're here," Harry suggested.

"Thank you so much!" she said, as I detected another German accent. "It's so beautiful in here."

"And warm!" Brenda added. "Good luck today, and come in if you need to take the chill off." Clara nodded as she got her coffee.

When they left, I began showing Brenda our procedure for taking sales. Her experience working at the White Gull Inn would be helpful.

Chapter 92

Rachael came back inside, and she nervously rattled off the many things that needed to be done.

"The band should've been here by now," she complained.

"It's all going to be okay," I reassured her. "People are coming here for a Christmas experience today, and they have no idea what to expect, so just enjoy."

"Harry is going nuts giving lots of orders, so I'd better get back out there," she said, turning toward the door.

"Then go and keep him company. Brenda and I can handle everything in here," I insisted.

"Did you see my list on the counter?" Rachael asked anxiously.

"Yes, yes, go!" I repeated with urgency.

As Rachael walked out the door, two ladies walked in to pay for their wreaths. Minutes later, I knew the party had begun when I heard the German band start up.

Kent eventually came in to check on Brenda, but he used getting a cup of coffee as an excuse. It was the first time I'd seen them interacting as a couple and found it interesting to watch.

The shop got busier and busier. Folks were bringing in their bratwurst sandwiches, which really made me yearn for a lunch break.

"Hey, Claire!" Ginger yelled from across the room. "This is my mother, Jane. She loves anything and everything Christmas, so she's soaking up this whole experience today. By the way, I introduced myself to Anna since I haven't been to club lately. What a sweetheart."

"I know," I nodded. "She really is. Did you taste her strudel?"

"Yes, and I think Mom nearly bought her out."

"This is such a fun and interesting place, Claire," Ginger's mother admired.

"I'm glad you're enjoying it," I responded. "Are there a lot of folks outside?"

"Oh, yes! We parked down the road, and the trolley dropped us off," she explained. "I want to see all of Rachael's barn quilts."

"Please look around while I help Rachael at the counter," I instructed.

"Oh, listen, Rachael!" I said to get her attention. "They're singing 'O Tannenbaum.' "

"I need to get out there," she said, heading to the door. "I'll tell Kent to send in some bratwurst sandwiches."

"Oh, good. I'm getting hungry!" As I said that, I noticed Cher had arrived.

"Look who I brought with me!" Carl blushed.

"We'd have been here sooner, but traffic on 42 was really slow and backed up," Carl explained. "This is a wonderful setup out here!" Cher beamed looking at him.

"How are you, Brenda?" Cher asked. "It looks like they quickly put you to work."

She nodded. "You'd better watch out, or they'll do the same to you guys," Brenda responded.

"We're willing to help," Cher noted.

Rachael came inside and described how a few folks were actually dancing to the music. Kent followed her with a platter of sandwiches and some nice mulled German wine for us.

"Not everyone gets this wine, so go in the back room and enjoy it," Kent encouraged.

"Thanks, Kent," I said with gratitude. "We're too busy for me to leave the counter, so I'll just eat mine here."

As I was eating, Lee and her husband, a cardiologist, came in the door. I hadn't met him before, so she introduced us as he paid for their Christmas tree.

"Thank you, Lee," I responded. "By the way, your work on the quilt is beautiful. Rachael loves it."

Chapter 93

The shop was filling up, and I was beginning to wonder whether Grayson and the two girls were going to show up.

The band came in to warm up as they sipped on some of the mulled wine Harry or someone had offered them. I saw Carl conversing with them, and then he came toward me.

"I told Cher this Christmas market is a grand idea," Carl complimented.

"It is!" I nodded. "This could really expand every year. By the way, who is minding the store today?"

He smiled. "No one," he said, shaking his head. "I decided it was slow enough for the boss to take off."

"Danke, Miss Stewart," one of the German players said as he was leaving.

"Bitte!" I yelled back. Cher and Carl looked at me strangely. "It means you're welcome," I explained.

"Let's go out and listen to them some more," suggested Cher. "You don't need me, Claire, do you?"

"Go! Brenda and I are doing just fine," I reassured her. "When Rachael comes back in, I'm going out to shop around. I wonder if Grayson will ever get here."

"The traffic is terrible, Claire," Carl reminded.

I returned to the counter where a lady was purchasing a lovely barn quilt of the Feathered Star, one of my favorites. Marta came in to use the restroom and admired it as well.

"You should see Anna with all those people out there," bragged Marta. "She's getting contact information on everyone for her new bakery."

"Smart, very smart!" I replied. "I hope she's getting lots of encouragement today."

"Well, I think we'll be out of strudel soon!"

"Wonderful for her, but bad news for me, I'm afraid. I hope to get out there soon to taste some."

Rachael came inside and was so excited that some of her coworkers from the Bayside Tavern had come out for the party. She commented that most had never seen her place before.

"I'll bet they miss you!" I claimed.

"I told them I'd be back after Christmas. They were so good to me after Charlie died."

"Is it okay if I run out to see things?" I asked Rachael. "I want to take some photos."

"Sure, go! Kent said he'd take some, too."

When I walked out of the barn, I saw the sweetest older couple waltzing to one of the German tunes. There wasn't much room, but they were having a ball. I could only imagine how crazy this place would be if Harry had a German biergarten.

"May I have this dance?" said a familiar voice behind me.

"Grayson! You made it!" I said with a big grin.

"Hello, Miss Stewart," Sadie chimed in, with Kelly by her side.

"Hey, girls! I'm so glad you came with Grayson to see this place," I replied.

"This reminds me of the Hallmark movies," Kelly noted. "They always have a Christmas tree farm like this where couples pick out a tree." We laughed and nodded.

"See those little trees leaning over there?" I asked Kelly. "They're free for the taking. I put one in my bedroom. Maybe you'd like a little one for yours."

"Oh, wow, cool!" Sadie voiced with interest. Kelly seemed excited by the idea, too.

"Thanks, Claire," Grayson said. He looked as excited about having a tree in Kelly's bedroom as he had about adopting Spot.

The band got our attention, and one member said they had a special treat for everyone.

"This is Anna Marie Meyer, who just moved here from Ludwigsburg, Germany," he announced. "She's going to lead us in the German version of 'O Tannenbaum,' so please join us."

Grayson put his arm around me as we watched Anna face the crowd that was now gathered around us. Brenda and Rachael even came out of the barn to participate.

Chapter 94

"Please join me!" Anna called out to the crowd. "If you don't know the German version, sing it in English."

O Tannenbaum, o Tannenbaum,
wie treu sind deine Blätter!
Du grünst nicht nur zur Sommerzeit,
Nein auch im Winter, wenn es schneit.
O Tannenbaum, o Tannenbaum,
wie treu sind deine Blätter!
O Tannenbaum, o Tannenbaum!
Du kannst mir sehr gefallen!
Wie oft hat nicht zur Weihnachtszeit
Ein Baum von dir mich hoch erfreut!
O Tannenbaum, o Tannenbaum!
Du kannst mir sehr gefallen!
O Tannenbaum, o Tannenbaum!
Dein Kleid will mich was lehren:
Die Hoffnung und Beständigkeit
Gibt Trost und Kraft zu jeder Zeit.
O Tannenbaum, o Tannenbaum!
Das soll dein Kleid mich lehren.

Everyone laughed and sang the best they could. Anna did an amazing job. Most sang the English version they knew. Grayson gave one of those manly whistles, which made me laugh.

Anna's face blushed, but she took a bow. Then Rachael gave her a hug for her good performance.

I followed Anna over to her tent with the intention of getting some strudel, but they were sold out.

"Oh, Claire. I'm so sorry. I'll bake some just for you real soon."

"I'm glad you had a good day," I said with encouragement. "I'll eventually get some strudel. But I hope I don't have to wait until you get your bakery open." She chuckled.

Grayson and I made a small purchase from Clara, who was selling jars of cherries, before heading back into the barn.

Kelly and Sadie were looking for Grayson, thinking he might want to leave, but he told them that Harry wanted him to stick around for a while. They didn't seem to mind.

"I'll let you get back to work here, as it looks like you're still busy," Grayson noted. "I'll see if I can help Kent or Harry."

I looked at my watch. Four o'clock. It felt like it was four hours later than that. What an exhausting day.

"You sure got a lot of compliments on your quilt," Brenda told Rachael.

"I owe the whole idea to Anna," Rachael replied modestly. "And wow, I had no idea she had such a lovely voice. She seems to be good at so many things."

I went back to taking sales when Brenda came over to me.

"What's all the champagne about?" Brenda asked with interest. "Kent just brought a bunch of it into the back room." I shrugged my shoulders.

Within the next fifteen minutes, the band stopped playing, and Anna and Marta came in to say they were ready to leave. They thanked Rachael and admitted they were exhausted.

The two girls were giggling in the back room having a good time. I heard them mention Billy's name a time or two.

Rachael came to me and indicated how wonderful the day's sales might be. Needless to say, she was very happy. She looked at the bare spot on the wall and wondered when she could restock.

Harry, Kent, Grayson, Carl, and Cher all came inside. Something was about to happen as Harry went over and hooked his arm around Rachael's.

"Attention, everyone!" Harry called out. "Rachael and I want to thank everyone for all your help today. It was a lot of fun, wasn't it, honey?" She nodded and laughed.

By then, the girls were curious about what was going on and came out from the back room with Kent, who brought out glasses for the champagne. What was going on?

"Rachael and I would like you to share a glass of champagne with us, not only to celebrate our first annual Tannenbaum party, but to celebrate our engagement to be married."

"Engagement?" I called out. Could it be? Everyone paused for him to say more.

Rachael spoke up next. "We couldn't think of when to tell all of you that Harry asked me to be his wife, and I accepted!" Everyone cheered. Hugs flowed freely around the room.

Chapter 95

Kent followed up by tapping on his champagne glass to get our attention.

"I'd like to confess that I knew about this major change in my father's life, and I couldn't be more pleased. I love Rachael, and they're a great match. Here's a toast to their happiness in the future."

"Hear, hear!" everyone cheered as they accepted a glass of champagne.

"I can't believe this!" Cher expressed as she came near me.

"I can," I nodded. "I've watched this happen before my very eyes."

"This is awesome," Brenda chimed in.

Grayson came over to stand by me.

"What do you make of that, Claire?" he sheepishly asked.

"I love it," I said, smiling. "I think Charlie would approve."

It was great to see all the merriment as they enjoyed the moment. I hadn't seen Rachael this happy in a long time. A bonus of her marrying Harry would be a better financial future for her, no doubt.

"I think we've had enough excitement, so the girls and I will be leaving," Grayson announced. "I'm glad we were here to share the news. I'm really happy for them."

"I am, too!" I said with delight.

Grayson kissed me on the forehead in front of the girls, and then off they went.

I thanked the girls for being good sports to come along as I walked to get my coat in the back room. I caught Rachael and Harry in an intimate moment, relieved their secret was out.

"Now, let me see this big rock up close and personal," I teased, getting a closer look.

It had to have been terribly expensive. The diamond was huge, but beautiful.

"I love it!" Rachael bragged.

"It's fabulous! You didn't announce when the big day would happen," I questioned.

"We're not sure," she added, blushing. "Kent will move into Harry's house, and Harry will move into mine. That's the long-range plan anyway. Kent is thrilled to have the extra space for his little family."

"I missed seeing the girls today," I noted. "Where were they?"

"We were too busy today for them to be around," Harry explained. "You'll see them here for our Christmas Eve party."

"Oh, that's next week." I realized. "I'll be here to work for sure. Congratulations again, you two. I wish you much happiness."

As I came out of the room, Kent was bringing in the Tannenbaum quilt.

"I guess I'd better save this for the party next year, don't you think?" he said, grinning.

"Gute Idee," I said in German. He laughed.

As I left that evening, the place still looked magical with all the lights. I had to smile at the thought of Anna's quilt bringing about such a party.

By the time I pulled up to my cabin, snowflakes were falling. With all my white lights, my cabin looked like a shining star in the woods. I still needed to make a firm decision on whether to purchase this little gem from Cher.

Puff was happy to see me after her time alone all day. I picked her up to give her a hug and went upstairs to the bedroom. My phone alerted me to a text from Cher.

[Cher]
What a great surprise at the party! Happy for them!

[Claire]
Happy for you, too! Fill me in on your appearance with Carl.

[Cher]
Stay tuned.

[Claire]
Hey, not fair!

Chapter 96

To Puff's dismay, I slept in later than usual. I lay awake planning my day, which needed to include a visit to the Pig. These constant days of snow had limited my visits to the grocery. The current light shower of snowflakes shouldn't be a problem if I left early this morning.

When I came down for my coffee, a UPS truck drove up my way. When he came to the door to hand me my box, I saw the return address was from Carole.

"Thank you!" I said with excitement.

I quickly opened the package. There were wrapped gifts that I'd have liked to put under the tree, but not with Puff living there. In the box were gifts from Carole, Linda, and my mother. A pang of homesickness came over me. Minutes later, the UPS driver returned to the door.

"Sorry, Miss Stewart, but I missed this package for you."

"Oh! Thank you. Have a Merry Christmas!"

The package was fairly large and a bit heavy. It was from Michael. How odd. We usually didn't exchange gifts. I tore the box open with vigor to see what was inside. It was a box full of men's ties with a note inside.

"Would you believe these are all Dad's ties? Mom sent them to me through the years thinking I would actually wear them, but I didn't have the heart to tell her I never did. I've heard of quilters making quilts out of ties and thought of you. Some of these are quite old. Maybe you can make Mom a quilt out of them, dear sister. Don't hate me. After all, it's a sweet memory of Dad. Merry Christmas, and hope to see you this summer."

I shook my head in disbelief. Dad died around twenty years ago, and this pile looked like Michael just threw them in a box as they arrived. I couldn't decide whether this was a curse or not. Where would I even store all these? As I dragged the box up my narrow staircase, I just knew my dad was laughing his head off.

I dressed as if I were going to the North Pole and headed out to do errands. My first stop was at the post office. As I looked at the Blue Horse nearby, I was tempted to make a stop, but with the snowflakes still coming down, I decided to stay focused.

On my way I passed through Ephraim, which always looked like a page in a storybook. The Moravian church up high on the hill made such a lovely background. I'd love to go there with Grayson one day.

The Pig parking lot was packed. Of course, another threat of bad weather brought everyone out for milk and bread. I managed to just get what I needed besides picking up a few things that were premade. As I was leaving, Lee was coming in.

"Lee, I just have to tell you that you really missed some excitement at the end of the Tannenbaum party," I teased. "Rachael and Harry announced their engagement!"

"Oh, my goodness! How wonderful. When will that happen?"

"They wouldn't say. I'm so happy for them. By the way, they put away the Tannenbaum quilt for next year's party."

"Great! The party was such a fun idea."

We both wished each other Merry Christmas and then got on our way.

When I arrived at Sister Bay, I took a minute to soak in all their beautiful Christmas decorations. On one side of the road was the Sister Bay Marina where Grayson kept one of his boats. We had enjoyed a lovely romantic dinner on the boat one night. Across the street was Al Johnson's restaurant, where I hoped to have lunch today. When I finally found a parking spot on the street, I went inside with a big appetite. I was lucky to get a table, so I quickly ordered the special of tomato bisque and a grilled ham and cheese sandwich. It was the perfect day for such a treat.

Despite the snow now sticking on the ground, I took my time and read emails during my lunch.

Chapter 97

After a delicious lunch, I went across the hall to where their wonderful gift shop was located. I loved browsing their clothing department, but everything was always too expensive for me. When I spotted a wonderful Scandinavian wool ski sweater in great colors of red, green, and blue, I took it off the shelf and looked at it with envy. I couldn't justify buying it for myself, but Cher would absolutely love it. She used to wear a similar one long ago. She was not one to spend money on her wardrobe, so I wanted to do it for her. Just as I justified the feather tree for Rachael and the Amish quilt for Ericka, I knew this sweater was meant for Cher. After all, it was Christmas!

As I checked out at their counter, I noticed some red catnip toys that I knew Puff would enjoy, so I purchased a couple of those as well. She was my only child, so to speak.

I went on my way feeling the Christmas spirit. Down the road was the Tannenbaum Holiday Shop, which I adored. Even if I walked out with nothing, I had to go there and look at every single thing. If I had a bigger place, I'd want a Christmas tree in every room.

As usual, there were lots of cars in the parking lot. When I entered the store, I experienced that magical feeling of Christmas that always came over me when I stepped inside. My favorite tree in the place was the Door County tree. I always checked to see what was new. I loved the helmet of the Green Bay Packers, so I bought one for me and one for Brenda. I had to think of a way to display all my Door County ornaments in one place. I'd thought about using a garland across the fireplace last year but never got around to doing that.

The staff was always friendly. I wanted to fill my arms with goodies, but where would it all go in my mini cabin? When I left, I was proud of the effort I'd made to control myself.

Arriving home, I was pleased with my purchases. As soon as I put my groceries away, I wrapped Cher's sweater, not knowing when I'd be able to give it to her.

The early darkness of the day told me it was time to build a fire and have a glass of wine. Puff was always happy to see me settle in so she could snuggle up next to me.

I was checking my emails on my phone when I heard a knock at the door. It was a soft knock, and I wasn't expecting anyone. When I could finally see who it was, I nearly fainted.

"Ava! For heaven's sake come in," I said in disbelief. "Are you okay?" She nodded and smiled. "Come in and sit. Where in the world have you been? It's such a shock to see you."

She took off her coat and slowly sat down as if she didn't know where to start with her explanation.

"I'm so touched by your concern, Claire," she began. "After all your persistence in trying to find me, I felt I needed to come and talk with you."

"I felt so bad after confronting you. I hope I wasn't the reason you went away. Are you in trouble?"

"Not with the law, if that's what you're thinking."

"Then trouble with what or who, for goodness' sake?" I asked with concern.

"My husband."

"Your husband? I thought you'd gotten divorced."

"I filed, but it isn't final yet. He's protesting big time and making my life hell."

"Well, don't let him," I firmly responded.

"You don't understand. He's an evil, controlling man. He'd cheated on me and I'd cheated on him, so our marriage had been rocky for a long time. I just couldn't take it anymore, so I left. He's threatened me with everything imaginable."

"He wants you to stay in the marriage even though you don't want him?"

She nodded. "It's not about caring for each other. It's about control. His last threat was more serious, which is why I had to hide somewhere. He could put me in jail."

"Jail?"

"He knows my history of sticky fingers, as you describe it. He said he'd report all the times he knew I'd stolen things. He covered up for me a time or two, so he feels he has enough to turn me in for jail time."

"Oh, Ava, I don't know what to say. I'm really sorry you're going through this."

"I didn't think anyone but him would notice my absence, but missing quilt club and the Tannenbaum party made my disappearance more noticeable. Thank goodness no one called to report me missing that I know of. I have a new cell number I want to give you. I disconnected my landline and other cell number."

Chapter 98

"Where did you go, Ava?"

"I'd rather not say because I can't risk him finding me. I'm hoping he thinks I left town."

"If you did, where would you go?"

"He knows I have friends in Chicago, so I'm hoping he's looking there."

"I've never seen him. Does he work?"

"He's in sales, so he does a fair amount of travel. That's how we both got in trouble in the first place. As time went on, we had little feeling left for each other."

"So, he doesn't love you at all?"

She burst into laughter. "No, and I'm not sure he ever did. He sure liked controlling me, though. He'll never agree to a divorce."

"It's not any of my business, but how are you surviving financially?"

"I've always had an investment that he can't get his hands on, and it infuriates him. Thanks to technology, it's kept secure for me."

I got up to offer her wine and something to eat. She quickly accepted the wine but not the food.

"Ava, you can't continue like this."

She looked down at the floor. "I know, but I also know I don't want to go to jail and end up with a record the rest of my life. Please believe me when I say that I've never kept anything that I've shoplifted."

"What could he really do if he found you somewhere, like the grocery store?"

"I've thought of that many times. The easiest thing for me to do would be to just pretend to give in and go back with him. But he knows that routine because I've done it many times."

"You're really not safe, Ava."

"He'll never find me where I'm staying. It's a safe and secure place, trust me." I couldn't help but wonder if she was in a romantic relationship of some kind.

"I really need to go. I can't thank you enough for being my friend. It took a lot of caring and courage to approach me like you did. Please keep this visit quiet from everyone. Who knows, I may be able to come back to quilt club. I miss it, and I love Marta. I know she'd take me back anytime."

"What can I do to be helpful?"

She smiled. "Continue to be my friend. And tell no one you saw me."

"I've never met anyone like you, Ava. I'll pray for you. Please stay safe."

"My hiding won't last forever. Here's my number. I'm talking more frequently to this God you told me about." I smiled and gave her a hug after she slipped me a piece of paper.

She took one more sip of wine and left. It was dark enough that I couldn't see what kind of vehicle she was driving.

I sat back down in front of the fire to think about what had just happened. I, too, had run away from a man, but this was so, so different. I put the fire out and went on up to bed.

I undressed and got comfy under the covers. Then I grabbed my phone to catch up on emails and texts. There was one addressed to Cher and me from the clerk's office. It read that their board meeting had been cancelled due to not having a quorum. Their next meeting wouldn't be until after the first of the year, when we'd be the first ones on the agenda.

I decided the delay wasn't a big deal. It would give us more time to prepare. I'm sure many members were away for the holidays.

Before I went to sleep, I sent Cher a quick text about checking her email in the morning.

Chapter 99

The next day, I tried to put Ava out of my mind. When I was changing the sheets on my bed, Cher called.

"I got the email from the clerk's office. I think it's just as well that it was postponed."

"I think so, too."

"I'm going in to help Carl with inventory today."

"Great! It appears the two of you are getting closer."

"Somewhat, yes, but he's still a mystery to me. I'm so happy for Harry and Rachael, though. It was all meant to be, wasn't it?"

"It was a great holiday surprise. They're perfectly matched, that's for sure!"

"I guess you and Grayson will be the next to announce an engagement."

"Not at all. We aren't even close to anything like that. So, when are you and I going to have Christmas and exchange gifts?"

"I promised Ericka I'd be with her and George on Christmas Eve. By the way, she's handling the radiation treatment pretty well so far, but she's dreading the chemo."

"I'm glad you'll be with her. I suppose at some point over Christmas I'll be with Grayson, but we have no plans just yet. I know when I'm at Rachael's Christmas Eve party, Grayson and Kelly will be with Marsha's family. Kelly gave me a bracelet with a cat charm on it as a Christmas gift. I thought that was pretty special."

"Sweet."

"Have you heard from Carole or Linda?"

"Yes. Evidently Austen is quite the gossip of the town. They didn't say what his current condition is."

"It's best I know nothing. I went to the Pig yesterday to get ingredients for some vegetable soup. I haven't had any in ages."

"Oh, that sounds so good. Well, I have to run. Enjoy playing Susie Homemaker today."

As I began the tasks in the kitchen with my colorful vegetables, I kept wondering if it were still possible to paint a quick watercolor for Grayson. I wanted it to be personal, so I got my phone to see if any photos would be helpful for ideas.

I scrolled and scrolled. I wasn't good at painting people, but I did take a lot of photos when we spent that evening on Sister Bay Marina. It was then that I saw a photo I had taken from inside the boat, looking out onto the water. The sunset made for a pretty background, and our wine glasses and bottle of wine were sitting in front of us on a table. It truly captured the moment. I hoped it would mean as much to him as it did to me.

I threw the veggies into the pot of broth and turned it on low. I went out to the porch, taking the photo with me. I sketched the scene with a smile on my face, which gave me encouragement.

As the afternoon went by, the lighting on the porch changed dramatically. I loved this porch so much. Who else has a studio as the very first room when you enter their house? I had to laugh at any doubt I'd felt about this cabin in the past. How could I ever let this place be owned by someone else? I don't think I could ever be without this cabin that I now call my home. Without hesitation, I called Cher at the gallery.

"Yes, Claire Bear," she answered.

"I'm sorry to bother you, but while I feel courageous, I want you to have the papers drawn up for me to buy the cabin."

She paused. "Okay. Let me go into the back room to talk." A minute later, she continued. "Remember, Claire, I'm in no hurry for a decision. We haven't even talked about a price."

"I know. I'll pay you whatever your asking price will be. The cabin is part of me now, and I can't imagine leaving." She hung up thinking I'd probably change my mind.

Chapter 100

I felt a huge sense of relief having made the decision about the cabin. If it were mine, I could do so many things to make it my own, like build a garage for my car. At this moment, I felt like it was mine already.

My veggie soup was delicious for dinner on a very chilly night. It made lots, so I froze some in containers. I put another log on the fire and covered up with my quilt. The quilt got Puff's attention, and she left her place under the tree to join me. I started to doze off at an early hour until my phone rang and startled me.

"Hello," I answered softly from my sleep.

"Oh, Claire, did I wake you? It's Grayson."

"I guess I got too comfy on the couch," I excused.

"I envy you. I just got home, and I'm beat as well. I got myself a beer and started thinking of you as I sat in front of our Christmas tree."

"That's nice."

"I can't believe it's almost Christmas. Would you have any interest in going to church Christmas morning with Mrs. Parker, Kelly, and me? I couldn't remember if you had plans."

"No plans, but I do want to go to church."

"Well, problem solved. I thought we could go back to my house for a little brunch afterward."

"Sounds wonderful! Can I bring anything?"

"No thanks. It'll be simple. We have an invitation to Christmas Eve dinner with Marsha's family the night before."

"It'll be a big day for you and Kelly!"

"Indeed! Is everything okay with you?"

"Yes, everything's fine."

"Well, then I'll let you get back to some shut-eye. I'll be right behind you once I finish this beer."

"I miss you!" I told him.

"I miss you, too!"

After we hung up, I sure wished he had said "I love you," but that's just where we were. We may never get to where those words are comfortable for us. I wasn't Marsha, and perhaps those words would just stay with her in his mind.

The next day I thought I might try my hand at making some Christmas cookies. I could take them as a hospitality gift to Grayson's as well as the Christmas Eve party at Rachael's.

I got out Carole's cookbook focused solely on cookies and paged through all the tempting varieties. Peanut butter cookies were always Michael's favorite. When I looked at the sugar cookie recipe, I had to dismiss it because I didn't have all the wonderful tin cookie cutouts that my family had used for years. I needed to ask Mom to keep them for me. My favorite was the Christmas tree shape, and Michael's was always the snowman. Once I turned to a recipe for chocolate chip cookies, I looked no further. There was no question those were the ones. It's funny how there didn't seem to be two recipes alike for such a simple cookie. Should I add nuts to some and not to others? Around noon, Cher called.

"Okay, you asked for it. My realtor has been contacted, and he'll get the papers ready for you to sign if you haven't changed your mind."

"That's great! I'm so excited."

"How do you know I'm not going to ask a million dollars for it?"

I laughed. "Because I think you're ready to unload this place and move on before you have to start doing some major repairs."

"Good point, Claire Bear. I'd better knock off a few bucks then." We laughed. "Would you like to come for dinner tonight to celebrate? It'll be our own Christmas celebration."

"Why, sure! What can I bring?"

"I'm the one getting rich here, so it's my treat."

"I'll bring your gift. Thanks for the idea."

I couldn't believe the excitement I was feeling when I hung up. Perhaps as soon as tomorrow, I could be the owner of this little cabin in the woods. It was just what I'd been saving my dream money from my Dad for. I wanted to shout the news to everyone, but it was a bit early for shouting. Instead, I needed to get the last batch of cookies out of the oven.

Chapter 101

Before I left the house that morning, I made a pretty plate of cookies to take to Cher's place. Her sweater wasn't wrapped to my satisfaction, but it would do.

"Come in! Merry Christmas!" she greeted.

"I'm happy to be here. What smells so good?"

"We're having a Thanksgiving dinner since we have so much to be thankful for! I have a turkey breast roasting and a few of the usual sides. This was a treat for me. I almost never cook anymore."

"Here are some Christmas cookies. I made them myself, mind you. They're from Carole's cookbook."

"You're kidding! I'm impressed. Thank you for going to the trouble. There isn't too much here that looks like Christmas, so these cookies will help," she joked.

"Your tree is very pretty."

"Let's have a glass of wine while I get this gravy going. You can look at those papers on the table to see what you think."

Doing as she suggested, it didn't take me long to notice the bottom line on the asking price for the cabin. It was much lower than I expected.

"Let's eat while everything is hot," Cher suggested.

"May I say grace?" I asked. She smiled and nodded.

"Thank you, God, for our amazing friendship. As we celebrate your birthday this Christmas, may we continue to have good health and love in the years to come. Bless our family members and friends who are not with us this evening. You know who they are and how much we truly miss them. In your name we pray. Amen."

I looked at Cher, and she had tears in her eyes.

"That was lovely, Claire Bear."

"Merry Christmas, Cher Bear."

We clinked our glasses and dug into the wonderful meal. It didn't take long for us to start remembering our Christmases of the past, and we laughed and laughed.

We left the messy table and went in by the Christmas tree and her gas fireplace. I was glad the cabin—soon to be *my* cabin—had a woodburning fireplace.

Cher gave me my present first. I was pleased to see it was one of the Door County afghans from Carl's gallery. I had almost purchased one for myself. The second gift was much more personal. It was an album she had kept up with photos and clippings of the cabin that was now going to belong to me. I clutched it close as I thanked her. I'd always treasure it.

Cher's eyes were as big as saucers when she opened up her sweater.

"You shouldn't have bought this for me because I know you paid way too much for it, but it's totally amazing and so Door County." I laughed. "I love it, I love it!" She stood up from the couch and held it close as she did a happy dance.

The gaiety continued until midnight. Before we said goodbye, we agreed to meet soon with her realtor, who was also a notary, to hand over my check.

I was on cloud nine when I came home. I had just received the best Christmas present of my life. I'd definitely continue the tradition Cher had started by updating the cabin memory book with any future changes I'd make.

Puff was already sound asleep on my bed. I wanted to wake her to tell her the good news about staying put in the cabin, but I thought it could wait. She was so smart that she'd likely figured it out on her own.

I crawled under the covers with such gratitude and joy. I didn't wake up until nine o'clock the next morning, which Puff didn't appreciate.

When I came down to the kitchen, it still smelled of homemade chocolate chip cookies. As I poured my coffee, I realized tomorrow was Christmas Eve and I'd be off to work for Rachael. I had to admit, I looked forward to the party that would take place after closing time.

Today I hoped to put a few finishing touches on Grayson's painting. I knew he'd be easy to please, but I wanted it to be just right. It was starting to look the way I'd envisioned, and I felt it captured that special evening we'd shared.

Chapter 102

As I walked about the cabin throughout the day, I made mental notes on what I'd change or add. It felt in some ways that I was seeing the cabin for the first time. Things were different now that it would be in my name instead of Cher's. I was sure Grayson would be open to giving advice, and George could likely help if I needed anything done.

I couldn't contain my excitement any longer about my big news, so I gave Grayson a call. Unfortunately, the call went to voice mail, so I just told him I'd gifted myself with the cabin as a Christmas present to myself. I knew he'd be happy for me. He'd told me before it would be a good investment.

With Rachael's party coming up, I decided to get busy preparing a large plate of the chocolate chip cookies to take with me. My concentration was broken by a return call from Grayson.

"Congratulations!"

"Thank you! Cher and I celebrated last night with dinner at her place. I know I'm doing the right thing with the cabin. Staying here just feels right. I do want to make some changes, like adding a garage."

"Well, that may not be as easy as you think, but I agree it would be nice to have one, especially with all our snow and ice here. The problem is that you're living in an area that has some restrictions."

"I know. I'm just dreaming right now. By the way, I'll bet Kelly is quite excited about Christmas. I hope she still likes her quilt."

"Oh, she's in one of her snits again. She made it clear she wasn't coming to church with me on Christmas morning."

"I'm sorry, Grayson. What's she upset about?"

"Nothing to be concerned about. This isn't my first rodeo with her. Mrs. Parker called and said she'll meet us at church. She likes to have access to her own driver."

"I see her point. It's her way of being independent."

We chatted a bit more, but I could tell there was something else really bothering Grayson.

I showered and went to bed early to get ready for my big day. There was always so much preparation for Christmas, and then it was over in a flash. I went to sleep thinking about my little cabin in the woods.

My red alarm clock went off way too early the next morning. Despite the darkness, I managed to put my feet on the floor and get going. Would Santa come to my little cabin in the woods tonight? I smiled at the thought of him squeezing down my chimney.

I dressed warmly since the barn got cold with folks coming in and out. Caffeine was a must, so I quickly poured myself half a cup of coffee, knowing there would be more at Rachael's. I looked at poor Puff and decided it was okay for her to have her little treat of catnip toys. She looked oddly at me as I laid them in front of her. Maybe she'd figure out they were toys while I was gone.

Once I was on the road, I looked forward to seeing my work family. Once again, I enjoyed the many Christmas lights along the drive.

"Merry Christmas!" I said cheerfully as I entered the warm barn that smelled of cedar.

"Merry Christmas to you!" Rachael repeated. "The coffee is ready, and you'll be pleased to hear that Anna brought us some strudel and fruitcake to enjoy."

"Wonderful! I've been curious about that fruitcake. It looks more like the stollen my mother used to make. I have great memories of eating that on special occasions. So, who else is working today?"

"Kent is on call but will come later for the party. I told Brenda to come anytime she'd like. I think she's really looking forward to it."

"I brought a plate of cookies that I actually made myself."

"You baked them?" I nodded and smiled.

"I know. Hard to believe. They're from my friend Carole's cookie book. By the way, you may want to sell her cookbooks here around Christmastime. Lots of folks will be baking cookies around the time they're buying their trees."

"Claire, your mind never stops churning with good intentions for our business. I told Harry I was going to ask you to be in charge of the barn gift area next year since you have such a gift for knowing what we should sell as add-ons." I looked at her in surprise. "We don't need all that space devoted to barn quilts. Most of the orders are special requests anyway."

Chapter 103

"You're serious, aren't you?"

"Yes! I'll be making more money, especially with the new Tannenbaum event. I just don't have time to order and keep track of inventory while I'm trying to make product for the shop."

"Well, I love Christmas, and I'm in the Christmas spirit, so I'll say yes. Now I have some good news to share with you." She stared at my hand like there should be a ring of some kind. "No, it's not that. I purchased the cabin from Cher! The thought of giving it up was too painful, so I decided I should own it. Cher gave me plenty of time to decide, and now I have."

"Oh, I'm so happy for you," Rachael said as she gave me a hug. "I have to admit, there were times I was worried you would go back to Missouri. This seals the deal on that, right?"

"I'm here to stay! You and so many others have helped in making Door County my home. Who would've thought that you and Harry would end up being part of my family? So, what does it feel like being engaged to that big teddy bear?"

"There are no words. I'll share more about that later, but we'd better get to work. You know the drill, so start with watering the tree. For lunch, I made ham salad sandwiches for us to eat in the back room. We'll have lots of food later. Harry is getting ready to grill chicken for tonight's party."

"Sounds great!"

Just as I'd imagined all the possibilities for the cabin once I owned it, I got to looking around the barn gift area and considering all the possibilities for Christmas sales. I could make a list right now of things customers would be interested in buying along with their tree.

Close to noon, Harry showed up in his Santa outfit. His generous build was perfect for the role, and so was his jolly personality. Rachael quickly told him about my purchase of the cabin, and he was elated. When she mentioned I'd have a new role as the new gift shop manager at the farm, he belted out a loud congratulations.

"I told Rachael she didn't need to go back to bartending any longer once we're married. I don't know if I convinced her, but if not, I'll bet you can."

"That's hard to say, Harry. She has a family at the Bayside, like I have a family here."

"You gals are so darned independent. I know better than to talk her into anything."

I nodded and smiled.

Around two o'clock, Brenda showed up with a corn casserole that she took to the back room for the potluck dinner. When she returned, she was nice enough to answer some questions from a lady about the barn quilts. When we were free of customers, I asked about her Christmas plans.

"So, are you and Kent going to be together for Christmas?"

"Not really. He wants me to meet the girls when he brings them in today. There's a Packers game coming up, so he hinted at getting tickets."

"Poor Harry. He'll never have tickets to games again now that you're willing to go with Kent," I teased.

It was getting close to closing time, so I instructed Brenda to help set up the tables and bring out the things we needed for the party. Folks started showing up early, so I tried to engage them in shopping while Brenda helped Rachael bring out the food. Some of the faces I remembered from last year. Out of the corner of my eye, I saw Kent introduce the girls to Brenda. Hopefully Cupid was doing his part in the matchmaking.

The merriment and Christmas music got louder and louder. Harry was quite the entertainer, and Rachael fit right in. As soon as all the food was on the table, Rachael got everyone's attention and thanked them for coming. Harry then chimed in and told them if they hadn't heard, Rachael had accepted his marriage proposal. The crowd roared and clapped with joy.

After enjoying a plate full of wonderful food, I told myself it was time to get home and rest my tootsies. When I put on my coat, Rachael approached and handed me an envelope.

"It's a Christmas bonus to let you know how much I appreciate you," Rachael said with a hug.

"Oh, no. It's not necessary," I said with surprise.

"You may need some extra cash now that you'll be a homeowner. Buy something wonderful, and have a very merry Christmas."

"Thank you so much, Rachael. We both have a lot to celebrate, don't we?"

Chapter 104

Coming home on Christmas Eve and seeing Puff as my only companion for the night was a lonely feeling. I took one swallow of wine and went upstairs to get in bed. I was worn out from the day.

I lay there thinking of Grayson with Marsha's family. Would he always want to spend time with them at the holiday? Tomorrow would be my turn for his attention. I thought of Mom and Bill, hoping they were both healthy and happy. Soon, I was out like a light.

Christmas morning came quickly. "Merry Christmas," I said to Puff, as if she cared about anything but her food at this hour.

I put on my robe, and after I made coffee, I treated myself to some of Anna's fruitcake. My phone rang, and I was not surprised to see it was Mom.

"Merry Christmas!" I answered. "How was your dinner last night?"

"It was very nice. Bill actually built a fire in my fireplace. It's been a long time since that's happened around here. It was a struggle for both of us, but it was worth it." She gave a little chuckle like there was more to the story.

"Did you still have firewood?"

"Plenty. It sure was nice to have that experience again. We may do it again sometime."

"I love a fire, too!"

"Have you opened my present yet?"

"I'm afraid not. I just finished breakfast."

"Well, go open it and let me know what you think."

I did just as she said and opened the box to find a lovely pink-and-red crocheted shawl.

"I love it, Mom. Thank you for making me something so special and so beautiful. I'll keep it here by the fire."

"I love my cherry apron and the Door County afghan. What a nice memory for me to have from my visit. Now, if I recall you're attending church today with Grayson?"

"Yes. Mrs. Parker is joining us, and then we'll go to Grayson's for brunch."

"How wonderful. I'll be thinking of you, dear. Please tell Grayson Merry Christmas."

"I will. I sure miss and love you! I'll let you know how it goes."

I held the afghan close, and sure enough, it smelled like Mom.

I went upstairs and decided to wear a tweed wool suit with my dressier boots for church. I wanted to look as conservative as I could.

When Grayson knocked at my door, I greeted him with a hug, which he wasn't expecting.

"Merry Christmas!"

"The same to you! You look beautiful as always."

"Thanks. Still no sign of Kelly, huh?" Grayson shook his head.

When we arrived in Ephraim at the Moravian Church, I noticed Mrs. Parker waiting for us. She kindly greeted me before we were seated near the rear of the tiny church. Tasteful greenery was everywhere, just as I had remembered it from last year.

Grayson sat between us, and the beautiful service led by the female pastor began. A children's choir sang a song called "Morning Star." Other special musicians added to the music as well. It was all quite touching yet still celebratory.

I caught myself watching Grayson throughout the service. He truly was a man of faith, and I was wishing I knew more about that aspect of his life.

Everyone was very friendly at the church, as had been my experience the first time.

As we left, we were handed a piece of traditional sugar cake. I wasn't sure why we were getting it but just accepted it and said thank you. Grayson gave me a quick explanation of the tradition of the sugar cake for Moravians on Christmas Day. The cake topping reminded me of monkey bread, which I'd eaten once as a kid. It looked cinnamony and sweet, and I looked forward to indulging in it later.

Grayson walked Mrs. Parker to her service car and agreed that we'd see her shortly at the house. On the way to Grayson's house, he was quiet like he had something on his mind. I wasn't in the mood to pry.

We arrived about the same time, and Mrs. Parker followed using her cane, which didn't appear to serve much use. Perhaps it just made her feel more secure.

"We're here, Kelly!" Grayson called out as we arrived.

Kelly came out of the kitchen and politely greeted us with little emotion.

"Kelly, I brought you a plate of Christmas cookies that I made," I said as I put them on the sideboard in the dining room. "Now, what can I do to help you?"

Grayson answered quickly for her and said the meal would be simple and served buffet style. He got us something to drink and suggested we take a seat. Something wasn't right.

"So, Grayson tells me your mother was unable to visit this Christmas," Mrs. Parker commented as we made our way to sit at the table.

"No, and I miss her," I replied. "I did talk with her this morning. My brother is supposed to be with her today."

Chapter 105

After Grayson filled our coffee cups, we helped ourselves to a simple selection of eggs Benedict, fresh fruit, small sausages, and a lovely assortment of pastries.

Making any conversation was awkward, and Kelly was not her cheery self like Grayson had alluded to.

"There is so much more I'd like to know about your church, Mrs. Parker," I noted. "I've been impressed so far."

"The history of the church is quite remarkable," she responded. "If you're interested in history, you should visit one of the oldest buildings in Door County that was built by Reverend Andras Inerson, who founded Ephraim with a group of Norwegian Moravians."

"It's interesting to note that the reverend built the house and barn all by himself," Grayson continued.

"Really!" I responded with interest. "I'd very much like to see it sometime."

"Kelly, did you have a good time with your relatives Christmas Eve?" Mrs. Parker asked to include Kelly in the conversation.

"Yes. It's always fun seeing everyone," she replied nicely. "You wouldn't believe all the presents that were exchanged."

"We definitely brought home more than we took," Grayson said with humor. "Kelly, before Mrs. Parker leaves today, you should show her the beautiful quilt Claire made for you." Kelly stared at her dad like it wasn't a good idea.

"How nice of you, Claire," expressed Mrs. Parker. "Grayson said you're quite a talented watercolor artist as well."

"He's too kind," I chuckled modestly. "I do enjoy both quilting and painting."

"Claire sells her work at the Door County Art Gallery on Main Street," Grayson added.

After another twenty minutes of awkward chatter, I just wanted the meal to be over.

"Well, Grayson, my car should be waiting for me about now," Mrs. Parker said after we all had finished eating. "I tire very easily, so if you all would excuse me, I'll be on my way. It's been a lovely Christmas morning. Claire, I hope you return to my church very soon."

"I'm sure I will," I said, getting up from my chair.

Grayson helped her with her coat and walked her to the car. It would've been nice for Kelly to have said goodbye to her instead of heading toward the kitchen.

I cleared some of the dishes from the table to be helpful.

"It was so nice to come here this morning, Kelly," I complimented.

"Dad suggested it," she replied.

"Where's Spot?" I asked, looking around. "Does he hide when folks come over like Puff does?"

"Dad insisted he stay upstairs," she said sadly.

"Kelly, I'll get all this later," Grayson said as he rejoined us from walking Mrs. Parker out.

"I don't mind," she answered. "You and Claire do your thing."

Grayson and I looked at each other and shrugged our shoulders.

"I'll have more coffee," I said cheerfully as I went back to the dining room.

In silence, Grayson and I both took our cups of coffee into the living room by the Christmas tree.

"Are we doing our thing yet?" I joked. We both burst into laughter.

"I'm so sorry about her behavior," Grayson said softly.

"I have a gift for you, but it's at the cabin," I noted.

"I have one for you as well. How about I come by around five o'clock this evening for a drink, and we'll exchange gifts?"

"I'd like that," I said as I watched Kelly go upstairs. Should I go up and say goodbye or not when I decide to leave?

"You just have to ignore Kelly," Grayson advised. "She's in a mood. She really loves that quilt you gave her. I don't know why she didn't show Mrs. Parker."

"Why don't you take me home, come back and help Kelly clean up the kitchen, and make nice with her? It's Christmas."

He smiled. Grayson said he'd do just that, and frankly, I was happy to be headed home.

Puff was waiting for me when I got back to the cabin. I picked her up and went over to make a fire. That was my way of telling her that I'd be home for a while. Kelly was not going to ruin my Christmas.

Chapter 106

As I changed clothes from my suit, my phone rang. It was Linda.

"Merry Christmas!" she greeted.

"Same to you, my friend."

"I just opened my gift from you, and I simply love the Door County afghan and the cherry print apron. If Carole didn't get the same thing, she's going to be mighty jealous."

I laughed. "I knew better and gave you the same gifts! Now, I haven't had a chance to open your present yet. I just got home from having brunch at Grayson's house."

"Carole has a lot of company today, so you may not hear from her, but I know she'll love this stuff."

"I don't suppose you've heard any scuttle on Austen, have you?"

"No. There's nothing new. By the way, Carole took your mother cookies yesterday, and she said she was very pleased."

"How sweet. I'm sure Michael will enjoy them as well. Thanks for calling, Linda. I can't wait to see you again."

We had no more than hung up when my phone rang again.

"Claire, it's Ava."

"Ava? My goodness, how are you?"

"I just wanted to wish you a Merry Christmas."

"Are you okay?"

"Yes, I'm in a safe place and having a nice day. I hope I'm not interrupting anything."

"No, it's fine."

"Thanks for being such a good friend. I hope you have a happy New Year."

"I wish you a better year as well."

She hung up on that note. I'm sure wherever she was, she was feeling very lonely. I couldn't let myself think about it.

The afternoon was nearly gone after all the phone calls. I went in the kitchen and made up a platter of appetizers for Grayson and me to have with our drinks.

Shortly after, Grayson was at my door. If he had a gift for me, it didn't show.

"Long time no see," he kidded. "Merry Christmas!"

"Same to you!" I said, kissing him on the cheek. "I made a fire, and I'll get you a glass of wine."

"How was the rest of your day?" he asked as I poured our wine.

"I think I wished everyone I know a Merry Christmas," I joked. "It was busy!"

"Did I just see Puff wearing a big red bow?" Grayson teased. "I can't believe she let you do that. I'm surprised Kelly didn't think of that for Spot."

I laughed. "Well, I knew Puff would want to dress for the occasion. I don't think a male cat would appreciate a bow, though. Hey, I have a plate of munchies here if you're interested."

"I'm really not hungry," he said sadly.

"Okay Grayson, something is eating at you. I could tell that you weren't yourself all day. Is it Kelly's behavior or something else?"

He got up and started pacing the floor. "She's acting like a baby," he said with disgust.

"Well, she's a teenager, and she has some raging hormones right now."

"I'm sorry, but she was downright rude today, and she continued to act that way even after I took you home."

"That's a shame. Is she telling you what's eating at her?"

"If I tell you, I don't want you to take it personally."

I was afraid of that. Why I did I ask? "It's about me, I take it?"

He took a deep breath. "When Kelly found out that the two of us were not having our usual ritual on Christmas morning, she threw a fit. When I told her I'd invited you and Mrs. Parker to church and brunch, she really got upset."

"I see. So, what was your former ritual?"

"Well, we'd wake up and go downstairs to open our presents together. Then we'd make hot chocolate and scrambled eggs. She'd do the hot chocolate, and I'd do the eggs. After breakfast, I'd make phone calls and read the paper while she'd have friends stop by. Our ritual was a way of comforting each other after Marsha died. Now Kelly's practically a grown woman, for heaven's sake. Why doesn't she understand that some things don't stay the same?"

"Oh, Grayson, I don't know what to say. I feel the pain for both of you."

"Well, I hope my little gift will make up for the rudeness you endured today," he said as he took a little gift box out of his coat pocket.

I moved closer to him as I accepted his gift. When I opened it, I saw a stunning diamond bracelet.

"Oh, Grayson, this is amazingly beautiful! It's too much!" He leaned over to kiss me and then helped me with the clasp as I put it on.

"I'll cherish this forever. My gift to you isn't bright and shiny like this one, but I hope you like it."

Chapter 107

Grayson's face lit up like a little kid's when he saw the painting.

"I hope this scene is what I think it is. I remember it well."

"I'm glad you recognize it."

"No question. I didn't realize you took this photo. I like it very much!" He leaned over and kissed me lightly on the lips.

"Once I came across the picture, I knew it was the scene I wanted to paint for you."

"I know exactly where I'm going to hang it, too."

"And where would that be?"

"It'll be on my office wall directly in front of me so that I see it every time I look up."

"I'm glad I've given you some joy today."

"You always bring me joy. I hope you can be patient with me as I deal with Kelly. I may not be able to see you quite as much until this blows over. She's really going through some things right now."

"Does she have any idea how close we've become?"

"No."

"Does she know you're here right now?"

He shook his head. "So, have you given any thought on what you'd like to do New Year's Eve?" The question caught me by surprise.

"Wow, I suppose it is getting close. What sounds good to you?"

"First, let me remind you that we have an invitation to the group's New Year's Day party over at John's house, but as far as us, I'd like a quiet, romantic dinner with my best girl, Claire Stewart." I smiled. "What do you say to that?"

"To be honest, I'm not sure I want to go to the house party. From what I observed last year, it's a guy party, and you would have more fun without me. Now, as far as having a romantic dinner with that best girl, I'm all for it."

"Okay. I'll start looking into it. If you're not going with me to John's house, I may skip it myself."

"How about some more wine or a bite to eat?"

"Just a tad more, please, but I really need to be on my way."

"Really?"

"You know I never want to leave here. But tonight's not the night to come in late."

"I understand. I do appreciate that you came over to make time for just the two of us. I really love my sparkling bracelet."

"And I love the painting. You're a talented lady, Miss Stewart."

As he stood up, he pulled me into his arms. It was good not to talk and just be held again. He suddenly pulled away.

"Falling in love with you shouldn't be this difficult, should it?"

I shook my head. "Funny, I don't find it difficult at all."

He grinned. "That's what I love about you. I need to go. I'll be in touch with you about New Year's Eve, okay?" I nodded as he gave me one last kiss.

I watched him leave with my painting under his arm. I had a sparkling piece of jewelry dangling from my wrist, but I felt sad. Our Merry Christmas wasn't all that merry.

I put out the fire and refrigerated my snacks that we didn't even touch. As soon as Puff saw me moving around, she knew I was getting ready to go upstairs.

I went up and quickly crawled under the covers for comfort. My heart felt empty, and now I was supposed to be patient until Kelly got over her snit. I should've known better than to fall in love with a widower who had a teenage daughter. Why did I think this would ever develop into something? I was tired of trying to analyze this crazy relationship. I put my feather-filled pillow over my head and went to sleep.

Chapter 108

When I woke up, I realized I still had on the bracelet that Grayson had given me. For some reason, I didn't feel warm and fuzzy about it. Perhaps it was a safe choice for him to make. If I had any sense, I should break up with this guy because of all the stress he's getting from Kelly. He'd get over me in a flash compared to grieving for his wife.

The sun was shining bright, and it gave me energy to think about my next painting. Cher interrupted my thoughts.

"So, I just have to know what Grayson gave you for Christmas. If you got engaged and didn't call to tell me right away, I'm really going to be upset and reconsider being your best friend."

I laughed. "You have a big imagination, my friend. No engagement, and no sign of one in the future. I did get a stunning diamond bracelet, however, which is still on my wrist."

"It sounds lovely, so why do you sound disappointed?"

"Oh, the bracelet was very expensive. There's nothing not to like about it."

As much as I wanted to, I couldn't share with her about how disappointed I was Christmas morning. I just wasn't in the mood to go into it all.

"Speaking of relationships, how's Carl, and how was your Christmas Eve?"

"No news regarding Carl. I'm going in tomorrow morning to help him finish inventory. Maybe we'll do something after that. George did the cooking at Ericka's house. He did a fine job, and Ericka went through the motions even though I know she didn't feel well. She truly does love that quilt we gave her, and I think the Christmas tree has helped her spirits, too."

"That's good to hear. Can I take her anything?"

"Don't bother. She has too much stuff right now and not much of an appetite. Her coworkers really went overboard."

"Do you think you'll be with Carl for New Year's Eve?"

"I'd like to hope, but he's moving slowly, and that's okay with me. How about you guys?"

"We're going to dinner. I turned down a house party with his friends, though. I just didn't enjoy last year's. I don't think I can answer any more questions to satisfy them. Anyway, now I'm sitting here at the kitchen table trying to decide which building I should paint next. Did you have a favorite?"

"Frankly, I thought the most beautiful sight was Noble Park. The color from all the quilts against the green grass at the white Noble House was striking. Did you get of photo of that?"

"I did! You've made a good observation there, my friend. I'll see if I have something that inspires me."

After we hung up, I started scrolling through my quilt show photos on my phone. I marked one that could possibly work, but I wasn't quite ready to start on it yet.

I went out to the porch and saw Brenda drive up.

"Hi, girlfriend," I shouted out.

"I'm on the way to work and a little early, so I thought I'd stop by. How was your Christmas?"

"Pretty good. How was yours?"

"My feet still hurt from working at the barn. It must be the concrete floor. You would think I'd be used to being on my feet."

"It was fun, and the feet do get a workout. I love the potluck they do with all their friends. I didn't stick around after I ate, did you?"

"Yeah, I tried to be helpful to Kent, who basically was the clean-up person."

"How did you like his girls?"

"Adorable and likely spoiled by Grandpa Harry, from what I can tell."

Chapter 109

"So, did you see him the next day?"

"No. That's their Christmas-with-Santa day. He did give me a little something funny, however."

"What?"

"A bobblehead of Aaron Rodgers."

I had to think for a second. "He's the quarterback for the Packers, right?"

"He is, and Kent knows I adore him. Those things aren't cheap, and it was a cute gesture, don't you think?"

"Absolutely!"

"I decided not to get him anything. I don't want him to get the wrong idea about our friendship."

"I should take your advice, Brenda."

"What do you mean by that?"

"Never mind."

"I was going to ask you if you'd heard of the book club at the library called Bittersweet Bookies. A friend from work asked me to go. They meet in the same room as your quilt club."

"I knew a book club met there. I like that name. I wish I had more time to read. You'd probably enjoy the club. I know you read a lot."

"I do. What else do I have to do? Good heavens, Claire! I just noticed that gorgeous thing on your wrist!"

"Oh, it's my Christmas present from Grayson."

"Land's, girl, it's stunning. Can you just imagine what he paid for that?"

"No, I can't imagine."

"I can see why you don't want to take it off. Well, I'd better get going. I hope you have a good day."

"I will," I said, watching her drive off.

It was so good seeing Brenda come back to life again now that Kent was in the picture. I poured myself another cup of coffee and began building a fire. On the coffee table was that sweet album that Cher gave me on the cabin's history. I took time to look at it once again. It was obvious that it was a labor of love for her, and I wanted to continue that tradition.

Feeling a bit depressed about Grayson, I went out to the porch to begin thinking about and even sketching what I could paint resembling Noble Park. I took my bracelet off and set it on the table. It didn't exactly give me good feelings right now, and it was distracting me. I knew myself well enough to know that when I was in this dark mood, creativity wasn't going to flow. I welcomed a call coming in from Carl.

"Claire, are you busy?"

"Not especially. Why?"

"I have a gentleman here in the gallery who would like to commission you to do a painting for him. He'd like to meet with you in person if that's possible."

"Why, sure. Give me about fifteen minutes, and I'll walk down to meet him."

"Great!"

My curiosity about the commission got me excited, so I touched up my makeup before putting on my coat to leave.

When I arrived, somewhat out of breath, I saw an elderly gentleman who was introduced to me as Mr. Adams. He was good-looking, well dressed, and charming.

"I like your watercolor work, Miss Stewart," he complimented. "I have a photo with me that was taken in Peninsula State Park. The photo has great value to me because I proposed to my wife fifty years ago right on that pier. She was afraid to walk all the way out to the edge, so at this particular spot, I asked her to marry me. It was a pretty, but windy, fall day, so the water was quite active, as you can see over here."

"Mr. Adams, this is such a sweet story," I responded. "Let me look closer at this photo. I think I know where this spot is. Even though your photo is black and white, I think I can make this work."

"Oh, Miss Stewart, I'd appreciate it so much," he said with a big grin. "I don't care what it costs. I like this size canvas over here. Can you work with that?"

"I'm sure I can," I said, looking at the 18″ by 14″ canvas.

"We'll take care of everything, Mr. Adams," Carl reassured him. "I'll give you a call when I have it here in the gallery."

"I'm forever grateful," he said, going out the door. Carl gave me a big grin.

Chapter 110

As I studied the photo and made some notes, a man started talking to Carl about a painting he recently brought to him.

"Oh, Claire, have you met Foster Collins, our most famous painter?" he joked. "Oh, I mean besides you, of course." We chuckled.

"*The* Foster Collins?" I repeated. I was stunned as I looked him over. "No, we haven't met, but I'm honored to meet you, Mr. Collins. I'm certainly an admirer of your work, even before I came to Door County." He grinned. "Did you bring something here to sell?"

"I'm sorry, I didn't get your name," he interrupted.

"Foster, this is Claire Stewart," Carl introduced. "She's a quilter and a painter who's fairly new with us. She's doing well with a series of Door County places."

I couldn't help but stare at this tall man with thick sandy-gray colored haired hair. I thought I detected a narrow mustache outlining his perfect smile, and somehow, he'd managed to keep his summer tan. I knew I was supposed to say something, but what?

"Nice to meet you, Claire," he said, extending a handshake. "Do you live here in the area?'

"Yes, very close by," I described. "Where do you live?"

"Green Bay, but I'm in the peninsula a lot," he noted. "If Carl has accepted your work, I compliment you greatly. I like the audience that Carl's gallery attracts."

"Claire just recently purchased a charming log cabin near here, so congratulations for her are in order."

"Wonderful," Foster responded politely. "Tell me more."

I blushed. "It has an enclosed front porch where I work," I explained. "The lighting is perfect for painting."

"It makes a difference, doesn't it?" Foster nodded as he seemed to examine my whole being.

"It was nice to meet you, Foster," I said nervously. "You've made my day."

"Thanks, Claire," Carl said. "Stop by again this week."

I nodded. "I will. Goodbye," I said like a giddy schoolgirl.

I couldn't wait to go home and google Foster Collins. I had no clue he lived in Wisconsin. Now that I think of it, I believe one of his paintings had showed a Wisconsin red barn in a field of green wheat. Carl had to be absolutely thrilled to have his work to sell. Wait until I tell Cher I met Foster Collins!

Now that I had Mr. Adams's work to do, I put away my sketch of Noble Park. Tomorrow I'd drive to the very scene where this long-ago proposal took place. I could only imagine how delighted Mrs. Adams would be with having that scene painted. I sat there staring at his photograph until my phone indicated an email had just come in. It was from Marta.

Marta announced we'd have our first meeting of the year on January 2 at the usual time. She didn't describe any agenda items. Hopefully we'd have another member to suggest to the group. The big question would be whether Ava decided to show up.

I had nothing in the fridge I wanted to eat for dinner that evening, and I hadn't gotten my mail that day, so I decided to leave the cabin again and try to do both.

I made the mistake of walking. It was getting colder, so by the time I arrived at the post office, I was pretty chilled. I picked up the latest edition of the *Pulse* newspaper while I was there.

I walked over to the Blue Horse, but it was already closed, so I went with my second choice.

I arrived at the counter of The Cookery and ordered some whitefish chowder and a spinach salad to go. As I waited, I looked at all their wonderful pastries I was tempted to take home, but then I realized I still had tons of cookies left.

With warm soup in the bag, I walked home in the brisk air as snowflakes started spitting about.

I went straight to my fire to warm up when I got home. The chowder was still warm. As I opened my mail, I took a spoonful to warm up.

A larger envelope had come from Carole. I ripped it open and saw it was a newspaper clipping. There, circled for me to see, it read, "Dr. Austen Page Takes an Early Retirement at the Age of Fifty-Eight."

Chapter 111

I took a deep breath and wondered why Austen thought retirement was necessary. He must not be adapting well to being in a wheelchair. He was always a vain and proud man, so perhaps this image of being disabled was too much for him. Now what would he do with his time? There was no point in calling Carole. This article pretty much said it all.

I ate my dinner thinking of my past with Austen. I didn't want that to continue consuming my thoughts, so I worked out a layout for the Peninsula Park painting when I was finished eating. I knew going to this spot at different times of the day would give me a unique perspective.

If the weather was pleasant tomorrow, I'd go first thing in the morning. I wanted to get this commission completed so I could start on my own work.

As I busied myself throughout the day, the thought of not hearing from Grayson lingered. I sure hoped he wouldn't cancel our plans for New Year's Eve. Would he share what we were doing with Kelly? What a struggle this must be for him. I'd never told him that he had to let go of his memories of Marsha. She'd always be part of his life because of Kelly. I knew it wasn't easy for either of them.

That evening, as I made a fire, I noticed snowflakes drifting like feathers out of a pillow. Would it stop snowing long enough for my adventure to the park in the morning?

I lay back once again admiring my Christmas tree while sipping some wine. My beloved tree would have to come down soon, and Puff and I weren't ready for that. My family's rule of leaving the tree up until New Year's Day was set in stone. Was I up to breaking that rule?

I had just put out the fire to head upstairs when Grayson called.

"Are you still up, Miss Stewart?"

"Not for long, Mr. Wills. How was your day?"

"Very busy. I just got home. Much of the staff is off for the holidays, so I had some incidentals to take care of."

"I see."

"I promised John I'd get back to him on whether we'd join all of them on New Year's Day. It's all up to you."

"I told you I was going to pass, but I don't see why you shouldn't join your friends as you always do, Grayson. Please thank them for including me, though. I sense that you may not want to go as well. Am I right?"

"Possibly. You're not going to back out on *our* plans, are you?"

"I wouldn't miss it for the world," I said in a happier tone. "Where are we going?"

"It's in the planning stages, but it'll be nice and quiet."

"Sounds good."

"How about I pick you up around seven o'clock?"

"Perfect. Are things a bit better at home?"

"Somewhat. I'll look forward to seeing you soon, then."

"Great." I felt like I had just made an appointment with a utility repair guy.

I went to bed trying not to think too hard about our relationship. I just needed to dwell on my trip to the park tomorrow.

When I woke up the next morning, I realized I was still connected to memories of my dream. I was in Peninsula Park in the same spot as Mr. Adams was, only it was Austen, of all people, who was proposing to me. I tried to protest, saying he was the wrong person, but then I woke up in my small bedroom in the cabin. The dream made me sit up and get control of the moment.

I followed Puff downstairs to breakfast and sat at the kitchen table staring at Mr. Adams's photograph once again. It appeared to be fall according to the bushes and trees. I, too, like Mrs. Adams, was not one to walk out onto the pier, but I'd do the best I could. The snow had stopped during the night, so I didn't see a problem in going to the park as planned.

I checked my phone and decided to send Carole a text, thanking her for sending me the newspaper.

[Claire]
Thanks for the paper. I was surprised by the news. I made some cookies from your cookbook, and they were delicious. Miss you! Have a happy New Year!

Chapter 112

The late morning was chilly when I pulled into the entrance of the park. I'm sure there would be very few visitors this time of year. I parked in the small camping area. Soon afterward, I found the path to the pier, which had a slight hook at the end. It took me ten minutes of talking myself into it, but I finally had the courage to go partway out onto the concrete pier.

The bonus of this view was the back side of Fish Creek against the bay. Another small island stood off to the right. I looked at the trees and bushes that now were covered in the light snow that had recently fallen. I'd have to turn them into fall foliage to match Mr. Adams's photo. I couldn't help but wonder if this proposal was in the heat of the moment for Mr. Adams or if he'd had it all planned. I suppose I should've asked him more questions. The cold air was now getting to me, so I returned to the car.

I decided to drive a little farther down the road since there wasn't any traffic in this park of 3,000 acres. Trails going every direction had a name and were well maintained. Mr. Adams told Carl that this park was the third largest in Wisconsin. I knew there was a graveyard in the park where the Noble family was buried, but that would have to wait for another trip. I turned around at another park site and headed home.

Since I'd become so cold, I decided to stop at the Blue Horse to grab a cup of hot coffee. It was late enough in the morning that Grayson wouldn't be there. I knew I looked terrible with no makeup, so I got in line to quickly order my latte and bagel to go. I was in and out pretty quickly and then headed to the post office to retrieve my mail.

When I arrived home, I took my morning treat to the porch, where I returned focus to the commission piece.

Around three o'clock in the afternoon, Cher interrupted me.

"Hey, Claire Bear. I think I can report that I have an official date," she said with expectation.

"With Carl?"

"Of course, Carl. Who else? It was a very casual ask, but an ask it was. He said, 'Why don't we go out for a celebration at Anderson's after we finish inventory?' "

"That's great, Cher Bear, and you can definitely call that a date. Grayson hasn't told me where we're going for New Year's Eve."

"Knowing Grayson, it'll be wonderful, I'm sure. By the way, Carl said you nearly flipped when you got to meet Foster Collins."

"I did! I couldn't wait to tell you. Have you met him?"

"Not really. He was in here before, but I didn't know who he was. He's quite a looker, if I recall. Carl is thrilled to be able to claim he's selling his work."

"I can only imagine! I wonder where he hangs out when he's in Door County?"

"I couldn't tell you, but Carl says he's a very private man. I think I still have an article about him somewhere."

"If you do, save it for me."

"I will. Well, I guess it's time we say Happy New Year to each other. I can't remember when I last had a date on New Year's Eve."

"I'm so happy for you. I'll be thinking of you at midnight, okay?"

"Deal! We have a big year waiting for us, my friend, with the quilt show. And that stressful board meeting will be here soon."

"Try not to think of that just yet. Just enjoy your evening with Carl."

"I will. I love you, Claire Bear."

"I love you too, Cher Bear. Happy New Year."

For a second, I wished I were spending the evening with my very best friend instead of Grayson.

Mom called just as I was getting back to my work.

"Hi, sweetie," she greeted.

"Good to hear from you, Mom. Are you calling to wish me a happy New Year?"

"Well, not really. Do you remember my friend Beulah Reed from church?"

"Why, sure. How is she?"

"She passed away last night, and I'm quite down about it."

"Oh, Mom. I'm so sorry. Was she sick?"

"A heart attack killed her, but she had other health issues over the years. She was always in charge of the quilting at church when I quilted there."

"I'm sorry you've experienced more loss. It really hasn't been that long since Hilda died, and I know how much you miss her."

"I know. Please tell Cher about it. The three of us became widows around the same time."

"I will. So, will you be with Bill on New Year's Eve?"

"No, but he'll come over for a little supper on New Year's Day. Will you be with Grayson?"

"Yes. We're just going to dinner. Please tell Bill Happy New Year for me."

"I will. I love you, sweetie."

"I love you, too, and I thank God every night for you."

"Keep praying, keep praying," she joked as we hung up.

Chapter 113

New Year's Eve morning was only twelve degrees, but sunny. There were drafts in the cabin that I'd ignored until now, but as the new owner, I'd have to do something about them.

As I straightened up the cabin for a possible visit from Grayson, I thought about what I should wear for this special evening. I had to be dressed nicely, but warm. That was the new norm in this county. I thought of my white cashmere sweater Austen had bought me years ago. It had accents of pearls, which would make it dressy enough for tonight.

I decided to stay in my robe while I worked a bit on the Peninsula painting. I wanted it to come across as romantic and soft. It was chilly on the porch, so I kept drinking coffee instead of having lunch. Tonight would be a fabulous dinner, I was sure.

Out of my window, I saw Cotsy Bittner come to my door.

"Hi there! Please come in out of the cold!"

"Happy New Year! Thanks for the invite, but I have too many things to do to come in."

"Well, Happy New Year to you and Dan!"

"I just wanted to remind you that we leave tomorrow for Florida, so you and Tom are in charge until we get back."

"Oh, Florida sounds so good right now. I'm still trying to get used to Door County winters."

"We're ready for warmer weather. Is everything okay with you?"

"It is. I can't thank you enough for the Christmas party invite. You do such a nice job."

"Thanks. Well, I'd better get going. I have so much to do. I envy you in that nice-looking, warm robe."

I grinned. "I suppose I'll have to change for dinner," I joked. She grinned.

After she left, I was thankful I had such good neighbors.

By four o'clock, I started the process of getting ready for my big night. I looked forward to a nice, hot shower. With Cher's addition of this marvelous bathroom, I had enough hot water from the water heater to last me a lifetime.

I took my time, thinking Grayson might notice the care I was taking. Should I try a new cologne tonight?

By six thirty, I was ready and feeling good about how I looked. It was the last day of the year, and I'd go out in my finest.

On time as always, Grayson arrived promptly at seven o'clock. The first thing I noticed was his red scarf, of course. I could tell he liked how I looked.

"I hope it'll be a special evening for you," he said as he helped me with my fur coat. "You'll want the hood up on this gorgeous fur with that wind out there. It's supposed to get down to nine degrees tonight."

"Well, I hope wherever we're going has a nice fire to keep us warm."

"As a matter of fact, it does," he answered with a wink.

Without describing our plans for the evening, we pulled into the English Inn right here in Fish Creek. I was pleased with his choice.

"I don't know if I told you that I have a friend who owns this place, so he guaranteed we'd have a nice quiet table to ourselves."

"How sweet. I love this place. I'm just glad it's not one of these tables out here by the firepits." He chuckled.

When we walked inside, we were greeted by a waiter who seemed to know we were coming. He took our coats and led us to a private table by a fireplace. There wasn't anyone seated nearby.

"My name is William, and I'll be your private server this evening," he announced formally. Wow. A private server!

Grayson's mood was improving by the minute. He commented about the perfect fire for us.

My handsome date made a suggestion of a red wine he wanted me to try, and I was more than willing. From there, a silver tray of various appetizers appeared without us even ordering them. William explained each one. Most were seafood combinations I'd never experienced.

"Why can't this just be our dinner, Grayson?" I teased. He agreed.

Our conversation was going well. Almost too well. There were no mentions of Kelly, which I'm sure was intentional. I didn't want to ruin anything, so I didn't mention her name either and continued to stroke his ego for planning such a pleasant evening.

William described the coming courses, which included beef and lobster with incredible sides I'd never tasted before.

I was getting so full, but I wanted to experience every single thing. The dessert we chose from the dessert platter was a simple crème brûlée with raspberries. Indigestion would surely appear about midnight, but it would be worth it. We were enjoying our coffee when Grayson said he had another surprise for me. I couldn't imagine what it was.

He insisted it was time to go on another adventure, and I should pull up my hood and bundle up. I was speechless. William said he had hot peppermint coffee that would accompany us. Surely, Grayson didn't want to sit by a firepit outdoors!

When William opened the door to go out, there stood a horse and carriage for us. I couldn't believe it!

"Just for you, my dear," Grayson flirted as I climbed in. "Don't worry—there are heated blankets, and William has a nice warm drink for us to enjoy along the ride."

"So, are you ready?" Grayson asked as he tucked the blanket around my lap.

"I am if you are," I reacted with disbelief. "This is unbelievable, Grayson!"

Grayson put his arm around me, and off we went with a gentle stride. We didn't get back on Highway 42 but instead took a dark back road with only the lights of the carriage to lead us. This was certainly a new experience for me. Grayson said we wouldn't be going far and that we should just relax and enjoy our drinks. Now and then, Grayson would squeeze my hand as if he were enjoying it more than I.

It appeared to me that we had made a large circle and ended up on the side of the English Inn when the carriage stopped.

"Oh Grayson, this was lovely, and such a romantic thing to do on New Year's Eve."

"I knew you would like it. I should've planned this for Christmas, I suppose. I'm pleased you're wearing the bracelet."

"I love it and have received many compliments on it. In fact, the night you gave it to me, I forgot to take it off and woke up with it on my wrist the next morning." He grinned as he reached inside his coat pocket.

"Well, I decided you needed something to go with that bracelet," he nervously said as he displayed a small black box. My heart sank. It was obviously a ring. When he opened the box, it was a large, bright, diamond ring glaring at me in the moonlight.

"Claire Stewart, I know this is unexpected, but I need to know if you'll marry me and be my wife forever and forever." His face showed desperation for an answer. "I love you with all my heart."

I stared at him wondering if he was really serious. This was totally unexpected, alright. Did I hear him correctly? I'll never forget the look on his face, waiting for an answer. I was speechless, but I had to reply somehow. Please, God, help me.

"Grayson, I, I … ."

WHITE GULL INN'S
Montmorency Cherry Coffee Cake

Yields 8 servings.

Topping:

1 cup brown sugar

1½ tablespoons cinnamon

½ cup chopped walnuts

Coffee cake:

2 cups sour cream

2 teaspoons baking soda

4 cups flour

1 tablespoon baking powder

1 cup (2 sticks) of softened butter

1½ cups granulated sugar

4 eggs

2 teaspoons vanilla extract

2 cups pitted, frozen Montmorency* or other tart cherries, thawed and drained

---

Preheat the oven to 350°F. Spray a 13 × 9 inch baking pan with nonstick cooking spray.

To make the topping, mix together the brown sugar, cinnamon, and walnuts in a small bowl; set aside.

Stir together the sour cream and baking soda in a small bowl. In a separate bowl, mix the flour and baking powder. In a medium mixing bowl, cream the butter and sugar. Add eggs to the butter and sugar mixture, one at a time. Stir in vanilla and beat until fluffy. Add sour cream and flour mixtures alternately to the creamed mixture; blend thoroughly.

Spread one-half of the batter in the prepared pan and cover with cherries. Sprinkle one-third of the reserved topping over the cherries. Spread the remaining half of the batter on top, and sprinkle the remaining two-thirds topping evenly over the cake. Bake 60–75 minutes. Cover with foil after 30 minutes if the cake is browning too quickly. Test for doneness by inserting a knife in the center. Serve warm.

Thanks to White Gull Inn in Fish Creek, Wisconsin, for serving such a delicious breakfast and for sharing this recipe with us.

* *For information on where frozen Montmorency cherries are sold near you, please contact Seaquist Orchards in Ellison Bay, Wisconsin, by emailing Robin Seaquist at robin@seaqistorchards.com.*

READER'S GUIDE:
The Tannenbaum Christmas Quilt

by Ann Hazelwood

1. Rachael asked Frances to organize a séance. Do you believe the dead can still reach us from the other side? What influences your beliefs?

2. Kelly goes from excitement about joining her dad and Claire for s'mores to moodiness and resentment toward Claire and Mrs. Parker sharing her dad at Christmas. How are those experiences different? Do you have traditions with your family that you hold firm to keeping?

3. Cher started a memory book of the cabin and passed it on to Claire. Have you inherited something that you want to continue keeping current or pass on? What is it, and why is it worth preserving?

4. Claire has mixed feelings about Austen throughout the novel. What influences her feelings at each stage? Have you had a relationship you've had a hard time putting in the past? Consider the similarities and differences between Claire's relationship with Austen and Grayson's relationship with Marsha.

5. Claire's mom visibly ages in the book. What's your relationship with your mother, and how has it changed over the years?

About the Author

Ann Hazelwood is a former shop owner and native of Saint Charles, Missouri. She's always adored quilting and is a certified quilt appraiser. She's the author of the wildly successful Colebridge Community series and considers writing one of her greatest passions. She has also published the Wine Country Quilt series and East Perry County series and is now writing the Door County Quilts series.

booksonthings.com

Cozy up with more quilting mysteries from Ann Hazelwood...

WINE COUNTRY QUILT SERIES

After quitting her boring editing job, aspiring writer Lily Rosenthal isn't sure what to do next. Her two biggest joys in life are collecting antique quilts and frequenting the area's beautiful wine country. The murder of a friend results in Lily acquiring the inventory of a local antique store. Murder, quilts, and vineyards serve as the inspiration as Lily embarks on a journey filled with laughs, loss, and red-and-white quilts.

THE DOOR COUNTY QUILT SERIES

Meet Claire Stewart, a new resident of Door County, Wisconsin. Claire is a watercolor quilt artist and joins a prestigious small quilting club when her best friend moves away. As she grows more comfortable after escaping a bad relationship, new ideas and surprises abound as friendships, quilting, and her love life all change for the better.

Want more? Visit us online at ctpub.com